Praise for *The Unwanteds*

"Combining elements of Harry Potter and The Hunger Games, fantasy readers will be drawn to this plot. . . . Don't expect this to stay long on your library shelves."

—*Library Media Connection*

"McMann has created a world of magical whimsy."

—*School Library Journal*

"Imagination runs wild in this creative adventure."

—#1 *New York Times* bestselling author Brandon Mull

"Reading *The Unwanteds* was like discovering a brilliant, lost children's classic—except it's never going to be lost, because the readers will never, ever forget the magic they'll experience in its pages."

—James A. Owen, author and illustrator of *Here, There Be Dragons*.

Read all of The Unwanteds adventures!

» » « «

Also by Lisa McMann

» » « «

LISA McMANN

THE UNWANTEDS
Island of Silence

Aladdin
NEW YORK   LONDON   TORONTO   SYDNEY   NEW DELHI

For Matt

» » « «

ALADDIN

An imprint of Simon & Schuster Children's Publishing Division
1230 Avenue of the Americas, New York, NY 10020
First Aladdin paperback edition July 2013
Copyright © 2012 by Lisa McMann
All rights reserved, including the right of reproduction in whole or in part in any form.
ALADDIN is a trademark of Simon & Schuster, Inc., and related logo
is a registered trademark of Simon & Schuster, Inc.
For information about special discounts for bulk purchases, please contact Simon & Schuster
Special Sales at 1-866-506-1949 or business@simonandschuster.com.
The Simon & Schuster Speakers Bureau can bring authors to your live event.
For more information or to book an event contact the Simon & Schuster Speakers Bureau
at 1-866-248-3049 or visit our website at www.simonspeakers.com.
Designed by Karin Paprocki
The text of this book was set in Truesdell Regular.
Manufactured in the United States of America 0117 OFF
10
The Library of Congress has cataloged the hardcover edition as follows:
McMann, Lisa. Island of silence / by Lisa McMann. — 1st Aladdin hardcover ed. p. cm. — (Unwanteds ; bk. 2)
Summary: As the Wanteds, Unwanteds, and Necessaries struggle to adjust to changes
in their society, Mr. Today begins training fourteen-year-old Alex to replace him as Artime's leader
one day while Alex's disgraced twin, Aaron, connives to take over Quill.
[1. Social problems—Fiction. 2. Self-confidence—Fiction. 3. Magic—Fiction. 4. Brothers—Fiction. 5. Twins—
Fiction. 6. Creative ability—Fiction.] I. Title. PZ7.M478757Isl 2012 [Fic]—dc23 2011029418
ISBN 978-1-4424-0771-8 (hc)   ISBN 978-1-4424-0772-5 (pbk)
ISBN 978-1-4424-0773-2 (eBook)

Acknowledgments

Many thanks to all the Unwanteds at Aladdin who put this book together, from the highly visible to those behind the scenes. Special thanks to my editor, Liesa Abrams, who helps me see all my plot and character blind spots, and to Stuart Smith and the entire sales team, whose early enthusiasm for this series was so encouraging. Thanks as always to my amazing agent, Michael Bourret, who is a Gibraltar-sized rock in my life. And heaps of thanks to my assistant, Casey, for keeping me organized.

I am in awe of Owen Richardson for his gorgeous artwork and Karin Paprocki for her stunning cover design. Together you've made Artimé come alive in ways I could only imagine. Lauren Forte, you never cease to amaze me with the attention and love you give my books, every single time. Thank you.

To the scores of booksellers talking about this series . . . I'm so grateful for the way you have embraced the first book and put it into the hands of your customers. Special thanks to Unwanteds Gayle Shanks, Brandi Stewart, and the awesome folks at Changing Hands; Daniel Goldin and the amazing staff at Boswell Book Company; Becky Anderson, Jan Dundon, and the Anderson's Book Shop team; Sally and Camille at Pooh's Corner; my local East Valley B&N booksellers, including Sibley and Missy, who have been there for me since the beginning; and to the B&N folks at my home-home store in Holland, Michigan. You all rock.

To the teachers and librarians who have book-talked The Unwanteds with the magic words, "sent to their deaths," I thank you. To the team of Ed, Cindy, and Lynn back home, I thank you. To amazing people like Paul Hankins (who waits at the mailbox), Mr. Schu, Sarah Andersen, Jillian Heise (Thanks, Paulette!), and all the others whose wise words I follow daily, thank you for doing what you do. You are changing lives.

Belated thanks to the inspirational authors of my youth, some living, some gone but not forgotten, whose fantastical worlds influenced the creation of mine: Roald Dahl, E. B. White, Madeleine L'Engle, C. S. Lewis, Norton Juster, and Julie (Andrews) Edwards. I'd call you all Unwanted too, but I'm afraid you'd punch my lights out. Instead, readers may find the occasional hat tip to you throughout the series.

Everlasting gratitude to my Unwanted family and friends who have offered so much support for my little stories. Matt, I wouldn't want to do this job without you in the opposite corner of the library. Kilian, your illustrations are wonderful. You and Kennedy helped inspire this series and I'm so grateful for your help with magic spells. You guys are truly the best—there are no better kids in all the land. All the land, I say!

To you, dear reader: it doesn't matter whether your creativity lies in the arts or in apologies, in sciences or in sports, in numbers or in nature. If you think for yourself, even the least bit, I assure you that you are most certainly doomed. Welcome to Artimé.

Contents

Exposed

The sun was low over the sea off the shore of Artimé, making the distant islands look like flaming drops of lava on the horizon. An enormous winged cheetah named Simber came into view, flying over the nearby jungle. Clinging to his stone back were four Unwanted teenagers: Alex Stowe, Meghan Ranger, Samheed Burkesh, and Lani Haluki, all slipping and sliding and shrieking while they tried desperately to hang on. As they approached the lawn, Simber dove, nearly losing Lani off his back, but at the last moment grabbing her around the waist with his tail.

Mr. Today looked up at them as he walked toward the

LISA McMANN

mansion from Artimé's entrance. An angry-faced, broken-looking woman walked alongside him. The head magician held up his hand to signal Simber, who immediately spanned his wings to catch the air, and floated to the ground in a slow, surprisingly gentle sort of way. The beast took a dozen long steps before coming to a full stop, and then he knelt to let his passengers down. The four slid off and flopped to the grass, breathless and laughing.

Simber growled. He stood again regally on all fours and started walking away. "Therrre, now leave me alone," he said, pretending like he hadn't enjoyed any of it.

"Thanks, Simber," Alex called after him. The wind had twisted Alex's dark brown hair into tangled curls. He raked his fingers through it. It was getting long, and Alex had good reason for not cutting it. He didn't want anyone to mistake him for his twin brother, Aaron, ever again. He stood up and reached out his hand.

Lani grabbed it and pulled herself to her feet. She adjusted her component vest, and then smoothed wisps of straight black hair back into her braid. "I almost died," she said matter-of-factly. "Good thing Simber caught me with his tail or I'd be

LISA McMANN

completely dead right now. Not sure I'm ever doing that again, Alex."

"We would have saved you," Alex said. "Right, guys? I would have, anyway."

When Meghan and Samheed didn't answer, Lani and Alex turned to look at them. Samheed's grin was gone. His face paled and he stared past the others, toward Mr. Today and the woman who accompanied him.

Meghan reached out for Samheed's arm. "What's wrong?" she whispered. But she knew. They all knew, once they followed Samheed's gaze. It was the same thing that had happened over and over again in the past months, ever since Mr. Today had removed the gate between Artimé and Quill. Now Wanteds and Necessaries could visit and even reside in the land they never knew existed, and see the children they had once condemned to death—the family members they had thought were long gone.

The old mage, his hand on the woman's elbow, stopped her several yards from the group of teens. He turned and spoke to her with an earnest look on his face. The wrinkles around her eyes grew deeper, and then she nodded reluctantly and

LISA McMANN

stood firm, crossing her arms and tapping one foot slowly on the footpath, as if she had to be somewhere. Mr. Today approached alone and stood in front of the four friends, a kindly, sympathetic look crinkling about his eyes, and he said in a gentle voice, "Samheed, my boy. Your mother has come by to see you."

Not All Tea and Roses

I n the months since Artimé and Quill had opened up their border for the first time, after the deadly battle that showed Quill that creativity could hold its own in a fight, there had been many instances such as the one currently facing Samheed. In fact, it was all Mr. Today could do to accomplish his normal magely duties, what with the newly installed door knocker to the mansion being clacked all the time by frightened-looking visitors, unaccustomed to the bright colors and wandering creatures of Artimé. Daily Mr. Today was met with Necessaries who wanted to escape their slavelike conditions in Quill and take up residence in the

LISA McMANN

magical world of Artimé. Even a Wanted or two who felt the urge to rebel and ride the cutting edge of society joined them. Besides, the food and the landscape of Artimé were definitely more appealing than the newly fractured goings-on in Quill.

But at this moment, Samheed stared at the mage, his eyes as wide as a beavop's at the hour before dawn. "What does she want?" he asked in a quiet voice. "I have nothing to say to her." And while his tone was solid, he trembled inside, because he knew why his mother had finally come.

"She didn't say," Mr. Today said, "but I assume she'd like to talk about your father."

Samheed nodded, and then stood on tiptoe to peer over the tall mage's shoulder. "She doesn't look happy," he said. "But then, I guess she never did." He glanced tentatively at Alex, and then at the girls. "What do you think?" he asked gruffly. Samheed was not one to enjoy asking for advice.

Meghan, her expression hard, spoke up first. "I think you should say no right off." She bit her lip to keep herself from saying more, and her eyes filled with angry tears. She blinked hard to disperse them. But she couldn't contain her thoughts.

"It's not worth it, Sam. It's not. All they do is tell you how much they wish you really were dead."

Alex looked earnestly at his best friend. "Aw, Meg," he said, shoving his hands into his pockets. He didn't know what else to add—nothing seemed to comfort her these days. She and Sean had gone into Quill to approach their parents early on, hoping to be welcomed. But while their parents seemed almost pleased to see Sean again after so many years, they held some sort of bitterness toward Meghan, blaming her for their sorry lives because she was the second Unwanted they'd produced, which made them outcasts in Quill. Meghan hadn't been the same since then.

All Alex knew was that his own parents hadn't come by looking for him, and that he hadn't gone into Quill to seek them out, either. It was an easy choice. He knew his parents put their full support behind Aaron because Aaron was a Wanted. And they always would—that was just the way Mr. and Mrs. Stowe were. Alex knew better than to expect a happy reunion. Or a reunion at all.

Lani touched Samheed's arm. "You'll never know unless

you talk to her. It might be okay," she said. But they all knew that hers was the rare example of things working out okay. Her mother and younger brother, Henry, were now living here in Artimé, while her father, Gunnar Haluki, the former spy and new high priest of Quill, resided in Quill's palace for the time being to govern, now that the former evil High Priest Justine was dead.

Samheed twisted the toe of his boot in the grass. "You guys don't understand," he said. "It's different for me."

"Sam, come on. You didn't have a choice," Lani said wearily, as if she'd said it more than once before. "And besides, it wasn't you. It was Mr. Appleblossom."

"Because of me."

Lani's eyes sparked. "If he hadn't done it, there'd only be three of us standing here right now."

No one could refute that, so they remained silent.

"Mr. Today?" Samheed asked, looking up. He searched the man's face for answers.

But Mr. Today had none. "The decision is yours alone," he said. "I'll stay with you if you choose to speak with your mother. And if you choose not to, I'll ask her to leave."

Samheed gazed out over the lawn to the strip of sand at the shore, thinking, his jaw set. He muttered bitterly under his breath and turned back to seek wisdom once again from the old mage's eyes. Finally, angrily, he kicked at the ground and shook his head at Mr. Today. "Tell her no."

Blindly he broke through his circle of friends and headed toward the shore. They watched him go, but no one followed. They knew Samheed well enough by now to let him brood alone.

That Mess Called Quill

Aaron Stowe stepped outside the university into the hot, gray morning and scanned the road toward the palace, the peak of which he could just barely see from this distance. This tallest point of the palace was bent just slightly to one side, almost as if it had to hunch over to fit under the barbed-wire ceiling of Quill, or perhaps it helped hold up this sky border along with the forty-foot-high walls that encircled the land.

Aaron remembered the times he'd spent in the palace as assistant secretary when the High Priest Justine was alive. Only months ago he'd had so much going for him—his highly praised creation of the Favored Farm for the Wanteds, the solution to the poor Quillitary vehicle performance, and the big fix for the water shortage throughout Quill. He'd had vast plans to work his way into senior governor status and someday rule the land. But all his hopes and aspirations were shattered by former Senior Governor Haluki, who had stripped Aaron of his title and all the privileges that went with it, sending him back to university like an ordinary Wanted.

Aaron cursed the name of Artimé and all that belonged to it, for it had opened up so much chaos and insanity into his structured, regulated world. The only good thing was that Haluki was being extremely cautious about making changes, and hadn't ventured to do much of anything yet. Though, Aaron mused, if Haluki did make a drastic change and Quill rebelled, Aaron might just have the faintest chance at becoming *something* once again.

He wrinkled up his nose. The smell outside was getting worse every day. Garbage piled up along the streets, and waste of all kinds was not getting buried properly. Quill was turning into a giant cesspool now that half the Necessaries had left their duties here and flocked to Artimé. None of the Wanteds would take over such menial, dirty tasks—that was sure. It was far beneath them. So things sat as they were until the remaining Necessaries could get around to it after their regular tasks were completed. It wouldn't be long, Aaron knew, before Quill was in real trouble. The only question was how Aaron could capitalize on this latest development now that his glorious leader was dead. He pinched the bridge of his nose, remembering. Wishing. *Dear High Priest Justine . . . if you only knew what they've done to us.* He felt a rare pang in his chest at the memory of her but stifled it immediately, knowing full well she'd have condemned anyone for feeling things.

Across the narrow road two men paused in their walk to look at the mess in the ditch. "I went to Haluki yesterday about this," one said to the other.

"Useless thug."

"Shh," the first said, looking over his shoulder. "He's the high priest."

"Still," said the second. "What's he doing about it? What's his big solution to this mess? S-s-songing?" He stumbled on the unfamiliar word.

"He suggested we clean it up ourselves," the first said,

picking his teeth with a makeshift toothpick and then tossing it onto the pile of junk. "And milk the cows, too, while we're at it. Can you imagine that?"

A group of three walkers approached and overheard the conversation. They congregated to offer their complaints as well. "He told me to pick my own corn if I want corn," one said. "Looked me right in the eye and said it." The others shook their heads in disbelief.

Just then a group of university boys brushed past Aaron on their way into the building. "Hello," Aaron said, but the boys ignored him, as everyone had done since the battle. Ever since people found out he'd had a hand in this whole mess. Aaron kept his expression cool. He looked down at the dirt and then he closed his eyes for a moment. With a heavy sigh, he turned and followed them inside.

Aaron sat down on the edge of the meager bed in his university dorm room, elbows propped on his knees, chin resting in his hands. He stared at the bare wall across from him, where there once was a door for a short amount of time in the middle of a fateful night. But the wall held no answers to his now frequently asked questions. What was to become of him? How could this have happened? Here he sat, powerless. Stripped of his title and his access to the palace, scorned by his classmates so much that he'd begun skipping classes, hated by Unwanteds far and wide for trying to impersonate his twin brother—who was apparently so beloved by them—in the heat of the battle. And dismissed, considered worthless by all the other governors.

Aaron felt his chest tighten in fury. He closed his eyes, concentrating, willing himself to be calm but failing miserably. He felt like shouting all the vilest words he could think of at the top of his voice. He felt like stringing up Alex, High Priest Haluki, and that freakishly genteel Mr. Today, and making them suffer the way he was suffering now.

A strange growling sound began in the back of Aaron's throat, almost like a roar, and it escaped with a loud huff of air. "Garr!" He gripped the fabric edge of his flimsy mattress and twisted it, tensing all the muscles in his body, his face growing very hot. It was both frightening and liberating to let such feelings happen, and he knew he should stop, but in this case there was no turning back. "Raaah!" he said this time. And then "GRRAAH!" He flipped over on the bed, facedown now, and

LISA McMANN

pounded it with his fists, trying to let out the uncontrollable noises into the thin blanket so that they were muffled. He couldn't let anyone hear him. He wasn't sure what they'd do.

And then his eyes began to sting. Like giant dusty craters in the most desolate part of Quill, his eyes, unaccustomed to tears, achingly filled and threatened to spill.

But he held them in. Heaving on the bed, emotion spewing forth in every breath, Aaron brought his hands to his closed lids and pressed back the tears. His throat ached and it felt like something was stuck there. "Calm down," he whispered. "Calm down." His breaths slowed, and he wiped his face. He lay there for a moment more, realizing the grave extent of personal weakness he'd just shown.

Quickly he got off the bed, ashamed of his behavior. He went to his bucket of tepid water and dipped his hand in. He splashed the water on his face, carelessly allowing the excess to drip on the floor, wasting it.

"Great land of Quill," he muttered. He dried his face with his sleeve. "Come on. Get a grip, Stowe."

He turned back to his bed to straighten out the blanket. And then he sat at his tiny table and opened his textbook on the history of Quill. A small headache had formed between his eyes, so he pushed his thumb and forefinger into the inner points of his brows, trying to massage the pain away. The words blurred, but one pulsing thought pressed through. His mantra. *I am strong! May Quill prevail with all I have in me!*

A moment later there was a knock on his door. He froze. Had someone heard him cry out?

"Who's there?" he asked.

Aaron heard a shuffle outside his door, and four armed Quillitary soldiers burst through the door into the room. Aaron stood immediately, his chair scraping the floor and nearly tipping over. His eyes widened. He'd met them all before.

"Former Assistant Secretary Aaron Stowe?" said the apparent leader in a gruff voice.

"Obviously."

"You're being terminated."

Aaron's heart leaped to his throat. Terminated? As in "sent to the Ancients Sector"? As in "put to sleep"? It couldn't be—they didn't do that to young, healthy Wanteds. He struggled to regain the confident demeanor he'd projected on these people just months before. "What do you mean?"

"Your presence is no longer required at the university."

Aaron shook his head. "I don't understand what you are saying."

"Pack your things," the man said icily, taking a step toward Aaron. "You are no longer welcome here."

Problems
Unforeseen

Every day more and more Necessaries invaded Artimé. Mr. Today insisted that the Unwanteds treat their new neighbors with the utmost respect, but it was difficult when they were turning up left and right, asking endless questions. "What's that noise coming from the bushes?" "Where exactly is the Great Lake of Boiling Oil?" "Do the creatures bite?" It was becoming annoying. Even Ms. Octavia, the octogator art instructor, occasionally chomped her teeth together at them when she couldn't take them staring any longer at her seven flowing appendages (the eighth one was still just a nub, in the process

LISA McMANN

of regenerating after having been lopped off in the battle).

And then there was the question of magic. Would the Necessaries be allowed to learn and perform it? What about attending classes? And using the tubes?

"All newcomers will be allowed the same rights as the Unwanteds," Mr. Today declared at his now-weekly address on the lawn. "It will become clear who is capable of magic and who is not. For those who are, we're exceedingly grateful to have you on our side should we ever be forced to fight again."

While the Necessaries looked on as if they'd been given the first gift of their lives, some of the Unwanteds grumbled. But Mr. Today only smiled at the grumblers and said lightly, "Let's not create a whole new class of Unwanteds, all right?" That seemed to change some Unwanteds' minds in a hurry.

Mr. Today appointed Alex's class of Unwanteds—twenty altogether—to be teachers and tour guides to the newcomers. "You all remember the transition well, and you know oodles more than the most recent group," he said. "Remember how strange it was those first days, and how confusing? I think your class will be of great help and comfort to them, and to me as well." His voice sounded tired.

Alex studied the man. His face was looking a bit drawn these days, and Alex wondered if Mr. Today was getting any sleep at all. "We'll take care of it," he said. The rest of the group murmured their compliance.

Mr. Today coupled his hands together. "Splendid," he said. "Meghan, why don't you and . . ." He tapped his finger to his lips, searching the group, his eyes finally landing on one of the less vocal Unwanteds. "Cole Wickett. Yes, Meghan and Cole, you two put your heads together and organize this mess for me, will you?"

Cole Wickett, unused to being singled out by the great mage, blushed profusely and nodded.

"Of course we will," said Meghan, her eyes actually lighting up at the task, and she looked eager for the first time in a month. She took after her favorite instructor, Ms. Morning, who was also Mr. Today's daughter, and a very organized woman. This was perfect for Meghan, as she knew she needed something challenging to occupy her mind these days.

"Wonderful." Mr. Today turned to Alex. "And I'd like to see you in my office after lunch, please."

Alex hadn't spent much time at all in Mr. Today's office

since the night Aaron had come through the magical 3-D doorway, except for occasional nighttime visits to check the blackboards. "Yes, sir," he said. So much had changed since then.

They dispersed, leaving Meghan and Cole to organize the orientation process for the newcomers.

"Look at them," Samheed said to Alex and Lani with eyes narrowed. "Don't they look nice together?"

Alex glanced at Meghan and Cole, and opened his mouth to agree, but Lani poked him in the ribs and gave him a knowing smile. He turned his quizzical look to her, instead, and mouthed, "What?"

Lani rolled her eyes. She motioned toward Samheed with her thumb, and then looked back at Meghan. "He's jealous," she mouthed back at him.

Alex squinted. "Huh?" he said aloud.

Lani sighed. "Nothing." She turned to Samheed. "Yes," she said. "They do look sort of cozy. I didn't know they were friends."

"He's Ms. Morning's student too. A drummer." Samheed kept watching Meghan over his shoulder and he nearly

LISA McMANN

stumbled over a platyprot. "Watch it, fuzzball," Samheed said to the magical bird.

The platyprot hopped and tumbled out of the way, mumbling, "Watch it, fuzzball. Watch it, fuzzball." Its voice mimicked Samheed's sarcasm. Two nearby Necessaries stared at it and backed away, confused.

Lani started to explain platyprots to the Necessaries, but then she stopped. She'd figured out the strange-looking birds just fine on her own. The new people would too. So instead she just offered them a reassuring smile, linked arms with Samheed and Alex, and pulled them along to the mansion for lunch.

Afterward Alex made his way to the foyer, where Simber towered motionless on his pedestal on one side of the door. On the other side stood Florence, another enormous living statue, who often led the Unwanteds in warrior training. Alex climbed the marble stairs to the upper level, past the brand-new hallway that Mr. Today had created in order to hold the newcomers, the families' hallway, the boys' hallway, and the girls' hallway (which he couldn't see), to the very last hallway off the balcony. A mostly secret hallway it was, since very few knew it was there. Samheed knew. Will Blair had been another who could see it back when he was alive.

Alex entered the wide, wood-planked hall and went past two sets of mysterious-looking doors to the place where the invisible glass wall sometimes stood. Alex gingerly reached his hand out, feeling for it, having once smashed into it quite ferociously and never wanting to do that again. But the glass was down, and Alex proceeded to the end of the hallway, where a giant picture window allowed one to overlook much of Artimé and the entrance to Quill.

On the right side of the hallway was a small kitchen with some strange mechanical-looking things and a tube that Mr. Today had said led to nasty places. And on the left was the door to Mr. Today's office, which stood open. The old magician looked up and smiled warmly when Alex approached.

"Ah! Hello again, my dear boy," Mr. Today said, leaning back in his chair and stretching his arms up over his head. Nimbly he propped his feet up on his desk and waved Alex into the room. "Sit down, sit down. I've been thinking about you quite a lot lately. Quite a lot indeed," he said. "You see, I believe you're the one person in all of Artimé who can help me."

LISA McMANN

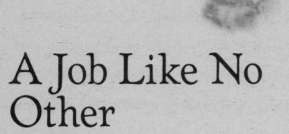

A Job Like No Other

O h, wow, really?" Alex asked with a nervous laugh. "Me?" He blinked, not knowing what else to say. He sat down a little straighter than usual in the chair and tried not to glance at the blackboards behind the old mage, but they were so tempting, flashing from scene to scene in Quill. Alex could ignore most of them, but he couldn't keep his eyes off the blackboard that showed the university, including his brother's dorm room.

"Yes, you," said Mr. Today, rocking slightly back and forth in his chair in a most comfortable manner. "I've thought and thought over the past months. Years, actually, but that was in a much broader sense, of course. I've been more focused these last months. Since that day in the boat, actually. And I'm quite sure."

Alex tried to follow what Mr. Today was saying, but truthfully he had no idea what they were talking about. "Mm-hmm," he said.

"And really, there are others that *could*, but none actually willing, you see. Like Claire, for instance—Ms. Morning. Completely able, completely unwilling." Mr. Today clucked his tongue.

"Ms. Morning." Alex nodded absently. He watched the blackboard when his brother's room came on the screen, and wished it would just freeze there. He stared at it and muttered, "Freeze." But the scene changed as always, rotating through a few different university views.

"Yes, and I don't blame her. She's seen enough, all right. But she'll be wonderful help. No doubt about that. Besides, I've just not had this knowing feeling about anybody else before now. "

Alex turned his attention back to Mr. Today. Sheepishly, he said, "I'm terribly sorry, Mr. Today. Um . . . what are we talking about, again? Ms. Morning is what?"

Mr. Today smiled and shuffled through papers on his desk. "Good question. What *are* we talking about, indeed? I should start again from the beginning this time, I imagine."

He chuckled to himself as he sometimes did when trying to explain very large, complicated things.

Alex, mystified, nodded.

"You see, Alex," Mr. Today said, and he abruptly stopped rocking his chair, took his feet off the desk, and leaned forward earnestly, "once we've made it through this lengthy transition period with the open border and the Necessaries and whatnot, I've decided that it's time I take a little holiday."

"A . . . a what? Where would you go? To Quill?" Alex thought he knew what a holiday was, but no one really talked about them here—definitely not in Quill, as there was nowhere to go, and not here, either, because no one desired to leave. Alex's first experience with the word was in Quill—a "holiday" was the day of the year that the Unwanteds were Purged. Here in Artimé they celebrated a holiday on the same day, but it was to welcome the Unwanteds. Alex didn't think Mr. Today meant it like either of those. But then there was the literature Alex had studied with Mr. Appleblossom in Actors' Studio. They'd read plays in which characters took holidays that consisted of weeks at a time. Characters would leave home to see the world.

"Dear me, no. Not Quill. I visit there often enough for my

LISA McMANN

weekly peace meeting with Gunnar." Mr. Today scratched his head. "No . . . I've been longing for quite some time now to go elsewhere." He ran his bony fingers through his shock of white hair, making it stand quite straight up, impressively defying gravity. "I want to visit the island where Justine and I grew up, before we left everything and started life here in Quill all those years ago."

Alex stared. "But . . ."

"And in order to do that, I'll need some help running things here." He tilted his head and looked pointedly at Alex.

"What, you mean . . . me?" Alex almost didn't say it, because it sounded so ludicrous.

"You, and others. But mostly you, yes."

"Why?"

Mr. Today smiled warmly. "Because, Alex. Don't you see? Don't you understand? Remember our conversation in the boat, when we were on the way to the palace during the battle?"

Alex struggled to remember, but that day was fuzzy in his mind from the severe injuries he'd sustained when Aaron had tried to kill him shortly after that ride.

"I told you that Justine was my twin. And I mentioned that I felt a certain closeness with you because of the twin connection, and the way we understand things. Do you remember that?"

"Oh." Alex nodded. "Yes, I remember."

"So now, over the years to come, I want to teach you everything about Artimé—how we got here, how I created things, how the world runs. This and that. Here and there. Then and now." He drummed his fingertips on the desk as if they were the musical accompaniment to this announcement.

Alex sat, stunned. "Wait. You want to teach all of that . . . to me." He almost laughed. "Why? I'm just a kid."

"Several reasons, really. Younger people learn faster and are able to retain more information in their brains, for one, so that makes your age absolutely ideal. And because I need a temporary replacement so I can take a vacation—I've worked every day for fifty years, after all. Every day. I think it's time for a break." His eyes were bright at the thought. "I'll also need a permanent replacement one day for obvious reasons," he said, pointing to his wrinkled face and tired eyes. "I'm not getting any younger."

Alex looked at Mr. Today in horror. He didn't want to think about that.

Seeing Alex's stricken face, Mr. Today smiled and continued

matter-of-factly. "Oh, I'll live at least another five or ten years, perhaps even more. I feel perfectly fine now, I assure you, but isn't this the best time for me to train someone? This is not a job to be learned overnight—it took me years to build Artimé to the grandness that you see here today, and it'll take quite some time to teach it all to you, especially when you're still studying with your instructors every day."

"But . . ." Alex hardly knew where to start.

Mr. Today went on. "And, well, obviously I know you are young and want some time for fun. Fourteen . . . you've hardly lived." He gazed thoughtfully somewhere beyond Alex for a moment. "We were fourteen when Justine and I discovered this island and began planning Quill." Abruptly he turned back to Alex. "But you'll have time to grow up and do other things too, of course. This is a long process and—"

Alex, feeling a bit overwhelmed, interrupted. "But I don't understand why somebody else can't do it. What about Ms. Morning?"

"As I mentioned earlier in my babbling, she's not interested. She is highly capable and will be a tremendous help to you while I am traveling, but she is not the future leader of Artimé."

"What about Ms. Octavia? Or Mr. Appleblossom, or Sean Ranger or any of the other adults?"

Mr. Today shook his head. "They have their own purposes and passions in life, in Artimé. They have other responsibilities—big ones, important ones. They love what they do. And besides, they are not suited for the role or I would have been working with them already."

"And you're saying I'm suited for the role?" Alex stared at Mr. Today.

"Perfectly."

"How can you possibly know that?" Alex wasn't trying to be offensive—he truly wanted to know.

"Alex, your brother, Aaron . . ." Mr. Today paused, preparing his words. "Consider this with me for a moment, and if I am wrong, I invite you to say so." He leaned forward. "I truly believe, my dear boy, that Aaron's power-hungry days are far from over. I think . . . I think you know that already."

Alex lowered his head.

"Am I wrong?" Mr. Today asked in a gentle voice.

"I don't know." But he knew that if he had to bet his life on it, he would bet that Mr. Today was totally correct. "No, you're right."

"The recent battle is done. But if we are honest with ourselves—and I think we always must be if we are to prevail—we'll admit that our battle with Quill was probably not the only one we'll ever see. It was simply the first. Justine is dead, but Aaron Stowe is as smart and determined as you are." He placed his hands on the desk before him and leaned toward Alex. With an urgent whisper, he said, "Don't you see, Alex? The Marcus and Justine battle is being reborn right now, this year, this very day. It's being reborn in you and Aaron."

Alex's eyes widened but he remained deathly still.

"And I'm very sorry it's happening," Mr. Today said. After a moment, he continued with great hope in his voice. "Be assured, my boy. Be assured! You are already doing so much better than I did. You've already proven yourself and your loyalty. Artimé needs you desperately. Alex, *you* are the one who knows Aaron best. And I hate to say this, but as long as he is alive, he is Artimé's most powerful enemy." Mr. Today looked into Alex's eyes. "Quite simply, we need you."

Alex shifted in his seat and looked away, staring instead at

Mr. Today's hands for a long moment. It was all too much. The pressure was blinding. He shook his head and said softly, "But Mr. Today, what if I don't want to have a lifelong battle with my brother?" He lifted his gaze once again.

The mage pressed his lips together, and then slowly pushed back from his intense pose and sat in his chair once again without a word, perhaps stunned by this, the simplest question he'd never considered.

Just then, over Mr. Today's shoulder, the university blackboard switched to Aaron's room. Out of habit, and despite the serious conversation at hand, Alex glanced at it. Then he leaned forward and stared at it hard. A second later he stood up in alarm. "What are they doing to him?"

Mr. Today, who had turned abruptly in his chair toward the blackboards when he saw that Alex's attention had been diverted, watched the scene. His jaw slacked in surprise. When the picture changed, Mr. Today bounded from his chair as if he were an energetic teenager and ran out of his office, across the hall, and into the kitchenette. "We'll talk again soon," he called out to Alex. With a grim look on his face, he stepped into the forbidden tube and disappeared.

Aaron the Streeted

Aaron Stowe, the Wanted, former assistant secretary to the High Priest Justine, former future senior governor, former future high priest of the great land of Quill, stared at the Quillitary soldiers encroaching upon him in the tiny room. And as much as he wanted to boom loudly at them, "Away from me, or the high priest will have your necks!" he knew—and worse, *they* knew—that he had no authority anymore.

Instead, in as big a voice as he could draw upon, which wasn't very big at all, he said, "I demand to know what you are doing here." Something crackled in his throat on the second

33 « Island of Silence

LISA McMANN

syllable of "demand," and the pitch stayed especially high for another two beats, which made two of the Quillitary soldiers snicker and repeat the words exactly as Aaron had said them.

Aaron took a step backward, feeling the heel of his shoe brush against the wall behind him. He had nowhere to go.

"Pack up his things!" the Quillitary leader ordered. "Get him out of here."

"No," Aaron whispered. His hands quivered, and he clenched them tight to stop it.

The soldiers pulled Aaron's change of clothing from the dresser drawer, gathered his washcloth, towel, his few toiletries, and his books, and they stuffed everything into Aaron's book bag. One soldier shoved the bag into Aaron's chest as hard as he could, slamming him against the wall and knocking the wind out of him. Aaron gasped and doubled over, trying to breathe, reaching desperately to grasp the bag as it fell, and just managing to slip his fingers around the strap and hang on. Two other soldiers flanked him, grabbed him by the arms, and pulled him back to his feet. They marched him out of his dorm room, down the hall, and out the university entrance. Other students scrambled to get out of their way, and then watched guardedly as one of their own top students was ousted in disgrace.

Once outside, the soldiers gave him a final shove. Aaron tripped and fell to the dirt road. He cowered near the ground for a moment as the soldiers climbed into their Quillitary vehicle and painstakingly brought it to life, screeching and groaning. When it finally *put-putted* down the road at a snail's pace, Aaron shakily rose to his feet. He dusted off his pants, picked up his book bag, and dusted that off too. And all the while he was thinking over and over, *Where am I to go now?*

When he had dusted off everything that could be dusted, he glanced over his shoulder at the people watching him from the university, and notched his chin just slightly higher in an attempt at regaining some dignity. He looked to his right toward the amphitheater and the Necessary housing quadrants where his parents lived, and then to the left, toward the Quillitary Sector and the palace.

Finally, summoning up a bit of courage, he turned to the right and started walking.

Alex the Ponderer

Alex watched the blackboard anxiously as bits of Aaron's ousting appeared before him. From Aaron's dormitory room to the lobby to the exterior of the building, Alex caught much of the story. And while Alex had known for a while that his twin could never be trusted again, he couldn't help feeling a twinge in his chest when he imagined how Aaron must feel.

When there was nothing more to see, and since Mr. Today didn't return, Alex eventually peeled his eyes away from the screens and went back to his regular class schedule, troubled though he was. Later that night Clive,

Alex's interactive blackboard, announced that a message had arrived from Mr. Today.

"Well, what is it?" Alex asked.

"All is well," Clive read.

"What's that supposed to mean?"

Clive just stared at Alex. "Well, Alex, I think it means everything has gone completely haywire."

"You know," Alex said, "I could do without the sarcasm once in a while."

"I do indeed know that." Clive smiled saucily and disappeared.

Still puzzled over the pithy report, yet feeling a tiny bit better about things, Alex fell asleep pondering the unusual discussion he'd had with Mr. Today.

He didn't tell his friends or anyone else about Mr. Today's sudden insistence that Alex would one day become Artimé's leader. But over the next days Alex began to notice something strange: an occasional toothy smile from Ms. Octavia; an encouraging glance from Mr. Appleblossom; a rare nod from Simber as Alex walked with his friends to the dining room one day.

"What was that about?" Lani asked Alex. Simber rarely acknowledged students when he was sitting at his post by the front door, for he was often quite occupied with sampling the air for anything unusual, listening for things that might indicate an attack was imminent. He took his job as Mr. Today's primary mansion guard very seriously.

Alex shrugged. "Maybe he has an itch. Could be fleas." He glanced back fearfully at Simber after he said it, remembering too late the statue's incredible sense of hearing. Simber narrowed his eyes at Alex. "Sorry," he mouthed at the giant beast. And he was sorry. He just didn't know how to handle Lani's question, or how to explain.

He also didn't know how to explain to Mr. Today that he would be happy to help in whatever way he could, but that Mr. Today had definitely made a grave mistake, and Alex would not be taking over any magely leadership roles now or in the future.

Later Alex and Lani headed to the somewhat accidentally hidden third floor of the library, which both Alex and Samheed had discovered last year. Lani and Meghan now knew about it as well, and the four often did their homework together there quite undisturbed but for the occasionally yawning tiki statue that had once saved Alex, and the blackboard with a rare announcement.

While Lani worked on history and literature, Alex created a list of reasons why he'd be absolutely, positively no good as the next leader of Artimé.

1. Just not great in all the various branches of the arts. Strong in painting/drawing/writing but weak in singing and only so-so in acting and performance.

2. Kind of a pathetic weakling. No muscles.

3. Almost ruined the world when the governors came last year. Would probably accidentally destroy it all single-handedly.

4. Not really into the lifelong family fight thing. Would rather ignore problems like Aaron because they will probably go away.

5. Not exactly fond of having to deal with any other problems, either.

6. Lack of confidence . . . after what happened last time.

LISA McMANN

Alex stared at the last one, remembering the pain of Aaron sending that deadly scatterclip at him. He rubbed the tiny scar on his chest, near his heart. It was still pink, and his skin was sensitive there. He'd been confident back then, almost cocky about his abilities. To be injured so badly by someone who did magic accidentally—it was a blow all right. And, actually, still a little bit too hard to talk about. He turned his pencil around to erase number six.

Lani looked up from her work and watched Alex wiping tiny bits of eraser off his notebook page. She reached across the table and tapped his hand. "What are you working on?"

He lifted his head and couldn't help but smile at the earnest look on her face. "Wow. Did you know that in the light from this table, your eyes are seriously bright blue?" he asked. "I wish paint came in that color."

Lani blushed. She pulled her hand back self-consciously. "Well, if anybody can make that color, it's you," she said. "Maybe you should work on that."

"Maybe I will," Alex said. He held her eyes for a moment longer, remembering the time he kissed her cheek during Magical Warrior Training. He smiled impishly and looked down at his notebook again, sobering as he read over his reasons. It didn't take much for him to realize that Lani or even Meghan or Samheed would make a much better ruler of Artimé than he.

After a moment he asked, still staring at his list, "Can I tell you a secret?"

"Sure."

"You have to promise not to say anything to anybody."

Lani hesitated. "Okay. I promise." She put her pencil down and folded her arms in front of her, ready to listen.

Alex looked up at her. He bit his lip.

"Well?" Lani prompted.

"I . . . well, you see, Mr. Today . . ." He couldn't say it. It sounded so insane. "Crud. Never mind. I'm sorry."

Lani frowned. "Okaaay."

"I shouldn't have said anything. It's just dumb anyway."

Lani shrugged. "Whatever." She pulled her book toward her and focused on it, and then—quite ceremoniously—turned her chair to the side so she wasn't facing Alex anymore.

Alex squeezed his eyes shut and muttered under his breath. And then he looked at her profile for a long moment. The way her hair parted at her shoulder, her olive skin tanned by the sun. Her perfect nose and lips. He flipped the page of his notebook and sketched her.

When he was finished, he wrote in tiny letters in the bottom right corner:

For Lani, for always.

Alexander Stowe

He pulled the page out of the notebook, took a tiny piece of translucent rubber from his pocket, dropped it on the center of the drawing, and said, "Preserve." The rubber melted and spread quickly to the edges, and the paper developed a glossy sheen that made it virtually indestructible.

Lani looked up when she heard Alex's magical utterance.

Alex slid the drawing over to her and watched as her eyes flitted over it, coming to rest on the words. She smiled then, studied it a moment longer, folded it carefully, and put it in her pocket.

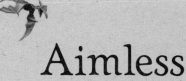

Aimless

It didn't take long for Aaron to realize that he could never go home to his parents—not if he wanted to retain a shred of class distinction. A Wanted going back to a Necessary family? It stank of defeat and mistaken classification. And while his feet carried him in the direction of the Necessary quadrants, Aaron knew that he would not stop there, nor would he indicate in any way that he was doing anything more than taking a walk for his own pleasure . . . in the odoriferous, scorching heat.

As night fell Aaron's feet grew tired. He approached the Necessary housing, unable to stop himself from stealing a

LISA McMANN

glimpse of number 54-43 as he passed by his family's row. It felt so familiar after years of walking home from school this way, yet that place was no longer home, nor could it ever be called home again. He increased his pace along the road and flipped up his shirt collar to partially shield his face, hoping none of his former neighbors would recognize him. But soon he discovered that the neighborhoods were all eerily quiet. *Everyone is in Artimé*, Aaron realized after a while.

Soon he left the housing quadrants behind and the land grew desolate. Late that evening he neared the well-lit entrance to the magical world and slowed his pace. Two stone gargoyles sat together on one side of the entrance, startling Aaron when they stood up and walked away.

Looking in, Aaron saw people and creatures on the lawn, laughing and having a good time. Eating and drinking and resting. A cool breeze blew through the opening, and Aaron closed his eyes, letting it wash over him. He swallowed hard, his throat parched. It would be so easy to sneak in and get something to eat and drink, he thought. Except for one minor problem.

He heard a snort and felt a hot, moist blast of air on his face.

He opened his eyes and stumbled backward, knowing from experience what it was.

Arija, one of four enormous, silky-furred, long-necked creatures called girrinos, whose duty it was to guard the entrance, knew Aaron by smell now and had smelled him coming. "You again," she said.

"What of it? I thought everyone was welcome here."

"If you meant us no harm, you'd be welcome. But we've seen no sign of that. What do you want?"

Aaron shrugged. "I'm just taking a walk."

"Looks like you're just standing."

"You have something against me standing in Quill now?"

"Not at all. Stand there all you like. Enjoy the fresh air." Arija sat down facing him, the ground shaking slightly when she did so. Her face was still at eye level with the boy. "You want to talk? Let's talk. What's new at the university? How are things going for you now? Are you enjoying the stench as much as the others who have decided to come here to stay?"

Aaron scowled. "Be quiet." He could see High Priest Haluki's family sitting on a blanket, eating and drinking, and a wave of fury swept through him.

"Ooh, such a mouth on you. Do you speak to your mother that way? I should hope not."

"Silence!" Aaron said.

Arija laughed merrily. "Such a demanding tone. I'm sure everyone pays great attention to you when you do that—all your minions. Where are they, by the way?" She tilted her head. "Didn't you travel with guards once upon a time?"

Without a word, Aaron cast a final furtive glance at the food and water inside the gate, and then he turned away from Arija and began walking once again.

"Sweet dreams," Arija called out.

Aaron clenched his fists and shoved them into his pockets, scratching his knuckles on the harsh fabric. He walked until he was out of sight of Artimé, cursing Haluki and Mr. Today and his own brother for being the cause of all the bad that had happened to him.

When there were no more lights to guide him in this remotest part of Quill, he moved off the road and sank to the ground against the wall to sleep. He stayed there in the shadow of the wall for two days.

» » « «

LISA McMANN

On the third morning Aaron ignored the few travelers passing by and staring at him. He got up and continued walking, quite weak for lack of water in this heat, but what else could he do? He began to search the ditches for anything that could be considered edible or drinkable, but he knew his chances of finding anything were terrible since it was against the law to throw away food, and there wasn't enough to eat or drink in Quill to make anyone wish to throw it away in the first place.

Aaron pondered it all from his new perspective of homeless and hungry—and he began to wonder why *anyone* would wish to stay in Quill when life looked so good in Artimé. If he were high priest, he knew what he'd do. He'd make Quill better than Artimé. He'd create more food—an abundance of food. And he'd utilize the ocean he never knew existed until a few months ago. Indeed, he had to question (but only slightly) the sanity of the High Priest Justine to keep such a thing a secret when it held so much potential. It was puzzling.

If Aaron were high priest, he'd create a way to make that nasty seawater drinkable. And he'd open up a passage to the water on this side of Quill and figure out if there was anything in the ocean—like some sort of chicken of the sea—that people

47 « Island of Silence

LISA McMANN

could actually eat. *Wouldn't that be something?* he thought. *An endless supply of food.* He grew nearly delirious at the thought.

As the day wore on, Aaron found himself on exactly the opposite side of the island from the university—near the Ancients Sector and burial area. There were a few people around, and Aaron wondered briefly if his father might be out digging graves today, but then realized it was late and all the Necessaries who'd stayed in Quill would have headed home by now, or out to do the jobs of the traitors who'd left.

Aaron stopped at the death post, a tall, branchless, dead tree trunk that had been anchored into the dirt and was leaning against the burial shed. On it were posted the most recent deaths. He took a long look at the list of names of the recently departed, though it wasn't very up to date since only teachers were allowed to write, and they didn't have time to stop at the Ancients Sector very often to update the list. Only the Wanteds got their names listed, but this list was longer than usual due to the battle with Artimé.

His eyes moved to General Blair's name, and then to the High Priest Justine's. Aaron stared at it reverently. His throat was scorched from thirst, but now it ached even more from the sorrow he knew he shouldn't feel. With significant effort in his weak state, he touched the letters of her name and closed his eyes. Using his well-trained mind and all the effort he had in him, he willed his sorrow to turn into bitterness, knowing that his bitterness would soon grow into a most unhealthy desire for revenge. And revenge was necessary now. After all that had happened in recent weeks, Aaron knew the truth: Revenge was the only thing that would keep him alive.

LISA McMANN

Meghan Rules

Meghan called the Necessaries to order on the lawn, clapping her hands to get their attention. The other nineteen Unwanteds from Alex's year stood in line nearby, feeling fairly important as the crowd gazed upon them with a certain amount of awe.

"Welcome," Meghan said. "We are delighted to have you here!"

Samheed poked Alex. "She sounds just like Mr. Today."

Alex grinned. "Definitely."

Lani shushed them.

"I'd like to start by introducing your group leaders," Meghan went on. She began calling the names alphabetically, and everyone stepped forward when their names were called. Alex glanced at Lani, whose face was hard.

"What's wrong?" Alex whispered.

"It reminds me of our Purge. Same names, same order," she said. "I don't like it."

"You're right," Alex said. And it did feel ominous.

Samheed, who overheard the conversation, said nothing, but his eyes were troubled. "Don't say anything to Meg," he said. "She'd feel bad. I'm sure she didn't mean it to be like that."

Alex and Lani nodded. When Samheed turned his attention to Meghan, who was assigning him his group, Lani elbowed Alex in the ribs. "See?"

"Ouch," Alex said, rubbing his side. "Why are you always doing that?"

"He likes her, you dolt. Can't you tell?"

"He does not," Alex said. He watched Samheed for a minute. "Does he?"

"Totally. Watch him glare at Cole Wickett. He's furious that Meg's spending so much time with him."

"Really?" Alex watched, and sure enough, when Cole went to the newly established groups to give out name tags, Samheed practically ripped them out of Cole's hand.

Lani grinned. "You need to spend more time noticing things. Less of this brooding and wandering aimlessly."

"But that's what I *do*," Alex said. "Are you trying to change me?"

"Never," Lani said, a mischievous look in her eye. "Okay, here goes me." Meghan called out the names of the Necessaries who would be in Lani's group.

Alex checked his watch. He had to meet Mr. Today in thirty minutes. He wasn't sure how much he'd be able to do with his group. Meghan called her own Necessaries, and then it was Alex's turn. But Meghan skipped over him.

He looked at Meghan, puzzled, trying to catch her eye. He caught Lani's raised eyebrow too. She was utterly too observant, he decided. It was almost annoying.

When Meghan finished with all the groups, Alex sidled up to her. "Did you forget my group?" he asked.

"What? No. Mr. Today said you were only going to be here

LISA McMANN

so the Necessaries would know who you are, but you weren't going to have a group."

"He said that?"

"No, I'm making it up." Meghan rolled her eyes.

"Well, I mean . . . what did he say exactly?" Alex asked.

"He told me you were meeting with him regularly now, and that you wouldn't have time to do both that and this. What's up, anyway?"

Alex glanced at Lani, who was straining to hear from several feet away while simultaneously trying to talk with her group. He felt bad not sharing news with his friends, but this afternoon he'd be telling Mr. Today that he couldn't be the new leader, so he didn't want to start any rumors when it was nothing anyway. "I don't know." He shrugged. "I guess I'll head over there, then."

He walked to the mansion, stopped in his room to get the notebook that contained his list of reasons why he wouldn't be a good leader, and then went to Mr. Today's office, which was empty. Alex wandered across the hall, made himself some tea in the kitchenette, and went back into the office, knowing he was a few minutes early. He looked eagerly at the university screen and saw that Aaron's room remained empty. Scanning the other blackboards, Alex saw no sign of his brother. He wondered if Aaron had gone home to their mother and father's house, or if he'd found some other place to live.

He turned away and looked around Mr. Today's office. On the walls were various odd bits of art, some of which Alex really felt drawn to, and other pieces that totally left him puzzled over Mr. Today's taste in paintings.

A voice from the far wall of the office nearly made Alex spill his tea.

"Anything new in Quill?"

All the Reasons Why Not

lex whirled around with a shout as Mr. Today entered from a door at the back of the office. Alex had never noticed the door before. A moment later its edges melted away and just the wall remained. "Oh, wow. Sorry, I didn't know about that door. You scared me," Alex said, letting out a breath of relief. "No, not much going on. Aaron's room is still empty. Do you know what happened?"

The mage adjusted the sleeves of his brightly colored robe. "Well, I know it wasn't High Priest Haluki who sent Aaron packing. It was probably the university or the Quillitary

LISA McMANN

thinking he could no longer be trusted. Everybody in Quill is more than a little paranoid right now."

Alex nodded. "Sounds like it." He bit his lip, not wanting to ask, but unable to stop himself. "So Aaron is . . . okay?"

Mr. Today walked toward Alex. "We're not sure where he is. According to Arija, he stopped by the entrance the other day and had a spirited conversation with her. But he didn't stay long."

Alex frowned. "Why would he come here?"

"I'm guessing he doesn't know where else to go."

"But we're sure he left?"

"Yes." Mr. Today pulled his chair out and sat down at his desk, inviting Alex to sit across from him. He pointed to Alex's notebook. "Oh, very nice—you must plan to take notes. I was hoping you would one day write a—"

"Uh, not exactly." Alex perched on the edge of the chair and opened the notebook to the page he needed. "It's just a list of things I have to tell you."

"Oh?" Mr. Today raised an eyebrow. "Well, then, go ahead."

"Um, you see, I've been thinking a lot about what you said

last week, and I've come up with some reasons for, um, not being able to do what you think I can do." Alex looked up. He didn't like how his hands were getting all sweaty.

"Go on," Mr. Today said.

"Okay, well, here," he said, and he handed the notebook to Mr. Today. "You can just read them yourself, I guess." He felt a little foolish, but he was determined to make his wishes clear.

Mr. Today peered at the paper, tapping his finger to his lips and nodding now and then as he read.

Alex wiped his clammy hands on his pants, jiggled his foot up and down, and waited.

Soon Mr. Today looked up. "Aha. I see," he said. "So what are you saying?"

"I'm saying that, um, that I'm kind of like Ms. Morning, I guess. I don't want the job. Yes, that's exactly it. The point, I mean. Of what I'm saying. That is." A pocket of air rushed from his lungs with a little squeak after he said it. He shifted gingerly in his seat and waited for Mr. Today's response.

The old mage smiled. "But I haven't even told you anything about it yet. Are you sure you want to make that decision so hastily? It might not be what you think."

LISA McMANN

Alex furrowed his brow. "I guess I'm just not a leader."

Mr. Today stood up and began to walk slowly about the office. "I understand," he said after a long minute of pacing. "And I accept your wishes. We should all do what we are passionate about."

Alex felt a rush of relief. "Yes. Totally. We—all of us should."

"Let me ask you, Alex, where do your passions lie?"

"My . . . ," Alex began. "My passions . . ." His voice trailed off, and then he closed his lips again and thought for a long moment. "I guess I'm not sure."

Mr. Today nodded thoughtfully. "Perhaps you can think about that over the next week and we can discuss it when we meet again."

Alex deflated. "Perhaps. I mean, yes, of course."

"But in the meantime, my dear boy, will you kindly indulge my old soul by letting me tell you what passions I see in you?"

"O-okay," Alex said, a bit suspicious but completely curious.

Mr. Today's eyes lit up. "Wonderful. Thank you." He stood, staring out the window for a moment, one hand raised slightly before him as if to deliver a soliloquy, but not the magical kind. He brought the outstretched hand inward to clutch the folds of his robe near his heart, and turned to face Alex. He began simply. "In you, Alex, I see a young man who loves to create and experiment with new spells. True enough?"

Alex nodded. He was always creating or trying new things—trapping clay that forms shackles around an enemy's wrists, ankles, or neck, origami dragons that can attack from a hundred feet away, and the 3-D door, something he was incredibly proud of, even though it had caused a lot of trouble. Very few Artiméans could make one of those—only Ms. Octavia, as far as Alex knew.

"I also see a loyal, fair-minded young man who cares about people and consistently wants to give them second chances when they mess up. Agreed?"

"I guess," Alex said. He thought about his once-enemy Samheed, and how close they had become. And Lani, how she used to drive him crazy. And then he thought about Aaron. "Maybe I give too many chances," he said. He looked at his hands.

"Forgiveness is not a negative trait." Mr. Today walked to

the window and looked out. "Not if one possesses common sense. Which you do," he said, turning and wagging his finger at the boy. "And it's a priceless gift, too, for common sense is not something one can just acquire at will. You either have it or you don't, as they say."

"Yeah," Alex said. "I suppose so." He looked up eagerly to see if Mr. Today had any more kind words to share.

"Alex, much of your strength lies in your honesty, in your courage in battle, in the way you inspire others to be better people—like Samheed, and believe it or not, like Aaron."

Alex snorted. "See? I'm a failure."

"Not at all. Aaron is fighting his own internal battle, and you very nearly swayed him once to join our side. Perhaps one day you'll try again, and who knows what can happen? No one else in Artimé has that power."

Alex was silent. Mr. Today moved back toward his desk and sat on the corner of it, facing Alex. He was wearing slippers today, Alex noted with a little grin.

After a time, Mr. Today spoke again. "I want to tell you a story, Alex."

Alex nibbled at his bottom lip, waiting. Wondering now if

Mr. Today really understood that Alex was turning him down.

"Simber," the old mage said.

Alex turned automatically to the door, expecting to see the beast.

Mr. Today shook his head. "No, he's not here. Simber was my first creation. Before there was Artimé, there was Simber."

In the Beginning

The old mage, still sitting on the corner of his desk, had a familiar faraway look in his eye as he thought about the beginning of Artimé. "I knew magic growing up—a few of us did, but we were largely an underground society on Warbler Island. Justine and I both could do it. I was better than she."

Alex sat up. "Wait—Warbler Island?"

Mr. Today nodded but didn't explain, choosing rather to continue with the story. "Once she and I moved here and we established Quill, the wall began to go up, which took years. Also during those early years, all the people were made

LISA McMANN

to forget their pasts and their magical abilities. And Justine instigated the Purge. You already know that eventually I became disillusioned with our motives and moved from Quill to this part of the island, and I lived in the little gray shack you saw when you first entered the gate."

Alex nodded. "And . . . you said something about Simber?"

"Ah, yes. One day I was down on the beach, feeling quite utterly alone in the world. I had suppressed my artistic tendencies, accepting Justine's belief that creativity was a sign of weakness. But that day we'd had a rare bit of rain, and the entire stretch of sand was damp. I began to sculpt an animal I'd once seen in a book as a child—a cheetah. It was the most stunning creature I'd ever seen, and I still remember that picture as if it were here in front of me.

"I worked to re-create it all day, getting the curve of its back and roll of its shoulders, the strength and proportion of its hind legs just right. Its face, its eyes—intelligent, powerful, fierce but caring eyes. And then, on a whim, becoming uniquely inspired, I added wings. Perhaps I was feeling a bit caged in myself." He chuckled softly, lost in the memory for a moment. "When I knew that I had perfected each part of the creature, I preserved that part with magic, making its surface almost completely indestructible," he said, smiling proudly. "And then, when I was quite finished, I brought it to life."

"Wow," Alex whispered. "Simber is made entirely of sand?"

"Indeed. Thus, Simber lacks the spots that a cheetah normally has."

Alex looked puzzled. "How did you bring him to life? I've never seen anyone do that before."

Mr. Today smiled as if he had a secret. He whispered, "That's because I've never taught it to anyone before."

Alex leaned forward, his eyes wide, his heart pounding in anticipation. "Will you teach it to me?" he asked.

The creator of all magical life in Artimé leaned forward as well. He pressed a finger to his lips for a long moment in consideration, his eyes flickering once to the wall and then back to Alex and remaining there, holding the breathless boy's gaze, until the weight of the question nearly toppled them both. Finally, Mr. Today whispered the answer.

"No."

The Slightest Clue

Alex's face fell. He looked away. "Oh." He felt heat rising to his cheeks.

Mr. Today's eyes were filled with pity. "I'm sorry," he said, and it came from somewhere deep, somewhere very sincere. "As much as I want to, my dear boy, I can't do it."

"It's okay." Alex wished he could disappear into the chair cushion. Why did he even ask? Why would he think Mr. Today would teach him when he wouldn't teach anyone else? It felt almost as bad as when Ms. Octavia told him he couldn't advance to Magical Warrior Training last year. He raised his eyes to the old mage. "It's because I said I didn't want to be the next leader of Artimé, isn't it?"

"Truthfully, yes," Mr. Today said, sitting back in his chair once again. "I made a promise to myself a long time ago that there would be certain spells, certain properties of our particular kind of magic that I would not teach to anyone but my successor. I fear these abilities could get into the hands of people who are incapable of using common sense, and who don't understand the value of that power." Mr. Today eased off the desk. "So as much as I trust you, I must save this particular secret for the right person. However," he said with a small smile, "I did give you the slightest clue."

"You did? What was it?"

But Mr. Today only smiled and changed the subject. "So, now you know the story of Simber, who remains one of my most incredible magical creations . . . and my dearest friend. His memory is impeccable, and everything he has experienced is captured in his inner senses—it didn't take him long at all to learn everything he knows. Such an amazing beast! He can see and hear better than any human or animal. He is capable of emotion, as you've witnessed more than once, and he is loyal to the end." He gave a wry smile and added, "You may have noticed that Simber cannot perform magic, though many of my other creations can. I didn't think of it at the time, him being my first, and now it's too late, but he hardly has need for it. The only other thing I didn't anticipate was that he would grow. I created him life-size, but he grew as if he were a newborn on that first day. I'm grateful for it now, but there was a time when I wondered if he'd ever stop."

"Wow," Alex said. "And did he? Stop, I mean? Or is he still growing?" He couldn't imagine Simber getting any bigger.

"Oh, he's stopped," Mr. Today said, laughing. "Thankfully."

"And you created Ms. Octavia too? Is she also made of sand?"

"Oh, Octavia—such a delightful creature," Mr. Today said, his hands clasped together. "No, she's not made of sand. She was a different sort of sculpture experiment. Simber is of the earth, Octavia is of the water. Clay, seaweed, lily pads, shells. That sort of thing."

"So her parts aren't . . . aren't real? Like, not from a real octopus and alligator?"

"Good heavens, no. I'd never behead a living creature to

LISA McMANN

create something magical. How heartless." Mr. Today clutched his robe dramatically. "No, she is purely fabricated. But I'm honored that you can't tell."

"I can't! Honest. She's amazing."

"Don't tell her I told you, but her eyeglasses are purely for show. She's quite vain about them." He chuckled.

Alex grinned. And then he grew thoughtful. "Why can't Ms. Octavia or Simber or Florence be the next leader of Artimé?" Alex asked.

Mr. Today was taken aback, as if the answer was obvious. "Why, *because* my dear boy. They were created by me. They exist only at my command."

Alex furrowed his brow. "So how do they die? Or don't they?"

"Aha! Another excellent question," Mr. Today said, smiling.

Alex waited, and when Mr. Today didn't speak, he said, "Aw, another secret?" Alex grinned in spite of his disappointment. He was glad Mr. Today wasn't mad at him for turning down the job. But now he wondered whom Mr. Today would choose instead—who would get to know the answers to these secrets? And he had to admit, the thought of one of his peers getting this information, getting to spend so much time learning from this most amazing person who created all of these incredible things, and who was getting ready to hand over the key to this world . . . well, that brought the slightest twinge of jealousy to Alex's heart. Like maybe he was missing out on the greatest opportunity of his life.

Thinking Like a Necessary

When Aaron left the Ancients Sector, full of newfound bitterness, his mind swimming with ideas, he realized what was the biggest, dumbest mistake he'd made so far. Now he walked with purpose, straight for the Favored Farm. How could he have forgotten his own creation? It must have been the disconnection between creating the idea of the farm, and actually doing the physical work of growing and harvesting. Wanteds were the thinkers, the creators, not the mindless pluckers and deliverers. If Aaron was going to be forced to walk for days with no one bringing him food or drink, he'd have to

LISA McMANN

start thinking differently. He'd have to think like a Necessary. He shuddered at the thought.

But at least he would eat.

It took him quite some time to get there. And he had forgotten about the wooden fence around the crops. But then he saw a soldier standing by the gate that led into the farm. Aaron mustered up as much authority as he could. "The high priest told me to pick my own corn if I wanted corn," Aaron said, repeating the complaint he'd heard days ago on the street outside the university. "So I'm here to pick my own food."

The Quillitary soldier eyed Aaron suspiciously for a moment, and then he stepped aside. "Limit is four items. Total, not each."

"All right." Aaron stepped into the garden and the smell of fresh fruits and vegetables was the most amazing thing he'd smelled in months. It nearly covered up the rotten stench from alongside the road. He inhaled, and then, trying not to seem too desperate, he quickly scanned the rows of the farm, digging through his memory for the layout he'd designed, wondering where the coconut trees and watermelon plants ended up.

Finally he found them on opposite ends of the farm. He

gathered up one of each and sat down under the coconut tree—a rare shady spot in Quill—but couldn't get the coconut to crack open, so he pounded his fist into the watermelon, finally breaking it, feeling like he also broke his hand in the process. But it didn't matter. He dug into the pink flesh and slurped it, seeds and all. It wasn't as refreshing as water, but it would have to do.

When finished, he wiped his sticky hands in the grass and his chin on his shirt, and tossed the watermelon rinds into a giant raspberry bush. Then he took two more watermelons and two ears of corn, leaving the useless coconut behind.

He made sure he had no signs of watermelon juice on his shirt, and then headed out past the guard, obediently showing the food. The soldier patted down Aaron's book bag and let him pass without a word.

When Aaron got to the street, he breathed a sigh of relief. As he wandered past the Quillitary housing sector, his arms aching from the weight of the watermelons, he stopped to rest and gaze at the governors' homes. They were the six best houses in Quill, not counting the high priest's palace. Aaron burned with anger when he thought about how his hopes to live in one of these one day had been so violently dashed.

He wondered if Governor Strang might be persuaded to be on Aaron's side—Strang had liked Aaron before everything fell apart. But Aaron hadn't seen him in a while. Perhaps he was home today. . . . But then Aaron looked at himself. Dirty. Smelly. Wandering aimlessly. He was sure the governors all knew about him being kicked out of the university. They were probably behind it, along with Haluki.

Aaron turned his gaze to Haluki's house as a drop of sweat made a shiny line from his temple to his jaw. Two buckets of water sat on the step by the door, having been delivered recently, no doubt. Tempting him. He swallowed reflexively, but the sticky sweetness of the watermelon had left his mouth drier than before. It was not worth trying to steal from a governor, much less the high priest, no matter how crazy with thirst he was. He'd be put in jail for years for that. Aaron narrowed his eyes, hating everything about that house and its occupants.

And then his eyes widened, and his hatred for the house trickled away. "Wait a second," he said softly. *If Mrs. Haluki and the two children are in Artimé, and High Priest Haluki is in the palace . . . who is living in the Halukis' house?*

"Great land of Quill," Aaron whispered. "That's it!"

Home Sweet Home

I t was agony for Aaron, waiting for dark, but he knew that would be the only way to properly sneak into the Haluki home. He wasn't about to blow it now. When it was quiet in the neighborhood, and all was clear, he went to the rear door to try a little trick he'd learned from Quillitary soldiers back when they liked him. The Quill doors tended to be a bit loose in their jambs during the driest months, and nearly every home had some sort of rot or termite infestation, so things were not as secure as they seemed.

Aaron lifted up on the door handle, moving the whole door an inch or so, and then wrenched it to the side. He heard the

LISA McMANN

rusted-out bottom hinge break free from the soft wood and clatter to the floor inside the house. One more wrench for the top hinge, and the door opened. Aaron grabbed his watermelons and went inside, setting them on the table. Then he maneuvered the door closed again and leaned against it, breathing hard. He had never been so light-headed in all his life.

He went to the front door, unlocked and opened it, and peered outside to make sure no one was about. When he was certain he wasn't being watched, he brought the precious water inside. In the kitchen he took a cup and, with a shaky hand, dipped it in and drank heartily. He dipped the cup in a second time, knowing he should try to preserve the water, but not caring at this particular moment. Two large buckets of water all to himself for an entire week—it was the best possible reward for all the punishment he'd taken recently.

When he had cleaned himself up, he made his way to a bedroom and collapsed on a mattress not unlike the kind he'd had at university, and fell asleep.

In the morning, when the sunlight streamed in through the dusty windows and the heat of the day was not yet upon the land of Quill, Aaron rose. He took stock of the Halukis' provisions, which were shockingly plentiful. They had an entire shelf of cooking and baking materials, a shelf containing large sacks of rice, beans, and peanuts, and a shelf of dried herbs and oils. Aaron stared at the abundance. Growing up in a Necessary house and then going straight to the university where his meals were served in a cafeteria, he'd had none of these extras just lying around.

Aaron glanced over his shoulder even though he knew no one was in the house. It was more out of habit, or perhaps because he knew he was doing something terribly against the law. Just being here made him worthy of a life in jail . . . or worse.

But he also felt strangely confident about not getting caught. It was clear from looking around that the Halukis had closed up the house as if leaving permanently—which rarely happened in the past before Artimé, except when the last of a family had been sent to the Ancients Sector. And even then, there was another family eagerly waiting to move in. But now with people vacating daily and moving to Artimé, and with all the added confusion in Quill these days, Aaron felt that if he were careful to come and go through the back door and limit his outdoor movement to after dark, he could get away with living here for quite some time.

He took a handful of peanuts and ate them as he surveyed his new living quarters. The kitchen and gathering space was twice as large as the entire home Aaron's parents lived in. There was a table with four sturdy chairs, and a sofa and two lounge chairs in the gathering area with soft cushions. *Who needs so many chairs?* he wondered as he tested them out. *A family of four needs four chairs at most.* Aaron furrowed his brow at the waste.

He wondered about all the homes that stood empty now in the Necessary quadrants. "All those extra furniture items just sitting there," he mused. "Beds, chairs, nonperishables, cooking equipment, waste-burying shovels . . ." Aaron moved through the house, noticing all the unnecessary things that the Halukis had, and he burned with anger once more.

"High Priest Haluki," Aaron said matter-of-factly, "one day you will beg me for your life." He moved down the short hallway. "And I will not give it back to you." He paused, a little surprised by the cold words that had just come out of his

LISA McMANN

mouth. But he cleared his head and continued on, entering a closed room that contained a desk and a large double-door closet. Aaron peered at the desk, noting a few books and papers. He stepped behind it to the closet and put his hands on the doorknobs.

When he pulled them open wide, he could only stare at the contents, completely baffled. His forehead wrinkled as he puzzled over the giant glass cylinder before him. He reached out tentatively to touch its surface, murmuring, "What in the name of Quill is this?"

A Skirmish

Coming toward the gate—everyone in Artimé still called it "the gate" out of habit even though the gate was no longer there—were two hulking, serious types from Quill. "Fresh out of the university?" Arija guessed to Tina, one of her companion girrinos, as the young men approached.

"Not wearing Quillitary garb, no book bags, a bit tired around the eyes but pale . . . ," Tina murmured. "Definitely indoor workers. Not old enough to have children in here, though." She and Arija stood, snorting a few times for effect.

LISA McMANN

The two stepped closer uneasily. "We're here to see our brothers," one said.

"What are your names?" Tina asked politely enough.

"Dred Crandall," said the taller one.

"Crawledge Prize," said the other, whose hair curled around his ears and dripped with sweat.

"And you're here to see . . . ?" Arija was skeptical. Crandall and Prize? They had the same last names as two of the governors. As far as she knew, the Halukis were the only governor's family here. But Arija certainly didn't know everyone in Artimé.

"Our brothers," Crandall said again, impatiently this time. He scratched a small scab on his neck.

Arija and Tina stood aside. "Do you know where to find them?"

"We'll find them," Prize said. He and Crandall passed through the opening and strode quickly to the footpath, looking a bit startled by the bright colors as they gazed left and right at the people milling around munching on breakfast pastries and strolling across the grass.

"Keep an eye on them," Arija said to the other two girrinos, whose names were Opal and Penelope. "Be ready to call for help if necessary."

Moments later, angry shouts rang out from the lawn near the mansion. Crandall and Prize had approached a group of Necessaries and were attempting to yank two of them away.

"Come on," Prize said, trying to get the Necessary to be quiet. "Your little vacation is over. You are required in Quadrant One."

"No! Stop! Help me!" the Necessary shouted, catching the attention of two teachers, Mr. Appleblossom and Ms. Claire Morning, who were enjoying a rather spirited discussion of musicals versus plays nearby.

Mr. Appleblossom bounded over and Ms. Morning kept up easily with her long strides.

"What's going on?" Ms. Morning asked, her normally kind voice quite curt this morning.

The Necessary tried to yank his arm away. "They're trying to force us back to work in Quill," he said, breathless.

"They have duties," said Crandall. He glared at the two teachers, who looked fairly harmless to him. He took a better

LISA McMANN

grip of the arm he was holding and turned toward the gate. "Come on," he growled.

Mr. Appleblossom spoke up. "Your pompousness and attitude is boor. Now kindly take yourselves right out the door."

Prize stared at the theater instructor. "What?" he asked, for Mr. Appleblossom's manner of speaking in rhyme took some getting used to.

"Out and out! Away, away, away! Do *not* return again another day!" Mr. Appleblossom gestured impatiently toward the gate and even stomped his foot.

Crandall, face turning red, let go of the Necessary and turned toward Mr. Appleblossom. He hovered over the little instructor, his hands balling into fists.

Mr. Appleblossom's eyes narrowed. A small smile played on Ms. Morning's lips as she watched.

Crandall glanced at Prize, and then they both looked at Mr. Appleblossom. Just as Crandall pulled his arm back to take a swing, he jumped back in surprise. "Ouch!" he cried out, spinning around. "Ow!" He looked this way and that, his eyes wild, his hands swatting at his body.

Soon Crawledge Prize was hopping and exclaiming in pain as well.

Ms. Morning's smile turned into a look of surprise, for she had not released a spell, and neither had Mr. Appleblossom as far as she could tell. As the two Wanteds gave up and ran for the gate, Ms. Morning spied the instigators, Cole Wickett and Meghan Ranger, who had been meeting on the lawn a short distance away and now came running toward them.

"Are you all right?" Meghan asked.

Mr. Appleblossom watched the two governors' sons until they were out of sight in Quill. He lifted his hand to his forehead and patted away any sweat that might have formed, though everyone suspected it was more of an act than a necessary gesture. "I'm well," he said, finally turning to the students. "The ruffians have fled to Quill." He turned to the Necessaries. "Now, you two friends are shaken quite, perhaps. A fizzy drink may calm you, if you will. Please, Claire? I must to class with these two chaps."

Meghan raised an eyebrow at being called a chap, but she knew Mr. Appleblossom often overlooked minor details in his quest for perfect rhymes, and like most students, she was okay with it.

"Of course, Siggy," Ms. Morning said. "Interesting choice of spells, Meghan. What did you use?"

"Oh, it wasn't me," Meghan said. "It was Cole's quick thinking."

Cole's face turned red. "Fire ants," he said. "It'll wear off in fifteen minutes or so."

"I doubt they'll try that again," Meghan said.

Ms. Morning nodded, but her face was troubled. "I'm glad it wasn't a permanent spell, or we might be in for more than we wished for." She led the Necessaries toward the mansion's kitchen while Mr. Appleblossom, Cole, and Meghan headed for the tubes to the theater.

A Mostly Normal Day

On rare occasions Alex was late for class, and this was one of those times. While Cole sent fire ants upon ruffians, Alex scrubbed his face and tried to run a comb through his tangled wet hair, but gave up as Clive chided him from the living area of his room.

"Late," Clive said every thirty seconds.

"Stuff it. I know." Alex shoved his books and notebook into his backpack and searched frantically for his component vest. He was presenting a new spell today in Actors' Studio so he needed it.

"Late."

"Seriously, Clive!" he said through clenched teeth. "I am aware of that."

Clive tilted his head. "What rhymes with Appleblossom?" he asked. "Not much. But I know what would be worse."

Alex ignored him.

"Orangeblossom," Clive said. He chuckled to himself. "Orangeblossom. Get it? Nothing rhymes with orange, so it would be . . ." Clive glanced at the clock in the corner of his screen. "Late," he said again.

Alex found his component vest and slipped it on. He grabbed his backpack and stepped into the tube. "Bye," he said sarcastically.

"Don't die," Clive said. He'd been saying that since the day of the battle with Quill, and since it had worked, Clive said it daily.

Alex didn't mind. He knew that deep down Clive was rather fond of him, and while normally quite annoying, the blackboard generally did whatever he could for the boy.

A moment later Alex stepped from the tube into the theater, where Mr. Appleblossom was already addressing the class. Alex slid into a seat next to Meghan.

"Shush," she said.

"I didn't say anyth—" Alex said, but Meghan glared at him. He sighed and set his backpack on the floor in front of him, pulling out his notebook and a pencil as quietly as he could.

Mr. Appleblossom, blind to Alex's lateness, waxed on. "In times like these I do despair this place, kerfuffles and commotion follow me. But one must hurly-burly through the race, for flicker, flap, and ruction ever be."

Alex blinked. He raised an eyebrow at Meghan but dared not speak.

She scribbled in his notebook, "There was a skirmish on the lawn this morning." She turned her attention back to the instructor.

Alex's eyes widened. He scribbled back. "Who's Flickerflap and Ruction?" He poked the corner of the notebook into Meghan's leg to get her attention.

Meghan let out a frustrated breath and read the note. "Shh!" she said, and pushed it away.

Alex, who hadn't said a word, wrote, "I AM NOT MAKING ANY NOISE, SO STOP SHUSHING ME!" He poked it into her leg again.

Meghan ignored him.

LISA McMANN

Alex gave up and listened as Mr. Appleblossom talked about their next production, *And Then Everyone Dies, The End*, another Appleblossom original—a musical comedy this time based loosely on the Purge, which sounded . . . kind of weird. Samheed, leaning forward in his seat, was nearly drooling over the lead part already.

After the announcement came "spells" time, wherein a few students introduced their latest theater spells to Mr. Appleblossom and the class. A few were fairly useless, but Alex and Lani tended to offer a decent lot that were sometimes practical for everyday life in theater, and sometimes potentially lethal, should Artimé be forced to fight again.

Today Lani's spell was a practical one. She said it was a seek spell, and explained that if an actor missed his cue and was unable to be found, Mr. Appleblossom only needed to touch something that the actor had created and say "seek" silently, and a ball of light would fetch the missing student. When the actor caught the ball of light it would explode, briefly displaying—like a picture—the created element that Mr. Appleblossom had touched. The wayward actor would then be able to decipher who was summoning, and simply follow the direction from whence the light came.

To demonstrate, Lani picked up one of Mr. Appleblossom's older scripts that he'd lent her. She closed her eyes, imagined the silent verbal component, and a bright ball of light shot out directly from the script to Mr. Appleblossom. It hovered until the instructor reached out for it, and then it exploded, and a lighted picture of *The Astonishing Adventures of Breakfast and Pearflower* appeared in the air. It melted away a moment later.

Mr. Appleblossom applauded. "A silent, lighted spell is all the rage," he cried out, "for it can be so dark behind the stage."

Lani grinned and sat down.

Alex's spell was a practical one, too, and not really one of his best, but he thought it would be quite popular in the right niche. He called it the prompter. It was a tiny intuitive earpiece that would whisper the words one needed when performing, in case of stage fright or confusion. "You only have to rehearse with it in place in your ear, and it will memorize the lines you say out loud, in the proper order. When you try to repeat the words later during a performance, it recognizes the context. If you get stuck, just touch the earpiece to signal that you need a prompt and it immediately whispers the next line into your ear." He demonstrated and offered others a try. "I've only made one so far. It took a while, but now that I have it figured out, I can make more when I have time."

"How very interesting, Mr. Stowe," Mr. Appleblossom said, but he looked concerned. "As long as all the actors here realize that this is not a substitute, you know, for the old-fashioned way to memorize." The little man tapped his foot threateningly.

"Of course, sir," Alex said. "Actors wouldn't be actors if they had to use it frequently. It's only supposed to be used for the occasional emergency prompt. In fact," he said, brightening up, "I think I can alter it so that if too many prompts are needed in a certain period of time, the earpiece shuts down."

Mr. Appleblossom smiled. "I think that alteration will work well. Congratulations—it's a brilliant spell."

After class the four friends met up and tubed to the dining room. "So what happened?" Alex asked once they got to a table with their food. "A fight? Who was fighting?"

Meghan spoke up. "Some Wanteds came by pretending to visit, so the girrinos let them in, but they were really here to, um, *encourage* their Necessaries to go back to Quill and work."

"Why'd you say 'encourage' all weird?"

"Because it was more like force. They were going to shackle them."

Alex's face grew troubled. "Oh, no."

Lani jumped in. "Mr. Appleblossom tried to settle it peacefully, but the Wanteds took a swipe at him, so Meghan and Cole totally sent them running with fire ant spells." She grinned.

"That's excellent," Alex said. "Nice work, Meg."

"It wasn't me," she said modestly. "It was Cole."

Samheed rolled his eyes and muttered, "He's lucky he didn't miss and hit Mr. A."

Meghan went on as if she hadn't heard Samheed. "The Wanteds were really furious. Mr. Appleblossom told us that he thinks we'll see more fights." She sighed and tossed what was left of her roll back onto her plate. "I thought this was all over. I don't want to do this war thing anymore."

Alex bit his lip. He didn't want to tell her what Mr. Today had said about the probability of that—he knew Meghan was still struggling to make sense of her family situation and she

LISA McMANN

didn't need more stuff to worry about. His thoughts turned back to his meeting with Mr. Today and he wondered whom Mr. Today would choose to be the future leader.

It looked as if he might need help sooner than anyone expected.

Born to Spy

O kay, Mr. Broody Pants. Spill it," Lani said to Alex as the four sat around a booth in the lounge one afternoon. Sean, who sometimes joined them for afternoon snacks, was nowhere to be found.

Samheed smirked. Meghan, swirling a mug of hot chocolate, tilted her head, puzzled.

"Spill what?" Alex looked crossly at her. "You always think you know things."

Lani grinned. "Aha!" she said. "I do know things. I'd make a great spy. So what's going on with you?" She slid toward him. "Tell us."

LISA McMANN

"Yeah," Meghan said. "I've been meaning to ask. What have you been talking to Mr. Today about? Is that what's up?"

"Nothing's up," Alex said. "Stop bugging me."

Samheed, watching all of this, crossed his arms over his chest and settled back in his seat as the girls stared Alex down. Alex flashed Samheed a helpless look, but Samheed just shrugged. "You're on your own."

Alex leaned back and let his head flop against the booth cushion. "Fine," he said with a sigh. "Mr. Today wants to take a holiday and he needs somebody to . . . I don't know. Sort of help Ms. Morning run the place, I guess."

"Ooh, a holiday," Meghan said dreamily. "Nobody ever does that! Where is there to go? I thought holidays were only in books."

Lani's lips parted in surprise. "So . . . he wants you?" she said softly.

"Well, he mentioned something like that, but I said no thanks." Alex turned to Meghan. "He wants to go back to the island where he grew up."

Samheed narrowed his eyes. "He wasn't born here?"

"I guess not," Alex said. He didn't know how much Mr. Today would want him to say, so he remained vague.

LISA McMANN

"Why did you say no?" Lani's eyes blazed.

Alex looked at her, surprised. "Because I'd be a terrible leader."

"What?" Meghan exclaimed. "No you wouldn't. Don't be so thick." She sat back on the seat. "Besides, this place practically runs itself by now, doesn't it? And it's just for a holiday. What's that, a few weeks maybe?"

Alex scowled at the table and said nothing.

Lani stared at Alex. Meghan looked at Samheed and then back at Alex.

"Oh. So, not a few weeks," Lani said. "Longer, then?"

Samheed leaned forward, elbows on the table. "All right, Stowe. What's this really all about?"

Alex, feeling a headache coming on, pressed his fingers to his temples. "For some stupid reason, Mr. Today thought I would make a good future leader. A permanent one for after he . . . you know . . . gets too old. Like in ten years. So he wanted to start training me a bit at a time now so I can help Ms. Morning while he's on his little holiday, and then slowly take over some other things because Ms. Morning doesn't want the job permanently. But I said no, because I'd stink at it, so that's that. Okay? Can we drop it?"

LISA McMANN

Samheed stared, mouth open.

Lani sat quiet, the corners of her lips twitching downward, eyes trained to a nebulous spot across the room.

Meghan, grinning, patted Alex's arm. "That is quite hilarious," she said. "Good one, Al."

Everyone was awkwardly silent. Meghan's smile slowly disappeared. She looked from face to face. "Not a joke?" she asked.

Alex shook his head slightly.

Lani nudged Samheed, indicating she wanted out of the booth. "I have to go," she said, her voice wavering. When Samheed saw the look on her face, he scrambled to his feet so she could slide out. She shoved past him and ran to the tubes, leaving the others staring, speechless.

Alex just sat there. "Did I miss something? What just happened?" he asked. "Is she sick?"

Megan shrugged, mystified.

Samheed, still standing, looked at Alex and finally shrugged. "I guess *I'll* go see if she's okay, then," he said. He turned, strode quickly to the tubes, and disappeared.

Throwing Stones

It took Samheed quite some time to find Lani after checking the mansion and ringing her blackboard to see if she was in her room. He jogged by the gate and asked the girrinos if they'd seen her, but they said only Sean Ranger and a few others had left Artimé that day.

Eventually he saw her outside by the shore. The sea was fairly calm today, and Lani was skipping stones over the water and letting the low waves wash up over her bare feet. Her toenails were painted fluorescent purple.

He walked over and stood next to her, not saying anything at first. He spied a few stones so he picked them up and wiped the sand off of them to see if they were good for throwing. When he had a handful, he offered them to Lani. "These look like they might skip," he said.

"Thanks," she said. She took them and gave one a try. It skidded over the water and she counted. "Seven. Not bad."

Samheed found a few more and tried one himself. His bounced once and plopped into the water with a glug.

"Twist your arm a little," she said. "Like it's a throwing star."

He did what she said and managed three skips. "Meh," he said. "I was never very good at this."

"You're dead-on with spells, though."

Samheed nodded. "True." When he was out of stones, he wiped the sand off his hands, took off his shoes, and rolled up his pant legs. "Wanna walk?" he said. He started walking slowly toward the jungle.

After a moment Lani caught up to him. They sloshed through the water side by side in silence for a long time, Samheed just thinking, watching the sand that stretched out immediately before him, and Lani with her eyes half-closed, face angled toward the sky.

When they got past the jungle to the lagoon where Ms. Morning's big white boat gleamed, Samheed pointed to an old downed log. "I sit here sometimes," he said. "Only when the platyprots aren't around, though. They're so annoying."

Lani grinned and sat down. "I know," she said.

Samheed sat next to her. "Are you ever tempted to give that boat a try?"

"Every time I see it," Lani said. "You?"

"Yeah."

They watched the water for a bit longer, and then Samheed spoke again. "So. Did you kill Justine?"

Lani looked at him in surprise. "What? Where did *that* come from?" she said with a little laugh.

"Well, did you?" Samheed asked. "You did, didn't you."

She looked away, trying to hide a grin. And then she shrugged one shoulder and tilted her head, looking out over the water.

Samheed regarded her for a moment, his esteem for her rising mightily, not only because she had the guts to kill the High Priest Justine, but that she managed to keep it to herself all this time.

LISA McMANN

"Well, you saved Mr. Today's life," she said. She leaned toward him and bumped her shoulder against his.

Samheed's eyes flickered. And for a time on a log in the small and quiet lagoon, next to the vast ocean that seemed to go on forever, the two, each silently remembering the parts that were played in battle with Quill, felt something enormous swell up inside them as they considered what *might* have happened without the courage of the other. Lani slid a glance his way, and he caught it, and couldn't help but share with her a little crooked smile.

But soon the moment passed, and before things could get awkward, Samheed shifted on the log and looked out over the water once again. "So, what's bothering you?" he asked, even though he thought he knew the answer.

Lani's smile faded. She clasped her hands together in front of her and slipped her arms around her legs, resting her chin on her knees. "Nothing much, really."

"Oh, right. That was obvious from the way you stormed out of the lounge, looking like you were going to hurl," Samheed said.

"Was it really?" Lani said sarcastically. She rolled her eyes, but Sam couldn't see it.

"I think you're required to tell me since I've been so nice for, like, a whole hour."

"That *is* quite an accomplishment."

"So?" Samheed asked. "Come on. Don't make me beg."

Lani closed her eyes for a moment and took a deep breath. "Okay, fine. It's just . . . I wasn't expecting Alex to say that. About Mr. Today, and the whole future leader thing."

Samheed nodded, careful not to interrupt her.

"I mean, Alex is great and I, you know, I really like him and stuff, but isn't there anyone else who might be a better choice? A stronger magician with more rounded skills? Somebody who would make a better teammate for Quill's new high priest? Someone who could really work in harmony with him, someone who understands him really well, and who would make this whole island really gel together? Somebody who really actually *wants* this job?"

Samheed cringed and stayed silent.

Lani sat up straight and turned to Samheed. "If Mr. Today is going to pick somebody young, well . . ." She looked out over the lagoon. "It should have been me, Sam." Her eyes filled and her bottom lip started to quiver. She held back the tears and swallowed hard. And then she whispered, "He was supposed to pick me."

Samheed bit his bottom lip and nodded. And then he turned and held an arm out awkwardly. She leaned in and rested her cheek on his shoulder as he patted her on the back. "Maybe since Alex doesn't want to do it, you could let Mr. Today know that you're interested," he said.

Lani just shook her head and sniffled. "I can't do that." She lifted her eyes and looked at Samheed in the dying light. "If he wanted me, he would have picked me."

A Very Different Gate

Day after day in his new home, Aaron plotted and planned, working tirelessly from the desk that had once been High Priest Haluki's. He'd scoured the drawers but come up empty-handed—the high priest had apparently packed up everything of importance and carried it with him to the palace. There was not much to be said for the giant glass cylinder in the closet behind him. It was the most curious thing, but seemingly useless, and there were no instructions or clues to hint at its purpose. It didn't take long for Aaron to forget about it entirely.

Every morning before sunrise Aaron snuck out of the house

and walked to the Favored Farm, careful to take a different path each day, listening to people's conversations while trying to be invisible. He noted that almost no Wanteds were taking advantage of the food at the Favored Farm. They were so unfamiliar with that kind of labor, he was sure they hadn't even thought of it. All their lives they'd had Necessaries delivering their food to them—they probably had no idea where food even came from.

Every day Aaron picked his four allotted items, sticking now to things that would keep fresh for more than a few days—beans of all kinds (he was glad to find the allotment for berries and legumes was a handful rather than just one), potatoes and onions, oranges, coconuts. He ate the foods that were about to go bad and kept the rest in the pantry.

Each week he set out his empty water buckets and they were filled without question. Perhaps in the chaos the Halukis hadn't been removed from the water list, or maybe there was no official list—when the water people came by with their cart, they simply filled the empty buckets. That was most likely the case here in the Wanted Sector.

Aaron went over his thoughts and ideas every night and

envisioned himself back in the palace. It would be a long journey, and if he really thought about it, he knew his chances of success were small. So he chose only to press onward, not think about it too much, and try not to mess it up. If all went well, it would still take years.

Early on the morning that his plan would take action, Aaron packed his book bag with a few handfuls of beans and a dozen oranges. He snuck out of the house before dawn and made his way up the road to the palace gate just as morning broke. He found a spot by the road to sit where the giant wall would provide him with shade until noon.

He waited. Occasionally a Quillitary vehicle lurched by, heading to or from the palace. Aaron turned away from them and tried not to draw attention to himself. He didn't think they'd do anything to him, but he didn't want to find out. It wasn't long before grumbling Wanteds walked up the road toward the palace, no doubt to air their grievances. Aaron stayed where he was, straining his ears to hear their conversations. When they glanced at him, he nodded politely but didn't say anything, and they kept walking.

Over the next hours Aaron watched and remained silent as

half a dozen more groups made their way to the palace. When the first groups returned, their grumbling was louder than ever. Aaron pulled an orange from his bag and peeled it slowly, watching and listening.

"We're supposed to live together peacefully? With *Unwanteds*? That's absurd!"

"Haluki has lost his mind."

"I fear for the future of Quill, I really do."

"What does he mean, live in harmony? What's harmony?"

"I want my Necessaries back!"

"We'll starve to death if we keep this up. Nobody's brought us a decent meal in weeks."

The voices faded.

Aaron popped a slice of the orange into his mouth and closed his eyes, letting the delicious juice trickle through his teeth and around his tongue. He chewed and swallowed, and then he opened his eyes to find an elderly woman staring at him.

"Oh, hello," he said.

"Where did you get that orange?"

Aaron wasn't about to tell her. "Would you like some?" He

tore half of it away and handed it to her. "How was your visit to the high priest? Any news?"

She eyed him warily. "You're that boy . . . ," she began, but the orange overpowered her thoughts. She reached for it. "Thank you," she said, her words sharp and clipped, but she tore into the orange and tried not to devour it in one mouthful. "There hasn't been much food delivered lately."

Aaron nodded sympathetically. "I know." He handed her the remaining slice. "What does the high priest say about it all? I'm sure he's doing everything he can to get our Necessaries back." Aaron looked off in the distance nonchalantly, but he was more than eager for a specific account from the palace.

The woman frowned. "He's not doing anything of the sort. All he can talk about is peace," she spat. "That's all fine with me as long as everyone knows their place. But High Priest Haluki sees no problem with Necessaries flocking to Artimé and staying there. And that's where I have to disagree."

Aaron gave her a concerned look. "But . . . ," he said, as if he were just thinking of it, "who is going to do the Necessaries' jobs if they don't come back? Isn't he going to force them to return?" His eyes flamed. "We'll all starve to death!"

"Exactly!" the woman said. "We'll die!"

Others returning from the palace slowed to listen, including two governors' sons whom Aaron knew as Crawledge and Prize. They recognized Aaron and at first regarded him with contempt, but soon focused instead on the orange slices in the woman's hand.

"What kind of leader lets his workers go free and his best people starve?" Aaron asked in a voice of wonderment, loud enough for everyone in sight to hear. "The High Priest Justine wouldn't have let this happen." He shook his head.

The small group of people nodded, some still skeptical of the speaker, but most were riled up enough to band together with anyone who thought the same thoughts as they.

"I wonder . . . ," Aaron said, but then he stopped and looked at the people. "Well, I shouldn't say anything. High Priest Haluki and the Quillitary have decided my ideas are worthless." He bent down to pick up his backpack, as if to leave.

"What ideas?" the original woman asked. "I suppose if you have some, it wouldn't hurt to hear them."

Aaron shook his head sadly. "No . . . it's nothing. I'm not to be trusted." He reached into his backpack and silently doled out oranges to everyone standing there. "I have some beans as well—I'm happy to share with everyone, as the *former* high priest would have expected."

Even the most reluctant ones stepped closer to Aaron now as he gave handfuls of beans to those standing there.

"I do miss the way things were," one of them ventured softly, as if afraid to be heard. "The High Priest Justine was a noble woman."

Aaron nodded solemnly. "Indeed she was." He smiled sympathetically at each face. "All we can do now is try to survive until someone comes to save us, I guess."

He touched the shoulder of the old woman. "I'll be here again a week from today. If I have found any extra food, I'll gladly share again."

With that, Aaron turned and walked away from the palace and the group of complainers, who now were silent and thoughtful as they looked down at the treasure in their hands, then up at the young former up-and-comer who had given them the means to survive.

As Aaron walked toward the Favored Farm to pick his daily food, contemplating just how well his work had gone that

LISA McMANN

morning, his thoughts were disturbed by approaching steps in the gravel and a familiar voice that sent shivers up his spine.

"Greetings, Aaron."

Aaron looked up, his eyes overwhelmed by the bright colors of the man's robe and his crazy shock of hair. Aaron scowled and slowed his pace, ready to defend himself if he needed to, but Mr. Today merely smiled brightly and kept walking toward the palace.

Righting Past Wrongs

Marcus Today entered the gray palace office of High Priest Haluki for their weekly peace meeting. "Hello, Gunnar, I brought you something," he said with a smile. He reached into a pocket of his robe and produced a tiny gargoyle statue. When he set it on the high priest's desk, it grew to the size of a cat. It blinked a few times and yawned, covering its mouth politely, its ears perking up. A sharp horn made Haluki think twice about patting it on the head.

With a flourish, Mr. Today said, "This is Matilda, an extra set of eyes and ears for you. She communicates instantaneously

LISA McMANN

with her counterpart, Charlie, back in Artimé. They'll be good to have around in case of trouble."

"How lovely!" said Haluki. "I think I've seen them before wandering around Artimé, down by the gate. Thank you—we can use all the help we can get."

"They tend to roam. But you mustn't worry about her. Matilda can take care of herself," Mr. Today said, chuckling. "You may wish to warn others not to get too close."

"I shall do that."

"She won't hurt you, however."

"For that I am ever grateful," murmured Haluki solemnly, looking at the statue.

Matilda nodded regally, as if she had just taken over as high priest of all the land.

Mr. Today taught his friend Gunnar a few hand signals that he could use to communicate with Matilda, and gave him a thin book that contained many more for him to study. And then he ran his fingers through his hair. "So. How are things?"

The high priest smiled, but his eyes had deep circles under them. "Marcus, all I can say is it's tremendously good to see a friendly face."

LISA McMANN

Mr. Today sat in a chair as Matilda slid off the edge of the desk, hung on for a brief moment, and dropped to the floor to explore. "Tough going?"

"Yes. The Wanteds have been streaming in every day with complaints. They're having such a difficult time figuring out how to care for themselves. The concept of picking fruit and vegetables appears to be beyond their realm of understanding. They want their slaves back."

"I don't blame them," Mr. Today said with a laugh. "What I wouldn't give to have a few slaves feeding me berries and carrying out my least favorite duties. Alas, they'll learn eventually. They aren't called intelligent for nothing. They'll figure it all out right before they starve."

"And . . . while I've hesitated greatly to make any drastic changes to Quill, wanting instead to ease slowly into a new society, my first major improvement is that I've let my governors go. We've been in constant dissent, they don't trust me, I don't trust them, and they don't share my vision for Quill."

"Hmm," Mr. Today said. "You'll pick a new team, though, won't you?"

"Yes, absolutely. I need to first figure out whom I can trust. I hope I haven't made a mistake."

"It would be a mistake to keep the advisors that you've hid many things from in the past, Gunnar. You are creating a new Quill now. You need new support. I think it will work out well in the end."

Gunnar smiled. "I hope you're right. Still, I'm eager to make changes—free the Ancients, open up the walls to the ocean, teach the Wanteds how to fend for themselves. But I feel I must handle the complaints and gain trust first. Each step feels like climbing a mountain." He shifted in his chair. "How are things in Artimé?"

"Slightly chaotic, but entirely manageable." Mr. Today considered telling Gunnar about the recent skirmish, but then decided the high priest had enough on his mind.

"Good." Haluki relaxed back in his chair. "Have you anything on the peace agenda today? I think it's a bit too soon to plan a friendly island-wide picnic and sports tournament." His eyes shone with mirth.

Mr. Today smiled. "I do, indeed," he said. "I've been thinking a lot lately, and I have a question for you."

"I will do my very best to answer it."

Mr. Today leaned forward. "About how many Quillens would you say remain alive from the original founders? Or did Justine, ah, get rid of them all?"

Gunnar closed his eyes, thinking. He tapped his finger against his chin as he counted silently. "There are six," he said after a moment. "Four are in the Ancients Sector. The other two barely escaped that fate due to Justine's death."

Mr. Today nodded. "And would you say they are with you or against you? Can you tell?"

"Hmm," the high priest mused. "They are across the board with their loyalties. The majority I'd say were devoted to Justine, but I imagine sometimes things change when one is ordered to die."

"I'll say," muttered Mr. Today. "Well, truth be told, Gunnar, I've got something eating at me and I feel a need to make it right. I'm wondering what you think."

"Sounds intriguing," Haluki said. He glanced at his door to confirm that they had privacy.

Mr. Today nodded. "You of all people know about my many mistakes over the years. And I've done my best to fix

115 « Island of Silence

things. But there's one error that remains. It's something that, if nothing were done to the wronged party, they should never know the difference. And if they are told of my wrongdoing, it could raise some hackles, perhaps cause more serious problems for the both of us, for the short term, anyway. But I will always have this mistake plaguing me, and that is the problem. I've stolen something that doesn't belong to me. And no matter the outcome, I feel I must make things right."

High Priest Haluki listened carefully as Mr. Today explained everything.

When he was finished, the high priest nodded. "Whatever the outcome, it's the right thing to do."

"We should call them together as a group and do it at once, don't you think?"

Haluki smiled. "I'll have my drivers gather them immediately."

Within an hour, the six remaining original founders of Quill sat in the high priest's palace, wondering what in Quill could have happened to cause them to be sprung from their various homes and from the Ancients Sector. It had been decades since they'd last seen Marcus. They peered at the high priest and Mr. Today, some of them still sharp, others not quite all there, but all of them fairly able-bodied.

"Two visits to the palace in one day," grumbled one woman. "Maybe you've finally come around to feeding us, High Priest."

"I've already told you how to find food, Mrs. Rattrapp," Gunnar said.

Three men sat silent, along with a woman who kept nodding off in her chair.

A final woman sat rigid. She glanced around the office, noting Matilda with narrowed eyes. But she remained silent.

Mr. Today stood before them. "Friends," he said, "you don't remember coming to Quill. Nor do you remember the water that surrounds the land, or the homes and people you left to be here." He looked around to gauge their reactions before continuing. "You also don't remember the magical abilities you all have. And that's my fault. Justine and I took those memories from you many years ago."

He watched them. The two alert women were the only ones who had any reaction at all. Slow-motion shock registered on their faces, along with a large dose of confusion. He was using words they hadn't heard before. "But I'm going to give you back your memories now. I'm so terribly sorry. I hope you can forgive me. I understand if you cannot."

He lifted his hand, and then paused when he caught the eye of the rigid, silent woman. It looked like she wanted to say something. "Yes?" Mr. Today asked gently.

"Will I remember my name?" she whispered.

Mr. Today nodded. "Yes, my dear Secretary. You'll have your name . . . right now." He waved his hand over the group.

The four from the Ancients Sector appeared slightly puzzled, but largely unaffected.

The grumbling Wanted woman's face turned red and she looked furious.

And the woman named Secretary burst into tears.

On the Lawn

Mr. Today walked the long route back to Artimé as he liked to do now, giving himself time alone to think about all that had just transpired. When he arrived on the lawn at sunset, he saw Alex, Meghan, Cole Wickett, and Samheed sitting by the water. He sat down with them.

"It's a beautiful sky tonight," he said, gazing over the water to where the islands could just barely be seen if one knew where to look. "How are things going? Are you managing studies along with your new duties helping the Necessaries?"

"Oh yes," Meghan said, always chipper in front of the

mage, even when she didn't feel like it inside. "Things are going well." She smiled sweetly at Mr. Today, remembering the first time they sat together on this lawn back when he had turned a flower into a music box. It felt like ages ago, though it had only been a year and a half. "It's still funny to realize all the things we didn't used to know." She laughed. "If that makes any sense."

Cole sat up straight. "It makes sense to me," he said, fairly toppling over with admiration for every word that left Meghan's lips.

Meghan didn't seem to notice Cole's attentions as she continued her update, but Samheed looked away in disgust. Alex squelched a grin. Once Lani had pointed out the love triangle, he'd been watching them closely, and found it hilarious that Meghan seemed entirely unaware of her suitors.

Alex elbowed Samheed. "Lighten up," he muttered. And then he said for all to hear, "Where's Lani? She's been scarce for days."

Samheed shrugged. "Probably working on something. Who knows." He shifted uneasily, knowing Lani was avoiding Alex, and turned his attention back to Mr. Today.

"And where's Sean?" Alex didn't seem to get the picture.

Samheed shrugged and put a finger to his lips, then pointed to Mr. Today.

"Well, that's wonderful, Meghan," Mr. Today was saying. He got to his feet. "Alex, I'll see you tomorrow as usual. The rest of you, thank you for your generous contributions to our Necessary guests. It means the world to me."

Alex joined the others in a round of good-byes, but wondered secretly why Mr. Today wanted to continue meeting with him when he clearly wasn't the leader Mr. Today was looking for.

"Did you tell him?" Samheed asked Alex after Mr. Today was gone.

"Yes, about five times."

"Why do you keep meeting with him, then?"

"I have no idea." Alex sighed. "I mean, I said I'd help out, so maybe that's why."

"Did you ever think about suggesting a different leader?"

Alex laughed. "Who, you?"

"No." Samheed scowled. "I don't want to do it either."

"Then who?"

"I don't know. Don't you think there's someone you know pretty well who would be a good partner for High Priest Haluki?"

LISA McMANN

"Well, sure. Lani. But she just seems mad that I said no. She hasn't said five words to me since I told you guys about it. So I don't think she'd want it, or she'd have said something."

Samheed flopped back on the grass and stared at the stars that were just beginning to pop out for the evening. He sighed and muttered, "Why does everything have to be so complicated?"

"You're asking me?" Alex said.

The next afternoon Alex made his way as usual to Mr. Today's office. When he stepped inside, he stopped abruptly. There he found Ms. Morning, dressed in riding jodhpurs, a vest, and a cap. Her long honey-colored hair was mussed as if she'd been out in the wind, and Alex wondered idly if Mr. Today had randomly created horses around Artimé or if there were just the magical kind that Samheed had once used.

She noticed his look and laughed. "Small group training on invisible steeds," she said.

"Ahh." Alex smiled and then noticed a stranger in the room.

On the far side of Ms. Morning sat a rigid elderly woman.

She startled when she saw Alex, and her face grew fearful.

"Oh, wow, I'm sorry," Alex said, his face flushing with embarrassment. He took a step backward. "Did I get my meeting time wrong?"

Ms. Morning smiled. "Not at all, Alex. You're right on time. I think we're all meeting together." She turned to the woman and patted her hand. "He's not who you think. This is Aaron Stowe's twin, Alex. The resemblance is startling, isn't it?"

"Yes," the woman said, still wary. "Quite." All Eva had ever wanted in life was her job, and a boy who looked exactly like the one facing her had been the one to take it away.

"Alex Stowe, please meet Eva Fathom."

Alex wiped his hands on his pants—he'd just finished working with chalks—and nearly tripped over the chair leg as he walked over and reached out a hand to the woman. "Good grief," he muttered at his own clumsiness, and then to the woman he said, "It's nice to meet you," thinking how strange it was that someone here in Artimé knew Aaron but not him.

Just then Mr. Today breezed in. "So terribly sorry to be late!" he said. "I was just checking in with Charlie, as I was a bit worried about how he's doing here without Matilda. But they are in constant communication, so neither is feeling too badly, much to my relief. And both understand their importance in helping us during these uncertain times. How are we all? Have we met?"

Alex nodded.

"We've met, Father, but I think we're all waiting for you to explain the connection," Ms. Morning said.

"Ahhh," Mr. Today said, rubbing his hands together and smiling. "Well, Claire, Alex, and my dear Secretary—oh, pardon me! My dear Eva—the meeting is somewhat coincidental, as Ms. Fathom is here as an old friend and a new resident and I'm excited to welcome her. And, incidentally, glad to know your magic has indeed been restored, Eva, because without it you wouldn't have been able to get into my office. So . . . well done," he said, extraordinarily pleased. "Well done. Additionally, you three are all part of my future plans. Claire, you and Alex will begin learning more and more about the nuts and bolts that hold this place together, as you've offered to cover things for me while I take a holiday, hum hum," he said with a little note of pleasure that he couldn't contain, "and the delightful Ms. Fathom would like to accompany me on my

LISA McMANN

holiday to the nearby islands and visit old friends, now that she remembers them. It's always nicer to travel with someone, don't you agree?"

As Ms. Morning and Alex had never traveled before, they only nodded politely, keeping their puzzlement at Mr. Today's strange statement to themselves, which people sometimes did with the mage. Ms. Morning said, "Oh, yes," to acknowledge that they were listening, but it didn't really matter since Mr. Today was talking excitedly now.

"Now, Alex, you said that you'd do your best to help out, correct?"

Alex shifted in his chair. "Sure, I guess," he said.

"Wonderful!" Mr. Today said. "Well then. Claire, Ms. Fathom will be staying here in Artimé from now on. Will you show her to her room?"

Eva Fathom, who'd said barely a word, had that anxious look about her eyes like most visitors from Quill. "It's a large place here," she said now, a bit uncertainly, as if doubting her decision to move in. "How will I find my room?"

"Never fear, never fear. Your door will magically call out to you. Just don't forget your name and you'll be all right."

LISA McMANN

The old mage grinned cheekily, which, after a beat, produced a reluctant chuckle from the former secretary to the High Priest Justine.

"All right," she said, warming up a bit. "I thank you for your hospitality. Are you sure I'll be . . . accepted here after the position I held?" She glanced again at Alex, whose resemblance to Aaron was so strong that she could hardly hold herself from showing him the contempt she felt deep inside.

"Perfectly accepted," Mr. Today assured her. "Alex may look like Aaron, but he is the opposite of his twin. And Alex has none of his twin's drive to take over anything at all, so please don't worry about him." He laughed and held out a hand.

Alex felt his smiling lips freeze into position. It was like everything continued around him, Eva Fathom getting up and Ms. Morning ushering her out the door, but Alex couldn't move as Mr. Today's words sank in. He knew Mr. Today meant to imply that Alex wasn't an evil person who was trying to take over anyone's position or land or community, but the way the words came out in that particular order felt like a fire-breathing origami dragon had attacked and penetrated Alex's chest, taking away his breath.

Door Number One

Mr. Today left the office to accompany Ms. Morning and Eva Fathom to the new Necessary hallway where Eva would be staying, giving Alex a few moments alone to recover, at least physically. By the time Mr. Today and Ms. Morning returned, Alex's frozen face had thawed and he'd coaxed himself into letting the sting go away. After all, it was true, wasn't it? Alex just didn't have the drive to become leader of Artimé. Was there something to be ashamed of because of that? Alex didn't think so. He sighed deeply and tried to relax in his chair, prepared to find out what he was supposed to do to help Mr. Today and Ms. Morning.

But when they returned, Mr. Today didn't sit. "Come with me," he said instead, and he turned abruptly, walking back out the door. He hastened up the mostly secret hallway to one of the two doors on the opposite wall. He paused dramatically as Alex and Ms. Morning caught up to him. "This isn't quite as exciting for Ms. Morning as she's been in here a time or two. But it's a fascinating place, and I think you'll enjoy it, Alex. I call it . . . the Museum of Large."

It was a door Alex had often wondered about—one of four doors in this part of the secret hallway that he'd never seen opened, nor anyone entering or exiting. He assumed the two doors on the same side of the hallway as Mr. Today's office were his private living quarters, which made sense when Alex remembered that Mr. Today had once come in through the back wall of the office. But the two on the kitchenette side of the hallway had remained a mystery until now.

All negative feelings forgotten, Alex watched eagerly as Mr. Today touched the handle and uttered a spell. "Door number one." The door swung open with a low creak and Mr. Today stepped aside.

Alex walked into the dimly lit room, squinting to see. His footsteps sounded louder than life, as if the room went on for quite a long way, and he could hear things whirring and clicking, and what was possibly a distant waterfall or a fountain.

Ms. Morning and Mr. Today entered behind him and closed the door, and just as Alex's eyes began to adjust, Mr. Today commanded light to appear. In an instant, torchlike lamps that were attached to the walls lit up one by one, chasing around the perimeter of what seemed like an endless room . . . or cave . . . or . . . Alex didn't know a name for it. He sucked in a breath as his eyes leaped from one large item to the next.

"Go on then, have a look around for a few minutes," Mr. Today said, chuckling. "You might not want to touch anything unless you're absolutely sure of what it is." Ms. Morning smiled, nearly as eager as Alex. It looked like a place where you could visit a hundred times and still never see everything.

Alex looked to his left along the wall. The length of it as far as he could see was covered in tall shelves. Books overflowed from them, some carelessly so, and none looked like they were in any particular order. There were giant maps and an enormous marble ball with etchings on it and a ring around it, floating on a bubbling fountain. In a way this part of the Museum of Large resembled the Artimé library, but this seemed more massive yet more intimate at the same time.

"What are all these books about?" Alex was secretly delighted to see them in such disarray. It felt very homey despite the vastness of this room. "And how is it possible that this room just goes on forever? It seems like it would bump into one of the other mansion hallways."

"The books—many of them penned by me—are about a lot of things. There are also duplicates of most of them in the library. As for the room size, it's magic like the lounge or the theater. It takes up no real physical space, which is why it doesn't encompass the entire upper level of the mansion."

Something looming to Alex's right caught his eye and made the boy turn toward it, away from the books. He gasped. Just dozens of steps away was an enormous statue of an elephant-like creature so large that it nearly touched the ceiling. Alex had seen a picture of elephants in the library, but this one was ridiculously huge and had two long, sharp tusks along with a smaller pair that gleamed. Alex looked at Mr. Today. "Is it alive?" he whispered.

Mr. Today put his hand on Alex's shoulder. "No. Sadly, I had to pull the magic from old Tater many years ago. He's a mastodon statue—a prehistoric sort of elephant that I'd seen a picture of once. I thought he'd be useful in moving things around, but I never did get his mind quite right in the creating process. He grew to this size in a matter of days and soon became violent with the domestic creatures. So I sent him to live in the jungle for a while, but it didn't suit him, and he began to destroy it—uprooting trees and wandering back to the lawn, scaring everyone. He grew quite beyond what I'd ever intended, and he was becoming vastly uncomfortable in his own skin, so to speak. And try as I might, there was nothing I could do to change his disposition. I had made a mistake, and the rest of Artimé was suffering for it."

Mr. Today reached out to pet the beast. He was only tall enough to reach the creature's knee, so he patted that. "It was a hard day, but in the end Tater requested it—he was incredibly unhappy, I could tell. Once the magic was gone from him I couldn't bear to destroy him completely, so he lives on in here as a little reminder. He was the last statue I made—I just couldn't stand to go through that again, so I stopped creating them."

LISA McMANN

Ms. Morning gave her father's hand a squeeze. He looked at her, his eyes the tiniest bit shiny with regret.

But Alex didn't notice the sentimental exchange—his gaze had already alighted on something new, and his jaw dropped. Standing near the middle of the room, beyond an old refurbished Quillitary vehicle and a gray shack that looked eerily familiar, was an enormous pirate ship, tilted slightly to its port side. It had three masts with beautiful yet ominous-looking sails, and a deep brown wooden hull that shone as if it had been polished endlessly. Magnetized, Alex moved toward it. When he got close, he put his hands on the hull, running his fingers along the smooth wood. And then he cocked his head and stood very quiet for a long moment.

He turned to Mr. Today. "Do you hear that?"

Mr. Today smiled and touched the hull. "Yes. I'm not sure what causes it."

"It's whispering, like it's coming from inside the boat."

Mr. Today nodded. "It's done that all along. I've never been able to understand what they're saying. Can you?"

Alex shook his head.

Ms. Morning, who had followed Alex, approached. "I think

they're speaking in a different language," she said. "I've tried to understand it but admittedly without luck as well. I meant to ask Siggy about a book on languages."

Alex looked puzzled. "Languages? You mean, not what we speak? Like animal language or something?"

Mr. Today smiled. "When I was a boy, people spoke different languages depending on where they lived. They may still do so, I don't know. I hope to find out."

Alex looked back at the ship. "So . . . what is it for? Did you make it?"

"No, I didn't actually make this. It washed up on the beach one day a few years ago—does that sound accurate, Claire?"

Ms. Morning pressed her lips together, thinking. "Yes, not more than five years ago, for sure."

Mr. Today went on. "There were two pirates inside, but they were already dead—there was nothing any of us could do to save them. They wore the strangest things around their necks. . . ." Mr. Today trailed off, remembering.

"But how did you get it up here in the . . . the Museum of Large?" He liked the name, though he didn't really know what a museum was, other than this.

Mr. Today snapped back to the present. "What? Oh, just magic," he said. "The transport spell—do you know it?"

Alex shook his head.

"No component necessary, just envision the item in the place you want it to go. Like this." He pulled a candy platyprot from his robe, plucked a tiny piece of lint off of it, closed his eyes, and whispered, "Transport."

The candy disappeared, and a moment later Alex felt something in his hand. He grinned and looked at the bright yellow candy, blew on it, and then popped the tasty treat into his mouth. "Cool," he said.

The candy in his mouth said a muffled, "Cool. Cool. Cool."

"It doesn't work with humans or living creatures, only objects," Mr. Today added. "Small things transport quite perfectly, but large things can be quite tricky to place properly, so if you're very particular about where you want something big to end up, you're better off moving it yourself."

"Why did you put the ship up here?"

"I was afraid our creatures would get hurt or trapped if I left it on the beach. And it was a tremendous eyesore. It was such a rotted mess, I wasn't sure it could be saved. But I've fixed it up now, good as new. This is where I do a lot of my thinking."

Ms. Morning nodded. "I remember when this washed up—it was in terrible shape! You've done so much with it. Are you planning to take this on your journey? I assumed you'd use the white boat."

"I've thought about it," Mr. Today said. "With a little magic I could handle this ship on my own. I'd have to change out the pirate flags for something more friendly-looking, of course."

Alex knew a little about pirates from Mr. Appleblossom, who had single-handedly performed (in double time) all the major roles of a pirate musical during Actors' Studio several weeks before. "I think you would make a great pirate," Alex said.

"Why, thank you, Alex," Mr. Today said. And then his eyes opened wide as if he'd just thought of something. "Have you noticed the whale yet?"

"Where?" Alex looked all around.

"On the other side of the ship." Mr. Today ushered Alex around the ship to where the skeleton of a whale stood on display, put together perfectly. "This is also not of my own creation. It's a real whale that landed on the beach and got stuck many, many years ago, when I was alone here. I couldn't use transport magic to get it back in the water because, like I said, that spell doesn't work on living creatures.

"Frantic, I tried everything I could think of to no avail," Mr. Today said with a sigh. "I guess magicians can't fix everything—at least this one couldn't, especially back in the early days." He scratched his head. "I might have been able to do something if it had happened now, though my healing spells still aren't very strong. Healing has never been one of my gifts." His voice was sad as he looked over the skeleton. "I stayed with it until the end. It was a hard moment, and it remains a difficult memory. I felt very helpless. I'd like to think the whale didn't blame me." He walked around to the mouth of the skeleton. "So very sorry about that," he said in a soft voice, as if the whale could hear him.

Alex, though sensitive of Mr. Today's feelings, couldn't stop his eyes from wandering. He stared hard through the whale skeleton at something strange on the other side. "What's that?" he asked, pointing. He ran around the other side and saw a giant, jagged piece of lightweight material with some yellow lettering on the side. There was a fanlike object attached to the front of it.

Mr. Today followed. "Oh, this! It came out of the sky one day," he said, a smile playing at his lips.

Alex stared at Mr. Today. "From the sky? Weird."

"Yes, it was very strange. It started out much larger, or so I'm told—Jim saw it, as did Simber and a few others. It fell into the water, quite far over the ocean. This piece washed ashore a day or two later."

Alex looked at Mr. Today, but he had no words to express his wonderment at all the unusual things this room contained. He looked around at everything—the enormous library, the ship, the mastodon statue, the whale skeleton, and the countless other things yet to be explored—and he asked as politely as he knew how, "Mr. Today, why do you keep all of this amazing stuff locked up in here? Don't you think others would like to see it?"

Mr. Today smiled and thought a moment before answering. "It seems a bit selfish of me, doesn't it? Indeed, it does. But these things are either too breakable or too big to display elsewhere, or they are my personal treasures. These items make up my existence, Alex. Much of my life was spent alone, and these things are witnesses to it. The library tells my story, the mastodon my mistakes, the ship my discoveries and my abilities to make old things new without magic, and the whale . . . my limitations, I suppose." He pressed a finger to his lips. "There are many other things in here, but perhaps we've seen enough for today."

Mr. Today motioned toward the door and the three began walking. "I wanted you to see this for a reason. If while I'm away you need to know something about my past, please do check the library here. You'll find history, magic, and mistakes galore. Do you remember the spell to get in?"

Alex thought back. "Door number one?" he asked.

"That's correct. And I needn't remind you to keep that to yourself. These things are precious to me. They are my treasures. I know you'll protect them and care for them, won't you?"

Alex nodded vehemently as they exited the room and pulled the door closed. "I'll protect them with my life," he said. And he meant it.

Cohorts

Day after day Aaron Stowe packed his book bag full of food early in the morning, snuck out of the Haluki house, and made it to the palace gate by sunrise. Each day after the first, he made friends with a few hungry Wanteds and told them to return the same day the following week. Each afternoon when he was finished with his work near the palace, he went to the Favored Farm to collect more food.

On Monday of his second week, a figure was waiting for him. Once he realized it wasn't someone out to harm him, Aaron smirked to himself—his plan was working. He approached

LISA McMANN

and recognized the figure as the elderly woman he'd met his first day at the gate.

"Greetings," Aaron said. "I'm glad to see you back. Have you a need for more food? I've brought you some like I promised."

"Aaron Stowe—isn't that your name?" the woman asked. She looked at him with an air of suspicion.

Aaron's eyes flickered. "I can't deny it. I was the assistant secretary to the High Priest Justine until her assassination. Then I was ousted from the palace despite my abilities to improve Quill, and now I struggle to get by like everyone. May I ask yours?"

The woman's eyes narrowed. "Gondoleery Rattrapp." She emphasized the second syllable of her last name quite forcefully, so that it sounded like "ruh-TRAP." "I'm one of the original founders of Quill," she said importantly. "And a bitter enemy of Artimé."

"Well met, Mrs. Rattrapp," Aaron said, hiding his shock at her boldness of speech, and offering a hand. When Gondoleery held out her hand in return, Aaron took it and bowed over it as if she were the high priest, which left the woman speechless for a moment.

"Gondoleery, please," she said when her voice returned to her.

Aaron smiled at her and rummaged through his bag. "Gondoleery, and you must call me Aaron. And now that we are friends, perhaps you'd like breakfast. I have some fresh fruit today and some peanuts."

Gondoleery eagerly accepted the food, and at the sight of it, a handful of passing strangers, including a few more familiar faces, approached. Aaron reached into his bag methodically and doled out food items one at a time to keep the suspense high, but kept his attention focused on Gondoleery.

The old woman ate a few bites and then spoke. "I came to talk to you about what you said last week—about your ideas. I doubt you've heard, but that fink Marcus Today informed the six remaining founders of Quill that he stole our early memories from us decades ago. Now he's supposedly sorry and he gave them back. So . . . I know everything."

Aaron couldn't hide his surprise. "What are you talking about?" The crowd around them grew.

Gondoleery continued. "Back when we all made our new society in Quill, we came from other places, all of us. Other islands, other communities."

Aaron had to hold in his disbelief. *Other islands?*

"Justine and Marcus traveled around—they both had long hair back then, and those ridiculous robes, which were actually more like ponchos . . ." She trailed off for a minute, lost in thought. "Anyway, they traveled around letting people know about the dangers of the world that would soon come to pass, and they offered us this wonderful opportunity for a safe and perfect society. I, being not quite twenty, jumped at the chance. What an adventure, I thought." She scowled at her wrinkled hands. "And after some time here, while we built the protective wall around our society, Marcus Today enacted his insidious plan. He stole our memories and brainwashed us into believing that we were surrounded by enemies."

Aaron, having lost all sense of decorum, could only stare. "He did that to you? Wait. Are you saying that he brainwashed the High Priest Justine as well?"

"He must have stolen her memory too," said Gondoleery. "She would never have lied to us—she was a good woman. She was my leader, and Marcus Today has robbed us all."

A fearful, thrilling sort of feeling pierced through Aaron's stomach as he worked his mind quickly over this surprising statement. What could it all mean? Ah, but he knew it was the ammunition he needed, and quite possibly his ticket to the palace. He needed to organize his thoughts and get his plan right from the first moment in order to build his team of followers.

As pressure built from the whispering group around them, Aaron thought for a moment longer. He composed himself, gazing off into the distance as if this weren't the most important conversation of his entire life, one that his entire success hinged upon. And then he nodded slowly. "You're right, of course," he said. "This is what I have discovered as well. Mr. Today has fooled us all. Look around!" He made eye contact with each person surrounding him. "Look at us! We have been completely duped by Marcus Today since the beginning of Quill, fooled by a deranged man who lives in a mansion and eats all he wants, and never needs or wants for anything. He has handpicked his constituents over time, deceiving his own twin sister into believing she was the supreme ruler. And then he caused her death when she—and I—," he added, "discovered his lies, so that these secrets would go to the grave with her."

He took a breath and let it out slowly. "But we are smart, and the truth is clear now: Quill is not the land of the Wanteds, and it never has been. Artimé is the land of the Wanteds, and we are the *true* Unwanteds, all of us."

And then he paused dramatically, waiting for complete silence, before he asked the ominous question. "My friends," he said in a dark and bitter voice, "how does it feel to be Unwanted?"

As the small crowd's shocked mumblings grew to complaints and anger, Aaron Stowe watched, concealing his delight. If he could keep the momentum going, revenge might be nearer than he'd ever dared to hope.

Misunderstandings

Alex shifted from one foot to the other as he waited near the steps outside of the girls' hallway in the mansion, staring at the blank wall and watching girl after girl pop out of it. Most ignored him, for it wasn't uncommon for a boy to be waiting there for one of the girls. But some gave him a quizzical look, curious as to whom he was waiting for.

Most of the students knew who Alex was. After all, he was the one who nearly wrecked everything by bumbling around Artimé during the governors' visit, and the one the Quillitary general singled out at the onset of the battle. Students knew

LISA McMANN

from gossip and whispers about his evil twin brother, and some mistrusted Alex for it. But Alex didn't think that was fair at all. Everyone still loved Mr. Today even though they now knew that Justine had been his twin. And half the Unwanteds had other siblings in Quill—why weren't those Unwanteds suspicious?

But Alex thought of none of this today. After a restless night and nearly two weeks of the silent treatment from Lani, Alex woke a bit bleary-eyed but determined to get on Lani's good side again. Because even though they fought sometimes, he liked her more than he dared to admit to anyone, and he was miserable when they weren't speaking.

Ten minutes passed, and Alex began to wonder if Lani had already gone downstairs. His mind wandered to breakfast, but getting things straight with Lani was even more important than food. Finally she burst through the wall wearing a pretty blue top that matched her eyes and reading from a book as she did almost every day.

"Lani," Alex said.

She turned her head, bewildered at first, a bit lost in her book, but then she saw him. "Oh," she said. "Hi." She glanced at the stairs, tempted to continue down them, but then bit her lip and stopped. "Hi," she said again. "I didn't see you there."

Alex smiled and pointed at the book. "I know."

They stood facing each other awkwardly, the top of the balustrade between them, others rushing past to get to breakfast before classes started.

"So . . . what's up?" Lani asked. "Are you going to breakfast?"

Alex swallowed hard. "I—no, I'm not. I want to talk to you."

Lani looked at the floor. "What about?"

"About why you're mad at me. Look, I'm sorry, okay?"

Lani closed her book and sighed. "What are you sorry about? Did Sam say something?"

"You talked to Samheed about me?" Disgusted, he shook his head. "No, I'm actually perceptive enough to know when you're mad at me all on my own, believe it or not." It came out harsher than he meant it. "You've been avoiding me for two weeks."

The crowd around them thinned as the last stragglers made their way downstairs. Alex glanced over the banister to the entryway below, where Florence and Simber stood in their

LISA McMANN

places focusing on the dining room, or perhaps pointedly *not* looking at the top of the stairs to give the two some privacy.

Lani put her foot on the top of the landing, lining her shoe up next to Alex's. "I know," she muttered. "You don't have to be sorry. It's not your fault."

"Well, I could have said yes," Alex admitted, "so in a way it's my fault, but I'm glad you see it from my perspective."

"Wait," Lani said slowly. "What?"

Alex's eyes widened. He got the feeling he had just done something wrong again. "What, what?"

"What are you apologizing for, exactly?" she asked, her free hand moving to her hip.

Alex could see the tension come back to her face, but he didn't know what else to say. "I—I'm apologizing because you wish I had told Mr. Today that I'd be the next leader . . . of . . ." He faltered.

Lani waited a moment, daring him with her eyes to say the next word. But there was no way he was going to do that. "Boys," she muttered before she turned on the ball of her foot and strode regally down the stairs.

"Crud," Alex whispered as he watched her silky hair

bouncing against her back at each step. He felt like poking his own eyes out. When she neared the bottom, she continued walking straight ahead to the massive front door. She opened it and walked out.

Florence glanced at Alex at the top of the stairs, trying to hide her amusement, but Simber stayed completely still except for his ears, which suddenly twitched and turned sharply, as if sensing something. Alex debated what to do for a moment, but then decided he didn't need to starve to death over it, so he headed down the stairs as well to grab some food to bring to class with him.

At the bottom of the steps, Simber tensed, and then quickly extended his wings, bumping Alex and knocking him flat, and scaring him a great deal.

"Attention!" Simber roared, jumping from his pedestal and charging to the door. "Florrrence, to the gate. Alex and everrryone else, come. We arrre underrr attack!"

The giant cat pushed through the door and bounded away, his rippling stone body a mere flash by the windows that overlooked the lawn. Florence bellowed a sharp, "Marcus!" that shook the entire mansion.

Alex took off out the door after Simber, the boy's hands automatically digging in his pockets for spell components. Lani had had a head start, and Alex's stomach twisted when he saw her—she wasn't wearing her component vest today. "Lani, wait!" he cried out, but she didn't hear him in all the noise between them.

Intruders

Alex ran toward the gate at top speed as a dozen others, including Ms. Morning and Sean Ranger, fluidly exited the mansion from all doorways. There was shouting and confusion, girrinos rearing up, and a number of screams. Simber thundered across the lawn, making the ground shake, and Alex could see at least fifteen Quillens running about and yelling, attacking the girrinos with long pieces of rusty metal. Lani stayed on the edge of the fight, ducking and shoving Wanteds, avoiding attack and trying not to get trampled, but unable to cast any spells without her components. Three girrinos took the brunt

LISA McMANN

of the attacks and the fourth contorted and shuddered on the ground, squealing and roaring in pain.

Alex shot off a series of scatterclips, catching one Wanted in a wide open space and sending him flying backward several hundred feet into the Quill wasteland until he hit up against something the scatterclips could stick into.

Ms. Morning ran up to the entrance, shooting spells and staring hard at the men and women who were attacking Artimé, trying to identify them. She ran up to one who was attacking the girrinos, disarmed him, and began to cast a spell when he turned. When she saw his face, she stopped mid-spell. Her mouth slacked open and the Wanted's eyes grew wide with recognition, and then with fear. He took a step back and held his hand up as if to protect himself or beg for mercy.

But there was no time for anyone to react further. Simber thudded to a stop at the gate and gave an earth-shattering roar. The Quillans took one look at the invincible beast and shrieked. They turned abruptly and fled down the dirt road toward Quill. Simber chased them several yards. Sean and Ms. Morning followed and stood in the road, watching them go. Ms. Morning's fingers covered her mouth as the man she'd disarmed looked back. Simber whirled around and stampeded back to the entrance, where Arija now lay completely still.

A crowd of Artiméans gathered around Arija, including Lani and Mr. Today, who knelt by the girrino's side. Alex, breathless, stopped at the edge of the crowd and peered through the spaces between people and creatures. All was eerily silent.

Mr. Today murmured something undetectable over and over again as he moved his hand over the girrino's neck. For several agonizing minutes he worked, and when he finally looked up, he had tears running into the deep wrinkles around his eyes. "I'm afraid—" His voice broke. He took a deep breath and rested his hand gently on Arija's soft fur. He shook his head. "I'm not able to save her."

Everything was silent for the tiniest moment as Mr. Today's words sank in. And then the remaining girrinos sent up a cry so loud, so sorrowful, that it broke the hearts of every hearted person and creature for miles.

When Aaron Stowe heard it from deep within Quill, he smiled.

A Grave Danger

As word spread around Artimé about the attack and the shocking death of sweet Arija, no one was surprised to find classes canceled and an order on all blackboards to report to the theater immediately.

Lani walked willingly with Alex now, the argument between them forgotten for the moment. The two entered the theater in shock, Alex putting his arm around Lani's shoulders, and Lani letting him, as they made their way to where they usually met their friends when there was a crisis.

Meghan and Samheed were there already, Meghan crying

and clutching Samheed's hand. The four of them stood, not saying much at all, each thinking about how weird and horrible it was to see somebody alive one moment, and see them dead the next.

Alex told Meghan and Samheed how it all had happened, and how Lani was fighting valiantly, and how Simber scared the Quillens off, but it had been too late. Samheed, in a rare moment reserved for such tragic occasions, nudged Lani and whispered gruffly, "I'm glad you're okay. Wear your stupid vest, okay?"

A moment later a ripple went round the room as humans and creatures bustled to get seated, or to find their spots in the air as Jim the winged tortoise did, for on the stage was Mr. Today waiting patiently for silence. After everyone had settled and the room was quiet, Mr. Today spoke.

"I wish to keep this brief," he said in a gravelly voice. He cleared his throat and began again. "I am deeply saddened by this attack. Arija was a friend to everyone, and she guarded our entry faithfully for many years. No one was more dedicated to the safety of Artimé than she."

Tears fell around the room.

"The attack makes it all too clear: Quill is struggling mightily to accept us—more than anyone had imagined. As much as our friend, High Priest Haluki, is doing to make this transition possible, it is still incredibly hard to introduce new ideas into a society that has been so set in its ways for all these years." He scanned the audience, now fuller than ever with hundreds of Necessaries and even a few Wanteds joining them. His eyes landed on Eva Fathom, near the front of the theater, and he smiled sadly. Her form seemed less rigid than before, her head bowed.

"Clearly, we didn't expect this kind of violent, organized attack. Clearly, we should have."

Just then Charlie the gargoyle meandered to the stage and approached Mr. Today. He made rapid gestures with his hands, as if speaking in a kind of sign language, and Mr. Today watched him with great attention. When Charlie had finished, Mr. Today thanked him, and the gargoyle left the stage and wandered back to the tubes.

"High Priest Haluki sends his deepest condolences. He was as shocked to hear of the tragedy as we were to witness it. He asks anyone involved in the skirmish who might have recognized a member of the party, whether Quillitary or otherwise, to please contact him."

At the back of the room, Ms. Morning twisted and worked a handkerchief. She didn't look up.

Mr. Today gave a tired sigh. "Ah, me. Here we are, back where it all started," he said, almost to himself. "You know what to expect this time. Florence will begin Magical Warrior Training with the new residents, and the rest of you will sharpen your skills once again.

"Simber will be stationed at the gate for now—he is there already. Tina, Opal, and Penelope will take some much needed time off to mourn their sister and leader. From this moment forward, everyone is to wear your fully stocked component vests at all times, stay tuned to your blackboards, and be prepared for battle at a moment's notice."

Lani glanced at Samheed, who was looking sidelong at her. She nodded and looked down at her hands in her lap.

Mr. Today asked, "Are there any questions?"

"Yes," came a loud voice. "I have a question." Sean Ranger stood up. "Mr. Today, why don't you put the gate back up? Haven't enough of us died?"

LISA McMANN

Mr. Today paused a long moment, and then he spoke. "I don't know anymore, Sean," he said simply. "I ask myself the same question daily."

"Is it pride? Because if it is, I think it's reckless." Sean stood his ground.

Mr. Today didn't seem offended. "Perhaps you're right. Thank you for speaking up. I'll consider it."

A murmur rose up in the crowd. Alex sat up in his seat, shocked and even a little angry. Before he knew what he was doing, Alex stood and said, "Mr. Today, how can you say that after everything you've taught us? You taught us that we shouldn't hide. You taught us that we have the right to exist and live freely! You saved us, and we have to save Artimé— that's the price we pay for getting a second chance to live." The room was quiet again. "And anyone who doesn't agree can just go somewhere else."

Sean Ranger's eyes flared as he sought and found Alex in the crowded theater. He opened his mouth to speak, but then one by one Samheed, Lani, and others around Alex stood in agreement.

Only Meghan stayed seated, looking from her brother to her

best friend and back to her brother again. Wearily she buried her face in her hands as the place erupted into arguments and accusations about who was right and what should be done.

Alex, in heated but respectful debate with someone two rows in front of him, glanced up at the stage to see Mr. Today watching him. Alex stopped midsentence, feeling bad about starting the argument and ruining Mr. Today's speech, but the old mage nodded at Alex and clasped his hands together. Alex thought he might even look a bit proud.

A surge of electricity rushed through Alex's blood, and he felt anew the absolute thrill of being saved by Mr. Today and Artimé, the challenge and luck of being alive—a feeling he hadn't felt since before his brother had nearly killed him. He smiled at Mr. Today, for the first time feeling less like student and teacher, and more like friends.

Almost as if they understood each other without needing words.

Sleepless Again

Whenever Alex couldn't sleep he took to wandering the mansion. Sometimes in the dark of the night he saw Samheed, who had a similar sleep problem. Tonight was one of those nights. They left their rooms almost simultaneously, Samheed firing off a snide comment to his blackboard, Stuart, as he closed his door, and Alex responding "I won't" to Clive's "Don't die" reminder. The two met up and walked together without a need to speak.

Like they had done in the past, both turned right when they hit the balcony, and right again to walk down the mostly secret hallway. It had become habit to check out the blackboards in Mr. Today's office every now and then. As they passed the door that led to the Museum of Large, Alex glanced at it, longing to go in again and explore.

Samheed noticed the look. "What's in there, anyway?" he asked. "Have you ever been in there? I tried the door once, but it's locked."

Alex just shrugged, not wanting to lie, and not knowing if he could tell Samheed the truth.

The glass wall was never in place anymore, but Alex was always cautious, sticking his foot out to make sure.

Samheed laughed softly. "I ran into that thing once too, you know. If you throw a scatterclip or an origami dragon down the hall, you can tell if it's up without having to inch along like that."

Alex sniffed. "I don't like to waste my components."

"Suit yourself. You look like a dork, though."

They entered Mr. Today's office and pulled chairs up to the blackboards, watching not much of anything in the dark. Alex knew that Mr. Today wouldn't mind them sitting in here watching. Not now. Not anymore. It was much less scary not having to worry about Mr. Today discovering them, Alex had to admit.

"I liked what you said at the assembly," Samheed said after a while. "I think you were right. What the heck happened to make Sean Ranger even ask that question? That didn't seem like him."

"I thought that was weird too, but he's been acting strange lately. Did you see him take off out of the theater after the meeting? He went straight for the gate and into Quill," Alex said as the blackboard focused on Aaron's old room. A new boy was there now, but Alex couldn't make out any features in the dark. "I think he and Meghan got gutted hard when they went to see their parents. Meg has seemed really preoccupied ever since they did that."

"Huh," Samheed said. "Meg told me once that when Sean was first Unwanted, her mother wandered around for a couple of years with a vacant look on her face, like she was having trouble getting over Sean. But she didn't have that same look for Meghan when she and Sean went back home to see them."

"Yeowch," Alex said. "She told me they seemed glad to see Sean. But her . . . not so much."

"That's pretty brutal. And a little too familiar."

Alex gave Samheed a sidelong look in the glow of the blackboards and the soft night lighting of the office. "Did your mother ever come back?"

"No. And I'm glad. I hope she . . . I hope she never does."

"Would you talk to her?"

"No." Samheed ripped his fingers through his hair. "I don't know. Maybe. Would you talk to your parents?"

Alex thought for a long moment. "Yes. But my parents won't come. They'll be on Aaron's side forever. He told me he never wanted to see them again, but that won't matter to my parents. They are Necessaries who want to be Wanteds. They'll starve to death before they come to our side. That's just the way they are."

They sat for a moment in silence.

"Hey, who's the new guy in Aaron's room?" Samheed asked.

"I dunno."

"Maybe Mr. Today is focusing on a different Wanted now. Spooky."

Alex sat up and leaned forward. "Do you think so?"

"No, not really. It's the same angle as before, and yeah,

look," he said, pointing at the knots of wood in their familiar places. "It's the same door. I think we both have that dumb door memorized."

Alex laughed. "Yes. I bet Mr. Today still has my 3-D drawing. It would be funny to go in and scare the new kid."

Samheed smiled evilly. But then he turned back to the blackboards. He wasn't about to be the bad guy again. "I wonder where Aaron is. Do you know?"

"No." Alex jiggled his foot. "And I don't like not knowing. It makes me nervous."

"I know. Me too."

They watched a moment more, seeing only a few unidentifiable people walking along the road. Alex squinted, trying to see if one was Aaron, but he couldn't be sure. A couple passed by, but all Alex could detect was an older woman with a young man of average height. It looked like Sean Ranger's profile—and was that his mother? He peered closer, but soon they walked out of sight. Alex sighed.

Samheed drummed the arm of his chair with his fingers. He stood up. "There's nothing happening. I'm going to get food."

"Yeah." Alex got to his feet too and followed Samheed out.

The two wandered back to the balcony and down the stairs. Alex looked at the empty spot where Simber used to stand. It was strange not having Simber to guard the mansion door at night. Impulsively Alex said, "I'm going for a walk. See you in the morning."

"Yeah, okay."

Alex went outside and stood at the seashore for a few moments, feeling the salty spray and tasting it on his lips. He sucked in an enormous breath and let it out as he thought about Arija, and about Mr. Today up on the stage, and the strange but welcome surge of electricity that had pulsed through him. It was still there, that feeling. It was like he'd been sick for so long he forgot what feeling well was like. But today, he remembered. He felt like running and doing push-ups. Instead he turned and jogged past the mansion toward the gate.

"Hello, Alex," Simber said without turning around.

"Hi." Alex came up alongside the great cat. He sat down in the grass and leaned up against the gray stone wall. He looked out to the road that encircled Quill, to the very place where he'd stood with Simber when Quill attacked. A visit to the gate

LISA McMANN

often conjured up strong feelings and vivid memories to those who passed through it. Alex shuddered as he thought about the other side.

"Arrre you cold?"

"No. Just remembering."

They sat in silence for a while, Simber's ears, eyes, and nostrils moving now and then.

"Can't sleep?" A steady, low, rumble-purr added comfort to the night noises. "Orrr doing something else tonight?"

"I haven't felt like doing much of anything lately," Alex said, surprising himself—he hadn't voiced that feeling before, but such was the power of the gate. "Not since . . . you know. Since that whole attack in Justine's palace."

Simber nodded.

Alex waved away a mosquito that had strayed in from Quill. "That was really hard, you know?"

"I rrrememberrr," Simber said in a way that made Alex feel a bit better about it all. "You nearrrly died as I was carrrying you home."

Alex let his head rest against the wall and he sighed.

"It's okay forrr you to feel that way," Simber said. "Yourrr body has rrrecoverrred, but yourrr mind also needs to rrrecoverrr."

Alex was quiet for a long moment. He pinched the bridge of his nose, feeling a headache coming on. "I just can't stand to think about another battle like that. About getting hit, and getting hurt like that again. You know?" He remembered how long it had taken to recover, how painful it was. "But," he said, almost with wonder at the words that were coming out, "if I had to, I'd do it again. I'd do it for Mr. Today and Artimé. For sure I would."

Then he looked at Simber and asked, "Do you think I have drive?"

Simber tilted his head, as if he were searching for the meaning behind the question. "The rrright question is, do *you* think you do?"

Alex pressed his lips together tightly and nodded. "I guess so. I think I do."

Simber almost smiled. "How does it feel?"

"It feels scary. Dangerous. It's a lot easier to just . . . be nothing. Ignore things."

For the first time since Alex had sat down, Simber looked at the boy. "Yes, it is."

"Mr. Today wanted me to lead. Like . . . when he's, you know, gone."

Simber turned his face back to Quill. "I know."

"I told him no."

"I know," the cheetah said again.

"Does he tell you everything?"

Simber smacked his chops. "Prrretty much."

"Oh."

"Rrright." Simber stood, walked to the road, and then returned, arching his back into an impossibly high arc, and then stretching out his hind legs as well, one at a time. "I feel as if therrre's something else you want to ask me."

Alex bit his lip. "I—I guess so. I mean . . ."

Simber sat on his haunches and waited patiently.

"I mean, who would . . . be there with me—for me— if I did it? Like, how you're there with him. Or, you know, would I just be alone? Or have to find my own . . . Because I don't . . . really . . . have anyone like that. Not at all." He thought about his friends, knowing of course they'd be there whenever he needed them, but they just didn't feel . . . big enough. And the job felt so cavernous, and Alex felt so . . . swallowed up by the thought.

Simber turned once again to face Alex. His eyes were warm and they glinted in the moonlight. "I am alrrready herrre forrr you, Alex. Wheneverrr you need me, as long as you need me. And even longerrr," he said. "It is my duty. But it's also my pleasurrre."

Blood rushed to Alex's face, but at the same time, warmth also flooded his chest. No one in Alex's memory had ever said words quite like that to him before.

Magic in Quill?

Aaron and Gondoleery met daily now by the gate to the high priest's palace, a most peculiar-looking pair, though to the casual onlooker they appeared simply to be a young man with his grandmother—a deceptively innocent combination. Thus they became nearly invisible to the Quillitary over time.

Every day the two were inseparable as they quietly coerced angry Wanteds and lured them with food to their way of thinking. Aaron, after a few days with Gondoleery, took a chance and told her where he was getting the food. He brought her with him to see the Favored Farm and showed her how easy it was to pick fruit and vegetables. And while Gondoleery had heard of this place from the high priest, she had no concept in her head of what it could be like, and had never gone to it because it was a Necessary job.

"This place reminds me of where I grew up. People planted things," Gondoleery said. She'd been thinking about her childhood a lot lately now that she had her memory back. "Each person grew their own, and brought the extras to a market once a week for the people who had no place to grow things. And those people would buy it," she said.

Aaron narrowed his eyes. "What's 'buy it' mean?"

"Exchange a valuable coin for it. The coins could trade for anything, and everyone wanted more coins, so that was the best thing to have."

"Strange," Aaron said, glancing over his shoulder to see if the guard was watching, and then shoving a handful of berries into his mouth and chewing thoughtfully. "You can't eat these coins, can you? So what good are they?"

"No, you can't eat them, but you can buy food with them, and other things."

Aaron shrugged, disinterested. "What else is there to need

except food? It sounds like extra work, trading coins for other things when you can just go get the other things."

Gondoleery wolfed down some grapes and nodded. "They kept making coins until everyone had hundreds and thousands of them, and then they weren't valuable at all anymore."

Aaron furrowed his brow trying to make sense of it, but it sounded completely crazy to him. And soon he forgot all about it. They picked their four items each that they were not stealing, showed them to the guard, and went on their way.

There was something else Aaron wanted to ask Gondoleery, and finally he ventured. "You said that when Mr. Today gave you back your memories, he also gave you back your magic. Does that mean you have magical powers, like Mr. Today and the Artiméans?"

Gondoleery hobbled along next to him. "Maybe," she said.

Aaron salivated. As much as he hated the creativity behind magic, it was still a powerful weapon to have on their side. "You aren't . . . sure?"

She narrowed her eyes at him. "I'm not sure of anything," she said, "including you. So I'm not going to answer that question."

Aaron bristled slightly. "Fair enough," he muttered. "I thought that you might have noticed how much trust I've put in you, how much food I've given you, and now I've showed you the secret of the Favored Farm, which is practically our own private stash. But no matter." He tried not to feel vulnerable, but he was suddenly afraid he'd made a big mistake in showing Gondoleery the farm.

"Keep doing what you're doing to upend Artimé and maybe one day I will tell you," the old woman said. As it stood, she wasn't quite sure what she could do magically. So far, it wasn't much. But Aaron didn't need to know that.

"I have no other plans than to do just that," Aaron said lightly. "We have ourselves quite a group of supporters now who have already enthusiastically made a mark on Artimé. Thirty-three at last count, including two governors' sons, which I'm very pleased about. I intend to grow our group to a majority in Quill so that we might take over the palace, get rid of Haluki and Artimé, and return to the beautiful peace we once had in Quill. Do I have your full support?"

"Of course," Gondoleery said. "You have my full support to restore Quill. But that doesn't mean you get all my secrets."

LISA McMANN

Aaron almost sniped back, "I don't want all your secrets—just the one!" but he held his tongue and nodded, returning his demeanor to caring and friendly.

As they approached the gate for the second time that day, Aaron saw a familiar figure waiting for them. They drew near, and Aaron held out his hand to the woman in greeting. "Ahh," he said grandly. "My dear Eva Fathom." He bowed over her fingertips. "What news do you bring us from the mansion?"

A New Spell

Alex, Lani, Meghan, and Samheed stood with hundreds of other Artiméans in two rows that stretched from the side lawn of the mansion all the way to the edge of the jungle. The rows faced each other, twenty yards apart, and Florence thunder-stepped between them, giving instructions on Advanced Magical Warrior Training.

She called this session "Advanced," though last year it was just called regular old ordinary Magical Warrior Training, because, after several very frustrating sessions with Necessaries and Unwanteds together, it became clear that certain new

LISA McMANN

Artiméans were in need of a very basic class. More of a let's-see-if-you-can-actually-pull-this-off-before-we-put-you-in-the-action sort of class.

Lani's little brother, Henry, ten years old but still about the size of a gargoyle (and, if you asked Lani, similar to a gargoyle in looks as well), was a quirky boy who asked a lot of questions and carried around a magnifying glass in case he needed to examine things, which he often stopped to do, to Lani's exasperation. But Henry was also exceptional at magic and took to it very quickly, so he joined the advanced class with his sister and her friends. They actually really liked the boy. He was clever and a hard worker and took his spells very seriously.

But Lani's mother was one such Artiméan who perhaps "needed improvement" in Florence's eyes. And there were many others—most of them adults, curiously enough, while the younger Necessaries were quite able to pick up the art organically. So the Beginning Magical Warrior Training class was born.

The beginners were originally assigned to watch the advanced students, taking notes and trying things, but after several accidents around the community, it was decided that they were no longer allowed to actually touch any components at this time.

So Alex and his friends waited patiently while Florence instructed the beginners, young and old alike, on what to watch for. Even Eva Fathom was there, watching with interest on the sidelines and taking notes.

Alex fingered the new heart-shaped component in his pocket, eager to give it a try. He was very proud of this particular creation—it was likely his most powerful spell yet, and he was already working on a lethal level spell to it. It scared and thrilled him just to think about it, and a little chill ran up his spine and quivered at the back of his neck. He hadn't felt this excited since . . . well, since the last time he began Magical Warrior Training. Maybe it was because he had worked so hard for it back then, or because he'd been somewhat unfairly held back from it originally, but deep down, Alex thought he knew what was so exciting about battle. It was because he was, to put it boldly, quite amazingly good at fighting.

He smiled to himself as he realized it. It was totally true. Alex was a great fighter, and he was also an excellent spell

LISA McMANN

builder—one of the best. Mr. Today said so. So did Simber, and Mr. Appleblossom, and Ms. Morning, and especially Ms. Octavia, who knew his skill level was far beyond many others his age.

"What are you smiling at?" Lani whispered.

Alex startled and looked at her. He grinned even bigger, and sort of goofily, because he realized that Lani was just as excellent in different ways. She was extremely stealthy and sly, and no one ever had to worry much about her—she could naturally get out of any pinch with her fast thinking and her intricate moves.

Lani grinned too. "What?" she asked again. And then she laughed. "Why are we smiling?"

Alex just looked at her, and his heart clutched and sputtered. "We're awesome," he said finally. "I'm smiling because we are awesome."

Lani laughed again and shook her head. "You are such a dork." But she said it in the sweetest way a girl could ever say it to a guy.

It was crazy. Alex felt like he was finally getting his energy back after the last battle, and he hadn't even known he'd lost it until this excitement surged through him these past few weeks. He bounced on his toes in anticipation, focused now on the Unwanted opposite him—a woman who'd been Purged about ten years ago, whom Alex had thought he'd seen around with a baby recently. He didn't know her name, but she flashed a cheeky grin at Alex and gave him a nod that said "Bring it."

As Florence counted down nearby, Alex put all his focus on the heart-shaped bit of clay between his fingers, and when she shouted "Fire!" Alex pulled his arm back, whispered, "Heart attack," and then sent it forward in the fluid motion of a true artist who knows that speed isn't important—only focus is.

The little heart left his fingers and sprouted tiny white wings, which gave it an incredible range. It sailed perfectly at the woman, who still grinned, knowing she'd get him back in a minute. It struck her in the chest.

With the smile melting from her lips, the woman's eyes grew wide, and she collapsed to the ground, her body in spasms. A few seconds later she stopped moving.

Alex gasped. The roar of the crowd around Alex sounded far away as all the others let go of their components and the row opposite them erupted into the strangest fits anyone had

LISA McMANN

ever seen. Some ran away screaming, some flew backward and were pinned to the great gray wall, others hopped around, and still others froze and didn't move.

There was complete silence from the beginner students, who watched in fear, and a momentary collective pause from Alex's row as they peered to see where their opponents ended up, and then a cheer. They ran immediately to their counterparts to release the spells. But Alex wasn't cheering.

He ran to the woman he'd hit. Her body had curled up on the ground, still and pale as death itself. Alex's stomach twisted in fear—*What if it was a little too strong?* He hurried to release the spell.

A tense moment passed and Florence approached. She looked at the woman and turned to Alex, alarmed. "What spell?"

"A new one," Alex said, ripping his fingers through his hair anxiously. "I call it 'heart attack.'" His own heart sank to his gut as Lani, Sam, Meghan, and a dozen other Unwanteds gathered around to see what the fuss was about.

Florence, never one to panic, patted Alex's shoulder. "Okay. It'll be fine. Look—she's coming around now."

The color slowly returned to the woman's cheeks and her eyelids fluttered. She rolled to her stomach, coughed, and pushed herself up on one elbow, a dazed look on her face.

Alex sucked in a breath and let it out in a loud, relieved whoosh. "Wow," he said. "Sorry about that." He held his hand out to her and she took it, getting up slowly. "Are you okay?"

After a minute she grinned weakly and shook her head in wonder at the boy. "That," she said, "was quite an experience." She coughed a few times as Florence examined her.

"I'm really sorry," Alex said again.

And then the woman looked Alex in the eye and said very seriously, "No, don't be. I mean it. That was intense. I'd do just about anything for you, Alex, if you'd make me a dozen of those." She straightened her vest and wiped a few blades of grass from her elbow. "As soon as possible, please. That's the worst spell I've ever seen. Or felt. Or . . . experienced. And by worst, I mean best."

Alex let out a rattled laugh, still slightly unnerved. "Okay, sure," he said. "No problem."

The woman held out her hand. "I'm Carina," she said. "Carina Fathom. You can find me in the family hallway."

Alex relaxed a bit when he heard her familiar last name. "Alex Stowe," he said, giving her hand a firm shake. "I'll make some for you, I promise."

The woman chuckled. "You're so modest. Don't you realize that everybody here knows who you are? In our hallway you're known as 'the guy to stand behind' if we ever have to go to battle again." She laughed. "That's a pretty big compliment."

Alex felt his face heat up. "Wow," he said, feeling extremely awkward. He thought he was still regarded as the one who had almost ruined everything.

He felt a heavy hand on his shoulder and looked up at Florence, who had a very pleased look on her face. "Okay, everybody," she said. "Back to work."

The crowd dispersed back to their rows, but Florence kept her hand on Alex's shoulder as they walked more slowly than the others and stopped halfway. When no one else was within listening distance, she faced him and spoke in a low voice. "You are a true warrior."

Alex blushed again and looked at the ground.

"I'm going to need two things from you, Alex."

"Yes?" he said, looking back up.

"A thousand heart attack components—after you supply your test victim first, of course—and your presence at a private magical weapons meeting with Ms. Octavia, Mr. Today, Simber, Ms. Morning, and me. Mr. Today's office, immediately after this session. Can you make that?"

The excitement inside of Alex grew until it nearly burst forth from his skin. "You got it," he said. He turned to run back to the line, and then he hesitated.

"Florence?"

"Yes?"

"Can I bring my friends? They're awfully good at spells too. We help each other a lot, and they have a lot of skills I don't have." He bit his lip, hoping he hadn't asked too much.

Florence narrowed her eyes. "Which ones? You mean the three you are so tight with? Haluki, Burkesh, Ranger, right?"

Alex nodded.

Florence considered it for a moment. And then she said, "I think that's a very good idea."

Alex grinned. "Thank you!"

He turned and was running back toward the shore to his spot where all the others waited patiently when something on

LISA McMANN

the water caught his eye. He stopped and squinted, bringing his hand to his forehead to shield the sun. His jaw dropped. "What the . . . ?" It was the strangest thing he'd ever seen. He shouldered past his friends and kept going.

Lani turned in surprise, and then she caught sight of it too. She sprinted after Alex and reached him just as he dove into the sea and swam out to it.

"Call Mr. Today," Alex shouted when he surfaced. "Hurry!" He reached for it and spun around on his back, kicking his feet and trying to pull the thing toward the shore. "Florence! Anybody! Help!"

Visitors

S amheed and Meghan both came running and helped Alex pull the thing ashore. They'd never seen anything like it, but it didn't take much to guess its purpose.

It was a makeshift raft of logs and vines. Several logs were missing, as if it had fallen apart along its tenuous journey. But that's not what the people of Artimé were looking at as they gathered around, for lying on the raft were two young people.

At least they looked somewhat human, but if pressed, one might have to admit to being unsure. A boy of ten or eleven, perhaps, and a girl a few years older, both completely still, eyes

LISA McMANN

closed. Their skin was badly sunburned, and they had very little more than that covering their bones.

But the most ominous feature was this: Each wore a most curious, sinister thing—a thick band made of metal thorns that weaved in and out of the skin around their necks.

Alex, who had cautiously stepped onto the raft and now kneeled between the two, stared at the girl with her parched lips and burned, peeling skin, the choker so embedded into her neck that it seemed part of her. Alex's stomach twisted at the thought of someone threading it into her skin. He reached out to touch it. "Who are you?" he whispered. But there was no time to puzzle over things.

Lani, who had immediately run to get Mr. Today, now returned at full speed, the old mage in her wake, his robe flying behind him. They had to break through the crowd that had rushed over at Alex's first frantic shout. Alex and Meghan kneeled around the two bodies as Samheed and a few others barked at everyone to back away and give them space to move.

Mr. Today dropped to his knees at the side of the girl and felt for a pulse.

Alex turned and put his head on the boy's chest. He held

his hand above the boy's nose and mouth. "I think he's alive," he said.

Mr. Today looked up. "The girl is too. Let's get them inside. Alex, remember the sick wing we created in the mansion where you spent so much time? I need you to re-create that for me immediately. I'm sending you the verbal component—check your pocket. Go!"

Florence ordered the crowd to go back to the lawn and continue with class. Alex had no idea how he was going to create a sick wing, but didn't hesitate. He sped to the mansion.

"Meghan, please find Ms. Morning and tell her we have sick and injured. She'll know what to do."

"Got it," Meghan said, and she took off.

"Samheed, can you pick up the boy, slowly and carefully please, and follow me?"

In the mansion Alex, still dripping wet, wriggled his hand into his pocket and pulled out the sodden note from Mr. Today. He stood between the front entrance and the dining room, read over the words, concentrating, and then took a deep breath to calm himself. He didn't want to mess this up. He held his shaking hand up to the wall and said, "Extend and heal, size small."

Nothing happened.

Alex muttered under his breath. And then, louder and more forcefully, "Come on, Stowe." He closed his eyes, took a deep breath, and shook his arms out to loosen them. "You can do this. Believe it." He let out the breath and opened his eyes. Concentrating, he allowed everything around him to fade to a blur and he stared hard at the wall. Then he held up his hand again, feeling the power it contained. He focused another second or two, and said it again, with great purpose and confidence. "Extend and heal, size small."

He held his pose, frozen and determined, staring at the wall. When it began to waver in front of him, he wasn't sure if he was about to faint or if it was really moving. It only took a second to find out.

The wall shimmered and then a piece the size of a doorway pushed back, first creating a space the size of a large closet, and then expanding in all directions until it neared the dimensions of Alex's room. From one newly formed wall, beds, tables, and chairs dropped down. Countertops and cupboards pushed out of another wall, and medical tools and supplies on carts grew up from the floor. Just as the last piece settled into place, the mansion door pushed open and Mr. Today and Samheed walked in, each carrying one of the strangers.

They hurried into the room and laid them on the beds. Mr. Today uttered a few healing spells over them in a calm, soothing voice. Soon Ms. Morning rushed in with a woman and man whom Alex recognized as nurses from when he spent time in here.

Alex, still standing in a puddle of water near the opening to the hospital wing, shuffled forward a few steps and stared into the room at the strangers. Where did they come from? Who were they? The girl, despite her sunburn and her pinched, starved look, had such a perfect, exotic face. And the boy's choker ornament must have been more recent—the skin around the thorns was swollen and scabbed over.

Alex imagined their story, their world. Had they been out rafting for fun and gotten swept away with the current? Were they out fishing and a storm came up? He pictured the exotic-looking girl trying to be strong as the two faced the huge sea alone, trying to act brave in front of the younger boy. Trying

LISA McMANN

to stay awake. And alive. He found himself drawn to her, admiring her, and he didn't even understand why.

A soft hand on his arm and a voice near his ear startled him back to reality. He turned and saw Lani. "Oh. Hey," he said weakly. "I didn't hear you come in."

The World Gets Bigger

Y ou should go change your clothes," Lani said. "I'll clean this up."

Alex looked down at the puddle under his feet. "Oh, wow. Yeah. Thanks. I'll be right back." He bounded up the stairs two at a time, entered the boys' hallway, and went into his room.

"What happened to you?" Clive said, his face pushing out from the blackboard.

Alex ran past Clive to his room. "Tell you in a second!" he said.

"One," Clive said. "Liar."

LISA McMANN

Alex changed his clothes and came back out, running a comb through his tangled mess of hair. "Two strangers on a raft landed on our beach," he said, breathing hard.

Clive's expression brightened. "Ooh," he said. "Where are they from? One of the islands out there? Not that I know much about the islands. I don't get to see anything but you." He sniffed. "I just hear things."

"Nobody knows. They're not conscious." He tossed the comb onto the bed and headed for the door. "I've got to go. Bye!"

Clive mumbled something incoherent as the door slammed and Alex bounded back down the stairs.

"Thanks," Alex said to Lani, who had cleaned up the water with a dry spell she made up on the fly.

"No problem," she said. "I tried to go in to see what's going on but Ms. Morning said we should just give them some space right now." She looked disappointed.

"Did you see the things around their necks?" Alex asked.

"Yeah, that's so strange."

"I wonder where they're from."

Lani shrugged. "Who knows?"

They walked out of the mansion and spied Meghan and Samheed at the shore by the raft. They headed toward them. Advanced Magical Warrior Training was still going on, but none of them felt like doing it right now. There was too much to talk about.

They examined the raft, but found no clues to its origin. "It's just a bunch of big sticks tied together," Lani said. "Anything on the other side?"

"No, just some slime," Samheed said. "I flipped it over already."

Alex looked out to sea. It was almost impossible to see the islands during the day unless you knew exactly where they were. They were most visible when the sun set behind them, highlighting the fact that they were stationary and the sea moved in swells all around. "I wonder . . . ," he said.

His friends followed his gaze. "I don't know where else they could have come from," Meghan said. "It's the only logical guess."

"Are there any other islands on the other side of ours?" Samheed asked. "Has anybody been all the way around Quill on the outside of the wall?"

"No," said Alex, who'd only been about a quarter of the way around Quill via boat when he'd gone to the palace with Mr. Today. "But I bet I know who has." He grinned. "Come on."

They walked quickly around the practicing students to the gate where Simber stood, stoic.

"I have a strrrange feeling you fourrr arrre up to no good," Simber remarked when they approached.

"We're totally innocent," Meghan said. "We were just wondering about the kids on the raft and where they might have come from."

"Harrrd to say," Simber said, sampling the air as he spoke.

"Are there islands on the other side of Quill? None of us has been all the way around," Alex said. "But you've flown up above the barbed-wire ceiling, haven't you? Have you been to the other side?"

"I have," Simber said. He raised an eyebrow, tempted to make them beg for his attention as cats are wont to do with humans, but gave in to their eager faces and continued. "Therrre arrre thrrree islands to the west—you can see two of them frrrom ourrr shorrre."

Alex and Samheed exchanged a glance. *Three?*

"And thrrree islands to the east." The giant cheetah brought his left front paw to his mouth and gnawed at a toenail for a moment. When he was finished, he said, "We'rrre exactly in the middle of a chain."

"Wow," Lani said, awed. When she wasn't riding on his back, she generally stayed several steps away from the statue, as they'd had their altercations in the past. One couldn't be too cautious, and she was never sure of Simber's mood.

"Seven islands," Alex said. "So the strangers could be from any one of them."

"But if you factor in the ocean's current," Lani said, "which is really strong right here, by the way, that would make it more likely for some and less likely for others." She'd just learned about currents from an old book up on the archives floor of the library, called *Bodies of Water*.

Samheed raised an eyebrow. "Okay, Smart Stuff, so which way does the current flow? Wait—don't answer that. I think I know from swimming out there."

Lani grinned at him. "Go for it."

"It flows . . . west." He hesitated. "No, I mean east."

"Which is it?" Alex said.

"East," Samheed said, sure this time. "I'm sure. The current flows east, which means it starts in the west and goes east. Because west is the direction the raft came from."

"That's the direction of the islands we can see. Right? Because that's where the sun sets."

"Right."

"So it's most likely one of those three out that way. Right, Lani?"

"That's my guess."

Simber coughed lightly and they all turned to look at him.

"Arrren't you supposed to be in class?" he said pointedly.

"We're skipping," Alex said proudly, feeling sneaky and brave at the same time.

"I can see that," Simber said. "Howeverrr, it doesn't feel quite rrright to congrrratulate you." The big cat stifled a smile.

Alex shrugged. "To understand the rules, one must first break the rules," he said wisely.

Lani gave him a quizzical look. "Who said that?" she asked.

"Me. Der," Alex said. "I made it up."

Samheed snorted. "Come on, guys. Before Simber decides to mutilate us."

LISA McMANN

Simber growled lightly as if in warning, but the four grinned.

"See you at the meeting," Simber said. "Maybe you should prrreparrre."

Alex's eyes widened. "Oh, crudbucket! I forgot all about it."

"Wait. You have *another* meeting?" Lani said, trying to contain her disgust. She'd made amends with Alex, but that still didn't make her like the fact that Mr. Today hadn't asked her to lead.

"We all do," Alex said. "You guys are coming too. I totally forgot to tell you—that's what Florence was talking to me about when the raft showed up."

Simber cleared his throat loudly, which startled the four into moving quickly away.

"Florence wants us four to come to the meeting about magical weapons today, right after class. I can't believe I forgot!" Alex began to trot toward the mansion. "Come on, we've got an hour—we need to bring our best spells and any other ideas we have."

The other three traded curious looks and pleased smiles as they broke into a run after Alex. They entered the mansion, headed straight past the new sick wing to the tubes, all shouting, "Library? Yes! Go!" at once. A moment later they disappeared.

LISA McMANN

Gathering Strength

As Aaron's following grew to thirty-five and then approached forty, they began meeting as a group in what seemed like it would be a most obvious place, but since people rarely traveled to the desolate areas of Quill, they were quite hidden in plain sight in a dusty field.

They met twice per week and they called themselves the Restorers. Aaron was the leader, Gondoleery Rattrapp was his rabble-rouser, and Eva Fathom, with the promise of her old job back once Aaron took over Quill, was the number-one spy.

"We have two objectives," Aaron said to the group at their

LISA McMANN

first meeting. "The first is to help Wanteds in need of food and turn them on to our ideas of restoring Quill to the way it used to be." Half the group nodded—restoring Quill was their job. Aaron had taken them, a few at a time, to the Favored Farm to show them where to find food not only for themselves, but also for others. Gondoleery's home became the headquarters for the food items, and Aaron moved some of the Halukis' supplies to her house as a way of showing her he trusted her. He desperately wanted to know more about her magical abilities. While she had eventually admitted she could do magic, she remained tight-lipped on the extent of it.

"The second objective is to cause chaos and fear in Artimé, which will make our Necessaries very interested in coming back home where it's safe." This time the other half of the group smirked. They loved this plan. Sneak attacks to instill fear—that was their idea of a good time. They collected items from their own homes and daily raided vacant homes in the Necessary quadrant, stealing everything they considered useful. Eva Fathom offered her home in Quill as the storing place for these things since she was now living as a secret agent in Artimé.

A few of Aaron's newest followers were from the Quillitary, dissatisfied over how things were being run since General Blair and Major Burkesh had been brutally murdered by the Unwanted—the major's own son—Samheed Burkesh. It was their goal to take the young man down at all costs.

At first these Quillitary members didn't trust Aaron, what with all the rumors going around. But once Aaron approached their broken-down Quillitary vehicle and showed them how to fix it, and then gave them some much-needed food, they reluctantly listened to what he had to say. And surprisingly, he made sense.

One Quillitary officer, Liam Healy, had been in on the most recent attack along with governors' teenage sons Dred Crandall and Crawledge Prize, and knew they had their work cut out for them. But Liam was willing and eager to lead the next charge.

Unfortunately, the giant stone monster, or whatever it was, was now stationed at the gate, and that left the Restorers puzzled about how to attack next.

Eva Fathom spoke up. "This afternoon around three o'clock, that monster, as you call it, will be absent from the gate for at least an hour."

Aaron grinned at his former adversary. "Well done, Eva." No wonder Justine had kept Secretary by her side all those years.

Eva smiled conspiratorially in return. "May Quill prevail with all I have in me," she said. The rest of them echoed the mantra. Hopefully, they would all get their lives back one day.

Liam Healy had been able to confiscate several Quillitary weapons, including two pellet guns that still worked, a large sack of gunpowder that no one knew what to do with, a long piece of rope, and several rusted metal knives. He handed them over to be stored with the rest in Eva's house, and then Crandall and Prize each presented Aaron with the most stunning score of them all—both had been able to sneak off with their fathers' pistols.

"We should save these for the ultimate battle with Artimé," Gondoleery said. "Not waste them in skirmishes."

"I agree," Aaron said. "But I'm not sure I like them sitting in Eva's unoccupied house with no one there to protect them." He scratched his head and looked around the room. "Who should keep them? My vote is for Gondoleery. Anyone second it?"

LISA McMANN

"Me?" Gondoleery exclaimed. "Why not you?"

"They are not safe with me. I fear Mrs. Haluki may return at any time, whether to live or to retrieve something on a whim—daily I leave the house exactly as I found it because of that fear, except, of course, for the food in the pantry. I just hope they don't remember the exact contents, living large as they are in Artimé. So it's that fear which prevents me from holding the pistols. I wouldn't want them falling into the wrong hands." He gave the old woman a meaningful look, and then said again, "Is there a second?"

"Second," said Eva. "They'd be no good with me, either."

"All in favor?"

"Aye!" said the Restorers in unison.

"Opposed?"

Silence.

"Then it is settled. The pistols go home with you, my dear Gondoleery."

"All right," she said, secretly pleased. "Now, what's our plan for three o'clock?"

Magical Weapons
Galore

Alex and Samheed waited impatiently in Mr. Today's office for the old mage, not because they were so eager to start the meeting, but because they'd realized a rather crucial problem—Meghan and Lani still couldn't see the mostly secret hallway, so they couldn't enter it. While the boys waited, Alex studied some of the pictures that hung on the wall. There was a series by one particular artist, it seemed, made up of dot designs that didn't look like much of anything at all, which was what made them so curious, not to mention hideous. He moved from one to another, but couldn't really understand why

LISA McMANN

they warranted placement in such special locations.

But art is subjective—Alex knew that as well as the next Unwanted. Mr. Today certainly had strange taste. Then again . . . one look at his robes would tell anyone that.

Finally Mr. Today breezed into the office through the back wall as he'd done before. "Greetings! Are the ladies coming as well?"

"They can't get in," both Alex and Samheed said at once.

"Good heavens, so they can't," Mr. Today mused. "Well then. We shall have to go elsewhere. Which works quite well, actually. We'll all meet at the gate. The girrinos are back from their mourning period and were going to take over for Simber during the meeting, but I've become nervous about them being there alone."

"Great," Alex said.

"Sounds good," Samheed said.

Mr. Today and the boys strode quickly out of the office and down the hallway, bursting through the wall, or so it seemed from the perspective of Lani and Meghan. "We're meeting at the gate," Alex told them.

They met Ms. Morning and Ms. Octavia on their way up

the stairs, and Florence at the entrance. The strange-looking party headed toward the gate just as Simber was saying good-bye to the girrinos.

The leaders decided on a spot a short distance from the gate so that Tina, Opal, and Penelope wouldn't be distracted by their discussion or accidentally hit by a wayward spell.

Mr. Today jumped right into the meeting. "First, a few business items," he said. "Alex, well done with the creation of the sick wing. You are officially one of the only students to successfully perform such a difficult spell without the use of a component."

Alex couldn't stop a wide grin from spreading across his face. "Thanks. That was cool how you sent me the verbal component." He blushed as his friends punched him in the shoulder or patted him on the back, and he bowed his head when Ms. Octavia gave him a very pleased nod.

"It was a new idea born from the urgency of the moment," Mr. Today said. "I rather liked it too."

He turned to the group. "As for the patients, they are alive and being treated," he went on. "But not responding to anything yet. Our hope is that they regain consciousness so that we might at least know from whence they've come." He lowered his voice. "The metal thorns around their necks are quite worrisome. I've seen it once before, when a ship landed on our shore. The dead men inside wore something similar around their necks. I admit I don't know what it means."

Alex remembered Mr. Today saying something about that in the Museum of Large.

"It sounds like it could be a rite of passage," Ms. Morning said. "Perhaps a sign of achievement."

"I'm glad we don't do that here when we achieve something," Meghan whispered.

"Me too," Lani said.

Alex and Samheed looked at each other and nodded.

"Whatever the case," Mr. Today went on, "we want to help these castaways find their way back home once they're quite well enough."

"What island do you think they're from?" Samheed asked.

"I can't begin to imagine. Warbler, the nearest one, was quite a paradise when we left it, and they did nothing of the sort back when I knew it. I can't fathom they'd have come from there." Mr. Today turned to Florence. "How goes the training?"

Florence smiled a rare smile. "My advanced students are excelling, but the beginners . . . well, the young ones are doing well, but the older folks just aren't making the connection between mind and magic. We'll keep trying."

"What about my old friend Eva?"

"She's the exception. She's doing very well. Her childhood magical abilities have come back quite naturally in our environment and she's very interested in learning. She's quite a delight. I'll probably move her up soon to work with her daughter Carina, who, by the way, would make an excellent group leader. She's quite skilled."

"Wonderful," Mr. Today said. He conjured up a pad and scribbled a few notes to himself. "And what do you and our resident experts have to show us today?"

"Well, Marcus, I invited these four because they have really taken spells to a new level. Their combined abilities are quite beyond anything I've seen before—though of course we've never had a focus as big as this on creating new spells, since we've obviously never needed to. Still, alone they are each excellent fighters, but together they are a team of innovators." As she was speaking, Florence waved the four to their feet.

"Why don't you show us what you've got? Explain first, then demonstrate."

Alex, who had been to many meetings with leaders, went first at the others' urging, as they were understandably nervous. Alex pulled a heart-shaped piece of clay from his vest and held it up.

"This is something I call 'heart attack.' With those words as the verbal component, the clay heart immediately grows wings and sails to your intended opponent's chest. Upon impact, it causes the enemy to collapse. Because of the wings, the spell has great distance and accuracy, and it's quite potent, rendering the attackee useless in less than half a minute, and quite dead-looking until the spell is released." Alex smiled and stepped back into the line. He looked at Samheed.

Samheed focused on Florence, which was easier than facing Mr. Today, since Florence was the instructor he was most used to talking to. He fished around in his vest and pulled out a small ball of rubber that looked like a tiny brain. "I just created this the other day," he said. "This is called 'dementia.' It renders the target completely confused and unable to cope with what's happening around him." He stepped back in line rather stiffly and turned to Meghan.

Meghan stepped forward with her component, a tiny aluminum spring. "This is what I call 'backward bobbly head.' It causes your opponent's head to turn a hundred and eighty degrees and bounce around, leaving him unable to command his body properly and unable to focus his eyes on anything." She moved back in line and grinned shakily.

Lani looked up, smooth and confident. "Hello," she said. "This is called 'pincushion.'" She held up a ladybug-size piece of stuffed fabric with a tiny pin sticking from it. "The opponent will feel as though a thousand needles are sinking into his skin, and any movement he makes from that point on will only worsen the effects, until the spell is released." She smiled pleasantly.

The instructors were very impressed and applauded for the students.

When they grew quiet again, Florence invited Ms. Morning, Ms. Octavia, and Mr. Today to volunteer as targets. They all agreed as if it were a wondrous adventure, for they rarely got the chance to attend Magical Warrior Training. Mr. Today stood opposite Alex, Florence took on Samheed, Ms. Octavia faced Meghan, and Ms. Morning stood across from Lani.

Florence confirmed all were ready to begin, and then she counted down. "Fire!" she cried.

The four attacked, and almost instantly Mr. Today collapsed to the ground, and Florence started groaning and acting completely confused, wandering around. Ms. Octavia's head spun around and her great alligator snout bobbled about uselessly. Ms. Morning let out a bloodcurdling scream as magical pins pierced into her.

Just then, a shout from the girrinos rang out. Simber turned sharply and rose to his feet. He bounded toward the gate. "Attackerrrs at the gate! Hurrry!"

The four friends, staring at their now-helpless instructors, hesitated and then ran after Simber, realizing there was no time to release the spells if they were to defeat the attack from Quill.

The four students drew components from their vests as they ran to the entrance, where the girrinos were already fighting mightily. Simber charged after several Quillans who tried to sneak past the gatekeepers. Alex, Samheed, Lani, and Meghan all fired and hit their targets, then pulled out another round and fired, knocking flat four more attackers, all the while hearing Ms. Morning screaming in the background, Florence stomping around like a giant robot, and a loud *sproing, sproing* coming from Ms. Octavia's bobbly head.

Others came running just as Simber chased the remaining attackers into Quill. When Alex saw that everyone had been contained, he hurried back to the instructors, releasing Ms. Morning first to stop the screaming, then the other ladies, and then finally he knelt down next to Mr. Today and released the heart attack spell. The old mage's face had gone gray. After several long, stressful moments of waiting, finally the man gulped in a breath and coughed quite savagely. He lay still for a moment, his eyes confused, and then slowly a wide grin crossed his face. He struggled to sit up, and then weakly he clapped Alex on the back.

"That's a keeper," he said, eyes wide. "Stunning." He shook his head as everyone else ran off to get a look at the enchanted attackers, two of whom were still screaming. "I really thought I was gone there for a moment, Alex. Make a note not to wait too long to release the spell on that one." He chuckled good-naturedly and held out a hand. Alex helped him to his feet. "Did anything exciting happen while I was out?"

Ms. Morning's Secret

O nce the eight remaining Quill opponents were disarmed, Alex put their arms into connecting clay shackles, and then the original spells were released.

Ms. Morning, back to her usual self, stood tapping one foot impatiently next to the heart attack victim, waiting for him to regain consciousness. A variety of Unwanteds took care of the other seven, prodding them toward the gate and sending them on their way, still connected. Mr. Today called on Charlie the gargoyle to communicate with Matilda at the palace, informing them that the high priest might find the prisoners along the road if he should choose to incarcerate them.

The instructors and the students, except for Ms. Morning, stood around in a circle discussing excitedly what had happened, when heart attack victim number one came to. He opened his eyes, sucked in a breath and coughed, and then looked up at his captor.

The two had exchanged glances once before, at the last attack, but he'd gotten away. Now, shackled and weak, he was trapped.

"Hello, Claire," he said, defeated. He coughed again.

"Liam," she said evenly.

He struggled to get up, and she did not help him. It took him several moments to finagle his way to his feet, his arms shackled as they were behind his back, and he toppled onto his face twice before he succeeded. Finally he stood up, wiping the gravel from his cheek with a shrug of his shoulder.

Ms. Morning stood with one hand on her hip, her eyes searching his face, betraying nothing. "Your family?" she asked.

"Both parents in the Ancients Sector," he said.

"I'm sorry," she said.

He appeared puzzled by the sentiment. "Why?"

"Because it's hard to watch your parents die."

"It's the way things are. Soon enough forgotten," he said.

"Maybe for you. For people like you."

"You say that with contempt."

"That surprises you? Look what you're doing to Artimé! It wasn't enough to kill us once?"

Liam stepped back, alarmed, but spoke in the calm, brainwashed voice of Quill, "*I* didn't kill you. I didn't kill anyone."

"No, of course not. No one is responsible," Ms. Morning said, her voice dripping with sarcasm and bitterness. "No one in Quill is responsible for any of your sickening ways. No one questions anything. No one has a conscience. I'm surprised you even remember me—aren't you programmed to forget?"

Liam stared at her. "You don't know what you're talking about," he said, but he didn't sound convinced. "Quill was a perfect land before Artimé was exposed. We just want our country back."

Claire's eyes blazed. "Everyone in here is your countryman. Did you ever think about it, Liam? Did you? After they took me away in chains, and we exchanged one last look—did you think I deserved that? Did you ever try to stop it? Or did you just accept that others knew better than you?"

Liam's lips parted, but he didn't speak.

Claire wasn't finished. "Did you even think about me afterward or did you just do as they told you to do? How is that human? Can you tell me how being forced to forget the ones you love is natural and good and right? Because I don't understand."

The small group of instructors and students had turned their attention to Ms. Morning and all now watched in silence.

Liam grew pale. "I—"

Ms. Morning lowered her voice. "Do you have a heart in there somewhere, Liam? You must, or the spell wouldn't have worked." She laughed bitterly. "I always held out hope for you. For twenty-five years I've thought, 'He's not like the others.' Yet here you are." She shook her head, caught between anger and tears. "You are disgusting."

With that, she turned abruptly and ran, nearly colliding with her somber students, to the nearest mansion door and disappeared inside it.

Samheed looked at Liam. "You really messed that up, didn't you." He grabbed Liam by the arm and pulled him toward the road to Quill, then shoved him in the direction of the palace. "You just put a big target on your back, buddy," Samheed called out. "Next time I see you . . ." He didn't finish the threat, making it even more ominous.

Liam didn't respond. He shuffled toward the palace, head down.

Along the way Liam passed Sean Ranger heading toward Artimé. Sean narrowed his eyes, but kept walking. Finally Liam caught up with the others. They took a side path to the housing quadrants and snuck to Gondoleery's house so she could release the spell on their shackles before Haluki or anyone else could track them down. And then they got back to work, harder than ever before.

The Mysterious Guests

Every day after Advanced Magical Warrior Training, Alex and Lani slipped into the hospital wing of the mansion to visit the strange collared guests, who remained unresponsive. Often Alex and Lani sat in chairs between their beds, wondering aloud what their story might be, while working feverishly to make new spell components. Mr. Today had put in a request for a thousand each of heart attack spells, backward bobbly heads, pincushions, dementia, and bee swarms, which was a Cole Wickett design that Alex had taken a strong liking to.

Alex and his cohorts now carried supplies with them

wherever they went so they could create components whenever they had a few extra moments, quite like someone might carry around a book, or a satchel full of knitting, to fill in the unexpected lulls of life.

On one such occasion Mr. Today came in and pulled up a chair next to Alex. They sat in silence for a while, Alex and Lani working, Mr. Today examining and admiring their products, and then Alex said out of the blue, "I think they were trying to escape."

Lani nodded as if she'd been thinking the same thing at that very moment. "Me too."

Mr. Today rubbed his chin thoughtfully, his fingers making a light scratching sound against the stubble. "What makes you say that?"

"It's the raft, I think," said Lani. "And they had nothing with them—no fishing supplies, no extra clothes. Who goes anywhere like that unless they're in a massive hurry? And who would attempt anything at all on a junky raft like theirs?"

"Good questions, all," mused the old mage. "Perhaps all their equipment was washed away in an unexpected storm."

Lani considered it. "Maybe."

"I wonder where they're from," Alex said for at least the tenth time since they'd drifted ashore. He stared at the girl.

"As do I," Mr. Today said. "I can only guess they're from one of the farther islands to the west, beyond Warbler."

Lani raised an eyebrow, and Alex leaned forward. "Have you ever been to those other islands?" he asked.

"Yes. The two distant ones were inhabited by somewhat primitive people, as I recall, thus perhaps more capable of doing something like this. . . ." He swept his hand toward the unconscious ones, indicating their thorny collars. "I came from the nearest, Warbler, a beautiful place. Tropical and sunny, but with more rain than Quill has gotten these past years. It has majestic rocks jutting up near the center of it, like someone's giant fist pushed a mountain through from the sea underneath. There's a freshwater stream running through Warbler, too, and beaches all around. The people were friendly and welcoming."

"It sounds dreamy," Lani said wistfully.

"It was. Perhaps we were foolish to leave, but we had our plans and ideas, you know. We couldn't have been convinced otherwise, even though we left some dear friends and family behind." He paused. "Eva Fathom grew up there as well. It was one of the places we were hoping to visit, but now . . ." He trailed off.

Alex frowned. "But now what?"

"I'm not sure this is a good time for me to leave after all."

The words hung in the air as if they wanted to be proven wrong, but Alex and Lani thought about everything—from the unconscious guests in the beds to the recent escalating attacks from Quill—and they couldn't come up with a way to do it.

"I haven't decided yet," Mr. Today went on, "but I can hardly forgive myself for the loss of Arija. What if someone were to be killed while I was off having a holiday? There's no room for forgiveness there."

"But Arija died doing the job she loved, the job she was created for," Lani said passionately. "If we all died doing the things we most believe in, we should die satisfied."

"All the more reason for me to stay, don't you think?" Mr. Today asked.

Alex was surprised to feel a little bit disappointed by Mr. Today's news. "I don't know about that," he said. "I bet these visitors will want to leave eventually, once they're well. Maybe while you're gone you can figure out what island they came from, so that we know how to get them home. I mean, if that's what they want." Alex thought some more. "And maybe . . . well, I don't know about this for sure, but maybe you could put the gate back up. For a short time, anyway. Just while you're gone." He hurried to add, "Not that Sean was right, or anything."

Mr. Today tilted his head curiously at Alex, and he hid a smile with his fingers. "Interesting way to look at it, Alex. I'll consider it."

"I mean," Alex continued, emphasizing various words as if he were just realizing his passion for the thought, "after all, I said I would help you and Ms. Morning. I think it'll be fine if you go."

Mr. Today scratched his chin again and then sighed. "We'll see. But there's no great urgency. Is there?"

Lani's Plan

There was something about the strange visitors that made Lani uneasy. And after the talk with Mr. Today and Alex, something about "no great urgency" just didn't sit right with her. She couldn't stop thinking about them. And she was quite certain that those two had been trying to escape.

That would virtually rule out the nearest island to the west, where Mr. Today had come from. Mr. Today had said that island was like paradise. Who would want to escape from a place like that? It only made Lani more and more curious to see it for herself.

The thought simmered inside of her for days, and at one point she even found herself back in the lagoon, staring at the gleaming white boat again, with dreams of an adventure dancing in her head. But she was smart enough to never do anything so adventurous alone.

Finally, one day at lunch, she brought it up. "Wouldn't it be fun to go on holiday like Mr. Today is going to do?"

Samheed raised an eyebrow. "I fink it could," he said, mouth full.

Meghan, who had been practically listless for days, said, "I guess I never thought about it."

"Oh, come *on*, you guys! What about you, Alex?"

Alex shook his head. "I have enough to worry about just preparing for Mr. Today to leave. I think he's getting more eager to do it. Could be any day now." He shoved a forkful of sweet rice into his mouth and chewed, wiped his lips, then pushed his chair back and stood. After he had swallowed, he checked his pockets to see if Mr. Today had given him any new spells to try, and then he shrugged apologetically. "And now I've got to go," he said.

"Boo," Lani said, slumping in her chair. "You're always

running off these days. We hardly ever see you."

"Yeah," Samheed said. "We haven't had a good adventure in months."

Meghan was silent, staring at her hands as if she hadn't even heard the conversation.

Alex blew out a disappointed breath. "I know," he said. "I'm sorry. It's just . . . there's really a ton of stuff to learn. It took Mr. Today years to do all this—there are some spells he's totally forgotten, so sometimes I spend hours looking through his journals. . . ." He trailed off, realizing he was telling secrets.

He scrambled to change the subject. "Meg, what's going on with you? You don't look so great. Are you all right? Did Cole Wickett and the Necessaries finally wear you out?" He laughed. "Cole Wickett and the Necessaries—hey, that would be a good name for one of Ms. Morning's student bands." He made a note to mention that to her the next time he saw her.

Meghan looked up at Alex and gave him a wan smile. "Sorry—I'm just distracted. Sean is acting really weird and I don't know what to do."

Alex hesitated. He knew he had to go, but decided Mr. Today would certainly excuse his lateness for the sake of a friend. He sat back down. Lani and Samheed turned their attention to Meghan too.

"What's going on?" Lani asked her.

Meghan's face was pale; she had dark circles under her eyes. Alex realized he hadn't really looked his friend in the eye in weeks. "What is it?"

Samheed just watched her and waited.

"It's Sean. . . . He's been going into Quill now and then. I think he's going back to see our parents."

Alex thought about it for a moment, and then shrugged. "Okay," he said. "Lots of others are doing that too. Why does it seem weird to you?"

Meghan shoved her plate aside, brought both elbows to the table, and propped her chin in her hands. "I guess what's wrong is that he hasn't actually told me he's doing it. When I asked him the other day where he'd been . . . he lied and said the jungle. But I know he was in Quill, and I watched him head toward our family's sector."

"So you think he's been visiting your parents without you? Why wouldn't he want you to know that?" Lani shook her head lightly, puzzled.

"That's what I'd like to know," said Meghan miserably. "I think maybe they really like him now." Her bottom lip quivered and she looked like she was about to cry. She slumped forward on the table and hid her face in her arms.

"Oh, Meg," Lani said. She got up and went over to Meghan, giving her shoulders a hug. "I'm sorry you're feeling bad. Maybe he's trying to patch things up for the both of you, and he's protecting you from their stupid way of thinking."

"Yeah," Samheed said. "I can see him doing that."

Alex frowned. He wasn't so sure. Not after the disagreement they'd had at the assembly. In fact, he hadn't seen Sean much at all since then, except sneaking around on the blackboards. "Are you sure he's visiting your parents and not doing something . . . else?" he asked, and then immediately regretted it when Samheed glared at him. Lani kicked him in the shin under the table. He struggled not to say "Ow!"

Meghan shrugged helplessly. "I don't know. All I know is that my parents will never forgive me for ruining their lives. 'Why didn't you try harder to be Wanted?' my mother kept asking me. She didn't see anything my way. It's like she gave Sean a free pass for his Purge, but blames me for being the second mark against them. Quill logic is so stupid!" She sucked in a shuddering sigh and let it out, laughing a little. "Good grief," she said, wiping a tear. "I'm fine, really. I'm just tired."

"You need a distraction," Lani said. "An adventure. A little holiday, maybe." Her eyes danced.

Samheed gave Lani a curious look.

Alex bit his lip and checked the clock. "So you're okay?" he asked, feeling like a jerk, but he was getting anxious about his meeting.

"Yeah, I'm fine," Meghan said. "Go on. Learn something amazing." She smiled.

"We'll take good care of her, don't worry," Lani said, grinning wider than she had in a while. "Have fun, Alex! We're going to go on an amazing adventure to cheer Meghan up."

Alex, who had already turned and started walking, looked over his shoulder, a pang of jealousy slicing through him. "I wish I could go," he said softly. "I really kind of miss you guys."

But Lani was already chattering excitedly and pulling Meghan and Samheed in the other direction, so they didn't hear him.

» » « «

While Alex hurried to Mr. Today's office, Lani spilled her plan to Meghan and Samheed as she guided them across the lawn.

"So, what do you think?" she asked as they half ran down to the shore toward the jungle. "Are you guys in?"

Meghan chuckled and let Lani pull her along. "I'll probably regret this, but okay. I'm so frazzled I don't really care what we do at this point. Sam?"

"Duh. I'm totally in. Why didn't we do this, like, a hundred years ago?" He grinned. "You're so conniving, Lani. I can't believe I didn't know this about you."

"It's because you were too busy thinking I was annoying, just like Alex thought."

"But how are we going to start it?" Meghan asked.

"Alex said it was magical. It shouldn't be too hard to figure out. He said that once Mr. Today said the spell, he just pointed the boat in the direction he wanted it to go and it went. No components or anything needed."

"Sounds easy enough," Samheed said. "If anybody can figure it out, it's us."

When they finally reached the lagoon, the three hesitated, looking at one another for a moment.

"Are you sure Mr. Today and Ms. Morning won't be mad?" Meghan asked.

"They never said we couldn't use the boat," Samheed said. "Mr. Today has only ever given us two rules. Besides, we're just going for a little ride. It's practically begging to be used."

Lani grinned. "If he doesn't want us to use it, I'm sure he has some sort of lock on it."

With an air of mischief, the three friends stripped off their shoes, rolled up their pants, and then waded out through the warm, shallow water to the gleaming boat.

Awake

Inside the mansion Alex started up the stairs to Mr. Today's office, but stopped short when he heard a buzz of voices in the hospital wing. There stood the mage along with a small throng of others, including the nurses, a few residents, Ms. Morning, and Eva Fathom, with whom Mr. Today was talking earnestly.

Alex turned around and headed toward them. "What's going on? Did something happen?" His chest tightened as he thought of the silent visitors. He hoped it wasn't bad news.

"The girl is awake," Ms. Morning said. She motioned for Alex to come in, and made a spot for him to stand near the bed. Alex approached, his stomach flipping with excitement, and wondered if all their questions would soon be answered.

He gazed down at the girl, who was now propped up on three fluffy pillows. But there was no way she could look comfortable with that necklace of metal thorns. Her face was turned away from Alex, toward the boy's bed, as if she were waiting, pleading for him to wake up too.

"She's scared," Ms. Morning said. "Too many adults swarming around. Maybe you can talk to her."

Alex nodded. "Hello there," he said softly. He reached out and touched the girl's arm to get her attention.

The girl turned her head sharply and reared up in the bed, staring at Alex, her face filled with fear.

Alex pulled his hand away and took a step back. When he saw her eyes, he sucked in a breath. The girl's irises were a deep golden orange, like a marigold thrust into the sunset—a color Alex had tried dozens of times to perfect. He heard a reaction behind him, but it seemed very far away as he focused on the visitor, mesmerized by her odd appearance, her glittering eyes piercing into his, the necklace of thorns moving almost fluidly with the turn of her head.

They held each other's gaze for a long moment, and the room fell silent. Alex's heart raced. He held his hands up to show her he wouldn't hurt her, and he smiled, hoping to appear friendly and not at all scary. "Hello," he said again.

She didn't move.

Alex's eyes flitted to the bedside table. "Would you like something to drink?" he asked. He moved slowly so he wouldn't startle her as he poured some water from a pitcher into a glass, and then offered it to her.

Her body tensed, and then she reached for it. She brought it to her nose with a shaky hand and sniffed at it carefully, her eyes never leaving Alex's. She opened her parched lips and sipped from it. And then she leaned forward, eyes narrowed, and spat the water into Alex's face.

"Whoa!" he cried, taking a step back. "What . . . the world!" He put his arm up to protect himself from further spewing. Then the girl opened her mouth as if to scream at him, but no sound came out. She struggled to get off the bed, her body tangled in the sheets and her neck band caught on a pillowcase. After a moment of shock the nurses reacted, coming to her side and soothing her. The girl gave another halfhearted attempt at escape, but then she sank back down, unable to do anything with so many people around. She turned away from Alex, closed her eyes, and pulled the blankets over her head.

Alex wiped his face with his sleeve and felt a strange urge to laugh now that the girl had settled down, but didn't think that would win him any points with anyone. So he held it in and looked to Ms. Morning for answers on what to do now. She beckoned to him to follow her out of the room. Mr. Today joined them and they climbed the stairs.

"Well, that was interesting," Mr. Today said, pulling a hankie from his robe pocket and handing it to Alex. "I'll bet you weren't expecting that."

Alex laughed and wiped his face. "No. But I'm glad she's awake, you know? I hope she doesn't give anyone any trouble." They turned down the mostly secret hallway.

"I imagine she was frightened to open her eyes in such a strange and different setting," Ms. Morning said. "She was so upset at first until she saw the boy. I'm guessing he's her little brother."

"Speaking of eyes, did you see hers?" Alex asked. They turned in to Mr. Today's office and sat down.

"Lovely, aren't they?" Mr. Today said. "They'd match well with my robe."

"Strikingly beautiful," Ms. Morning said, looking at Alex. "I've never seen eyes that color before."

"Me neither," Alex said, and he was surprised to feel his face grow warm while he thought about her. He hurried to think of something else to say. "Are the boy's eyes that orangey-gold color too? I mean, has anybody checked?"

"Yes, I believe once the nurses saw hers, they checked the boy, and his are the same," Mr. Today said. "It's very curious. I spoke with Eva Fathom and she said it wasn't a trait common to our home island, as far as she knew."

Alex wondered for the millionth time what kind of place the two visitors could be from. It sounded like it must have been one of the more distant islands, based on what Mr. Today and Eva Fathom remembered.

Mr. Today continued, breaking into Alex's thoughts. "I'm more than troubled by the metal neck bands, and now by the fact that the girl was unable to make a sound with her voice. I'm feeling a nagging sense that all is not right outside our little world."

He took a deep breath. "And because of that consternation, I've decided to take a short trip after all. At the suggestion of trusted individuals, including you, Alex, as well as Sean Ranger and Eva Fathom, I'm going to replace the gate to Artimé temporarily to protect everyone while I'm gone. I've got my weekly peace meeting tonight with Gunnar, so I'll let him know then what my plan is. After that I'll return to the mansion to take care of a few things and pack, and leave in the morning with Eva. Just for a couple of days, perhaps three, while we investigate." He paused and looked at Ms. Morning and Alex. "What do you think? Are you ready to hold down the fort for me?"

Allies or Enemies?

The sprightly Eva Fathom, former secretary to the High Priest Justine, smiled warmly at the girrinos at the gate as she strolled past them on her way into Quill. She walked alone for a short time until she was out of sight of Artimé, and then she was joined by a young, reddish-haired man who appeared to have been waiting for her.

"What's going on?" he asked.

"I've convinced him to put the gate back up. He and I are leaving first thing tomorrow for a few days."

The young man was silent for a long moment. "I'm worried."

"Don't be. All is well. The plan is solid."

"And Aaron?"

"This is sooner than he's expecting, but he's as prepared as he can be."

"Will you tell him about the gate?"

Eva Fathom looked at the young man warily, as if the question were some sort of test. She responded in turn, "Would you?"

The young man scowled.

They walked a few minutes in silence. The wavering heat hung low on the road in front of them, forming a mirage, from which a figure emerged.

"I should go," the young man said.

Eva nodded. "Good luck," she said.

"You too. I hope you know what you are doing."

Annoyed, Eva responded, "I should say the same to you, Mr. Ranger."

He turned off at a footpath, a shortcut to the housing quadrants. Eva kept walking toward Quill and the approaching figure.

"Hello, Aaron," Eva said brightly when the two met up. "What news?"

"Our army is growing, and we are all working feverishly to create adequate weapons."

"Will you be ready for an attack tomorrow?"

Aaron hesitated. "So soon?"

"It was a split-second decision. I think we should take it. I'll be leaving with Marcus in the morning."

Aaron hid his alarm. He thought for a moment, and murmured, "Of course. Well done. We're always ready."

"Excellent." The old woman pulled a handful of small clay hearts from her pocket and held them out to Aaron.

Aaron narrowed his eyes. "What about the thin metal clips—scatterclips, they call them? That's what I wanted. What are these?" He picked one up and examined it. "They don't look very fierce."

"It's the component for a spell called 'heart attack,'" Eva said. "Your brother made them for my daughter at her request. She claims it's the best spell Artimé has ever had. So I stole some."

"Have you tried it?"

"No. I didn't want to waste any."

"Is it lethal?"

Eva Fathom hesitated. "Of course it is. It must be, if it's the most powerful spell ever created."

"Well, what's their . . . what's the little *saying* that goes with it?" Aaron's annoyance grew. He had plainly instructed Eva to bring him scatterclips since he knew their power and how to use them. And he hated that he couldn't think of the word the Artiméans used. It made him feel uncomfortable and ill-prepared. With this sudden opportunity, he wasn't sure if he could pull everything together by tomorrow. But he'd have to.

"Heart attack," she said. "Throw it at the person, it grows wings or some such thing and strikes your opponent in the chest. He then collapses. And . . . is dead." She glanced over her shoulder and pressed her lips together.

"You kept one for yourself, I hope. The only way we'll gain the power we need is by getting rid of all the key players, especially Mr. Today. He'll never expect it from you." Aaron smiled. "He'll never know what hit him if you do it right."

"That's the plan," Eva said. "I'll take care of him, don't worry. I'm more worried about you mucking things up."

Aaron narrowed his eyes but said nothing. It was just the challenge he needed. He might be up working all night,

LISA McMANN

but tomorrow . . . tomorrow he'd be turning Artimé into a disaster zone, causing Necessaries to flock back to Quill, and once again he'd climb his way up the ruling ranks when the Quillens saw how he'd saved them.

And, if all went well, he'd also rid the world of Alex, Mr. Today, and all of their stupid Unwanted friends, once and for all.

Meanwhile

The white boat flew over the waves, almost as if it were skimming the surface, giving Samheed, Meghan, and Lani a smooth and most enjoyable ride. It had been a cinch to start it—the instructions and spells were posted right next to the compass, practically begging them to take it for a ride.

"This is more fun than flying on Simber's back," Lani shouted from the helm. She turned the wheel slowly from one side to the other, leaving a lazy S wake behind them.

Meghan agreed.. Her face, now rosy from the wind and sun, looked decidedly healthier than just hours before. She

LISA McMANN

stood on the seat next to Lani, gripping the top edge of the windshield and letting the wind rush past her, trying not to smile too much in case there were bugs.

"It's not bad," Samheed said. He sat in a seat near the back of the boat, leaning forward and gripping his stomach. His face looked anything but healthy. "Can you stop going back and forth like that, though?"

Lani glanced over her shoulder and straightened out the wheel immediately. "Sorry—hey, you're not about to glug up your lunch, are you?" She slowed the speed a hair as well. "Because if you do, try going for anywhere except inside the boat, right?"

Samheed scowled. "I'm fine. Just stop the spinning already."

The girls exchanged smirks but kindly left poor Samheed to suffer the queasies in private.

After a quarter of an hour or so, Meghan scanned the horizon and turned to Lani in surprise. "Are you aiming for the island?"

Lani shrugged. "I thought we could get near it. See what's there."

Meghan squinted. "What if people are there? That would

be so weird." They'd never seen people from other lands before the two visitors landed on the shores of Artimé. They'd never even known there were other lands, or other people, until recently.

"Yeah," Lani said. "This is where Mr. Today came from. He said it was beautiful and the people were nice." She stared ahead at the looming island, every now and then looking back over her shoulder so she would know how to get back to Artimé. She watched the compass too, having learned a little bit about sailing in her vast amounts of reading.

After a while, Samheed got up and walked to where the girls were. He stood behind Lani, taking mental notes on how she was driving.

"Feeling better?" Lani asked kindly.

"Yes, now that we've stopped rocking side to side," he said. "Thanks." He looked around at the vast ocean, then ahead at the island. "It's so strange to see it getting bigger," he said.

Lani nodded. She didn't quite understand the feelings that were swirling around inside her stomach. She was nervous and excited. And scared, too. But most of all she was intrigued to learn more, as was often the case with her. She couldn't get

LISA McMANN

enough stories of other worlds, like the ones they'd read in her literature class and Actors' Studio, and the ones that she'd made up and told to friends and neighbors back in Quill, which got her sent away. Now she was determined to see another new world for herself, rather than just read about it, or make it up in her head. It was a lofty goal, and it was happening right now.

By midafternoon they drew close enough to see that there were few visible rocks along the shore and lots of sand. There was no lawn, no mansion, no people or creatures walking about as far as they could tell. Just a length of beach and a grove of palm trees behind, and then the land built up toward the middle of the island, where enormous rocks rose grandly into the air. Water tumbled from the rocks and rich green vegetation grew thick and tall all around.

Lani slowed the boat and they drifted toward the island. It was so quiet that they couldn't even hear the calm lap of the waves on the beach. The three began to whisper without realizing it as they grew near, perhaps feeling the sacredness of their discovery, realizing this truly was the same paradise that Mr. Today had talked about. It was pure beauty to look at.

There was no thought now of Mr. Today or Claire Morning

perhaps being upset that they'd borrowed the boat without asking. No imagination of what might be happening back in Artimé at this very moment. And only a little trepidation from these adventurers regarding the unknown. There was just this one beautiful cove they were in, blissful and quiet, warm sun and light breeze, rocking gently on waves.

It was exactly what Meghan needed. She closed her eyes and breathed in the tropical scent. It was almost like Artimé, but after a few hours at sea it felt fresh and new. And splendidly free of Sean and her mean, stupid parents, and all the stresses that hung on her back in Artimé. She felt like a new, energized Meghan. A bold, invigorated Meghan without a care here in this new place.

"Let's go ashore," she whispered.

Lani and Samheed stared at her.

"What?" Lani asked, incredulous.

"I mean it," Meghan said. "Let's go. Let's do it."

Lani and Samheed caught glances and stared for a moment, trying to get a sense of how the other was feeling. Was it a reckless move? Samheed worked his jaw, his eyes intense, reading hers. Lani couldn't look away. She knew there were risks. What if it wasn't as nice as Mr. Today remembered it?

"Well?" Meghan said, breaking the stare-off.

Lani and Samheed looked at Meghan, then back at each other. Lani started laughing lightly, trying to get Samheed to soften the intensity around his eyes that they all knew so well. "I'm game," she said. She reached out her hand and brushed his elbow, trying to communicate without saying blatantly, *I think this would be good for Meghan.* "Sam? Are you in?"

"Guys, I don't know. We don't know anything about this place. What if the strangers came from here?"

"Mr. Today said this was a good place. It's exactly as he described it to me and Alex—the rock formation in the middle, the waterfall, the beauty of it all . . ." Lani bit her lip.

Samheed closed his eyes and sighed, shaking his head the smallest bit. "Okay," he said finally.

Meghan's grin was payment enough to make everyone feel like they'd just made the best decision of their lives.

Speeding Up

There were a baker's dozen thoughts whipping through Alex's head when Mr. Today asked him and Ms. Morning if they were ready to take over Artimé. His first thought: *NO!* His second: *Well, it's only for a short time.* His third: *NO, NO, NO!* His fourth: *At least he's putting the gate up.* His fifth: *Absolutely NO WAY!* And so on and so forth, all the way to thirteen.

The good news was that Alex was obviously maturing to the point where he didn't have to say all of these things out loud in order to process them. That was a relief for all involved, and, in a strange little way, it gave him some confidence in himself.

LISA McMANN

The bad news was that Alex's stomach churned, and he very nearly felt light-headed at the thought of something going horribly wrong, so much that he had to resist the urge to stand and leave the room.

"We're in good shape, Father. Aren't we, Alex?" Ms. Morning gave Alex a look that told him exactly what to say.

"Fine shape," Alex said, his voice cracking under the pressure of her stare.

"Good!" said Mr. Today, practically giddy. "Simber, Florence, Octavia, and all of your friends will of course be on hand for whatever you may need. I expect things will go on quite as they do when I am present. You truly won't even notice I'm gone. Artimé is a well-oiled machine. And if anything should happen, you know how to fight . . . and how to read. I've given you every command I can think of, and both the library and Museum of Large hold additional clues that I'm sure will help you, should you be attacked while I'm away. But," he said triumphantly, "that won't happen, because of the gate." He very nearly hummed with excitement.

"That sounds lovely, Father."

Alex gulped and nodded.

"I'll gather up some students and we'll make you a takeaway lunch for tomorrow—how exotic!" Ms. Morning said. "We'll pack up the boat tonight with every supply you could possibly need so you'll be all ready in the morning."

Mr. Today beamed with happiness. "Delightful. Simply a dream." His eyes grew moist for a moment. "While we will be out exploring on serious business, I must tell you, Alex— getting away is something I've longed to do since the walls went up. I've never felt more confident than I do now that Artimé will be in the best hands with you and Claire." He reached out and took Alex's hand, shaking it solemnly. "Thank you."

Alex wanted to say, "But I don't know half of how to run this place!" He wanted to say, "There's so much you haven't explained!" He wanted to say, "Please don't go. Please don't go!"

Instead, he did his best to smile confidently. He reached out and hugged the old man, patting his back quite hard a few times in the embrace. Mr. Today chuckled, the laugh rattling soundly in his chest. Finally Alex came up with what he thought were the perfectly grown-up words to say. He released the embrace

LISA McMANN

and looked at the mage. "I hope you find everything you are looking for, sir. Thank you for believing in me." He smiled, and some of his jitters went away.

Mr. Today nodded solemnly. "Never forget, my boy. I chose you for this. There will always be times we struggle, make bad decisions, even fail. What's important is not that we fail, but that we learn and grow. And that we know that there is always someone out there who believes in us."

Alex nodded.

Mr. Today continued. "Whatever problems you may face, you must know this: I do believe in you."

Alex nodded, eyes shining, not trusting his voice to speak. He looked down at the ground, a smile forcing its way to his lips, feeling proud and sheepish at the same time. He stepped back as if to escape from the strong circle of emotion that surrounded Mr. Today. And as his leader continued to gaze proudly at him, Alex finally said, "Okay, okay. It's just a few days. Sheesh."

Ms. Morning and Mr. Today's voices pealed in laughter through the office and down the mostly secret hallway. The man wiped the mist from his eyes. "Well said, indeed." With a mischievous glance, he said, "Come, let's go create a gate and tell Artimé of our plans. We'll put a big crown on your head so the Necessaries know whom to bother with their trifles while I'm gone."

This time it was Alex who laughed.

When Mr. Today called all of Artimé to a meeting on the lawn to explain the reason for the newly reinstalled gate and his impending absence, Alex gazed out at the crowd of people. Such good people here in Artimé—even the former Necessaries, who were struggling to fit in and help out. He looked around from face to face, unable to tell a difference between the groups.

As he looked he began to search for his friends, wishing he'd had a chance to give them the scoop before the rest of Artimé heard. But he grew troubled when he noticed from his place next to Mr. Today that his three closest friends were nowhere to be found. It was strange. He scanned the audience more carefully, and realized there were a few others missing too, like Sean Ranger. And Eva Fathom.

Suddenly something seemed terribly . . . off.

Making Preparations

There really wasn't time to wait until darkness fell in Quill—Aaron needed to get busy right away. Still, he didn't want to bring any attention to himself or to any of the homes of the others who'd recently joined the Restorers—some of the Quillens were nervous enough as it was, and many of them were doing this without the knowledge or support of their families. So their options were limited.

Aaron managed to round up everybody and split them into groups to be less obvious, sending a few from each group first to Gondoleery Rattrapp's house to get supplies and weapons, then having them disperse as unobtrusively as possible to their respective meeting spots. If the Quillitary saw too many people gathering together or walking together, they'd certainly be suspicious. Aaron didn't need that.

So he had no choice but to use the Halukis' home as a meeting spot, as much as he didn't want to. But there were so few residents roaming the streets in the governors' row most days that he hoped for the best. At the very worst, if he were caught outside the home, he'd claim to be on a delivery and no one would likely know the difference.

He, along with Eva Fathom, Liam Healy, a woman named Bethesda Dia Gloria, and Crawledge Prize, one by one snuck into the back door of the Haluki house and spread out their goods, including half of the magical items that Eva Fathom had been confiscating for him for the past few weeks. Aaron agreed with Eva that it made sense to use magic if they had the ability, though he despised the creativity behind it. Still, they were powerful weapons, which had been easy enough to see when Aaron brought Alex down.

Gondoleery Rattrapp, who in recent days often sat at her kitchen table alone, staring at her fingers and pondering over her childhood and the magic of her youth, had the other half of the magical weapons—and Aaron discovered that she seemed to be even better than Eva at picking up on magical spells. Gondoleery's plan had been to spend some time teaching her team how to use the magical components to see if any of them were at all competent. But the older Quillens had a significant disadvantage, they'd found. Their creativity was virtually nonexistent, and that translated into a big fat zero in the magical ability department. It hadn't taken long for Eva to give up entirely on anybody over the age of twenty-five, and the more impatient Gondoleery threw the towel in on the entire lot of them and went back to her kitchen table to brood over the components. Which was quite fine with Aaron. He didn't want too many people knowing how to do it, anyway.

Inside the Haluki house, no one had time to gawk at the size and amenities that came with the governorship, though they each noticed. Instead they began to assess and clean their weapons, and create new sharp weapons from the odds and ends of metal pieces they'd found or stolen over the past weeks. All the while Aaron paced and muttered to himself, trying to figure out the perfect plan.

It's too soon, a voice in his head kept telling him. *It's a perfect situation but we're not ready yet. Be smart!* Aaron tried to ignore it, but the more he tried, the louder it got. He began to doubt himself.

"Eva," he said sharply. "I need a word with you."

Eva Fathom narrowed her eyes at the way he ordered her around. She finished what she was doing, and then when she was good and ready to do so, she set her weapon down and slowly walked over to Aaron. He swiped the back of his hand impatiently across his forehead, wiping the sweat from it.

Eva approached, folding her arms across her chest. She'd taken a lot of orders in her life, and it bothered her that some peach-fuzz-faced boy was trying to tell her what to do. "What is it?"

Aaron took her by the shoulder and turned her away from the others, and began walking with her. "You're sure you have the guts to kill off the old guy? Just do the heart attack magic thing and throw his body into the ocean, right?"

Eva stiffened. "Why are you doubting me?"

"I'm not!" Aaron said in a harsh whisper. "I'm doubting me. I don't think we have enough weapons or people yet to

LISA McMANN

make this successful. But we're certainly messed up if the old man survives."

Eva didn't much care for Aaron's continual negative remarks about Marcus's age, seeing as she was a year or two older than Marcus herself. But now was not the time to quibble. "It's all part of the plan," she said. "I'll take care of him."

"You keep saying that. You'll . . . take care of him." Aaron averted his eyes and wondered if he could really trust her to do the dirtiest of all deeds. "You mean you'll *kill* him. Right?"

Paradise

We probably shouldn't stay long," Samheed said. He slipped out of his sandals and took off his component vest, and then he hesitated, looking at it. "Should we wear these?"

Lani, who'd been intent on studying the island for several minutes, knew instinctively what Samheed was talking about without having to avert her gaze. She'd thought of the same thing a moment earlier, and thus had time to think. "The paper components will be ruined, and the clay components will melt in the water and make a mess in our pockets." She turned her gaze to her friends. "Besides, I don't think there's anybody living on this island anymore. I haven't seen or heard a single thing."

"We could bring just the metal and rubber components with us in case we need them," Meghan said. "And leave the vests here."

Samheed nodded. "That sounds good." He took out a few scatterclips and dementia spells and slid them into his pants pocket, leaving his vest on the boat seat. The others did the same.

Lani cast the magical anchor spell, as was laid out in the instructions by the captain's wheel, and felt a slight tug of the boat when the waves tried to wash them closer in. Satisfied, she slipped off her shoes as well. "I wish we'd thought to bring swimsuits, or at least other clothes to change into later."

Meghan shrugged and climbed over the side of the boat. "We'll dry." She jumped in with a big splash and when she surfaced, she said, "It's all part of the adventure! Come on, you guys!"

Samheed and Lani needed no more urging. They joined

Meghan in the water, forgetting to be quiet now and striking out in the cool water toward the shore. When they could reach the bottom, they began wading toward the beautiful sand that sparkled before them. As they neared they began to run, splashing in the shallow water. Meghan collapsed on the wet sand, and Lani fell next to her, causing Samheed to trip over her leg and fall down too.

"Ahhh," Meghan said, the waves lapping at her feet. "This feels good." Little ocean bugs scurried about on the sand, being water-lifted to other places without a moment's notice.

Lani wrung her long hair out and playfully slapped Samheed in the face with the ends of it.

"Watch it," Samheed growled, but he had to admit getting to hang around with two creative, smart, talented girls on a beautiful beach was not his idea of a bad time at all.

The three of them lounged on the shore, eyes closed. It wasn't much different from lying on the beach of Artimé, but when they thought of the adventure they'd taken to get here, it seemed somehow very special.

Suddenly Lani sat up. "Something's weird," she said.

LISA McMANN

Meghan shielded her eyes with her hand. "What's weird?"

Samheed sat up too. "I was just thinking that same thing."

"It's too quiet," Lani said. "I mean, there's no sound at all since we reached the shore except for our own voices."

"No birds, no tree frogs . . . I can understand. But no noise from the waves? That's strange." Samheed knitted his brows. "I'm not sure about this place."

Lani looked at him, concerned. She glanced at Meghan, who had risen to an elbow now. "Huh," Meghan said.

As the three of them looked at one another, they wondered if they should perhaps heed the worrisome grip of fear in their chests and run at their highest speed away from the strangely quiet island. But there was no time to process the thought, for a moment later they each felt a sharp, severe poke between their shoulder blades. Without even a chance to cry out or see what had hit them, Meghan, Lani, and Samheed exchanged an identical look of terror before their bodies went limp and they dropped back to the sand, unconscious.

Missing

Once the meeting adjourned and Mr. Today went back inside to prepare his notes for the peace meeting, Alex set off to find his friends, at first methodical and measured in his motions. But then, when it became apparent that they were not in their rooms, the lounge, the dining hall, or the third floor of the library, he moved hurriedly, to no avail.

"Why arrre you rrrunning arrround like that?" asked Simber from his usual post inside the mansion, slightly annoyed by the boy's constant slamming of the front door and whisking about through nearby tubes and flying up and down

LISA McMANN

stairs. "I'm trrrying to catch up on my sleep now that the gate is up again."

"Have you seen Samheed, Meg, and Lani?" He said it so quickly that it sounded like one word, *SammyMeghanLani.* "Did they go into Quill? Did we lock them out by mistake?" He was frantic and sweaty, his hair sticking to his forehead as he ran around.

"Calm down," Simber said. "I'm sure Marrrcus made arrrangements forrr that. Did you check with the girrrinos?"

"Not yet . . . So, they might not be locked out for days?"

"I'm cerrrtain that Marrrcus has thought of that since many of ourrr rrresidents come and go now. Likely the ladies at the gate will hearrr them knock and someone—perrrhaps even you—will have to let them in. Did Marrrcus give you the spell forrr the gate?"

Alex hesitated. "Well, yes. I guess so. He did it with me standing there, anyway."

"Therrre," Simber said. "You see? Now you must think like the leaderrr, not wait for him to give you instrrructions."

Alex stared at Simber.

Simber, suddenly patient, continued. "So, at this point,

what you might be thinking about all on yourrr own would be to go down to the gate and tell the girrrinos to summon you if any of ourrr fine Arrrtiméans need to be let in."

Alex blinked. "Oh. Right. Of course." He stood a moment longer, then, with a slight nudge from the cheetah's stone paw, he stumbled outside and ran to the gate to do what a leader might do.

When Alex returned to Simber, he started chattering excitedly about how, when he got there, someone was already waiting to come back in, and so he let them in and it all worked perfectly. But then he noticed Ms. Morning walking up, her forehead wrinkled into a worried frown, looking up at Simber, and he stopped talking immediately and started listening.

"The boat is missing," she said to Simber. "Have you seen it or heard of anyone's plans to use it today? I'd like to load it up for Father's trip."

"No, I haven't. You'rrre surrre it hasn't been swept away?"

Ms. Morning shook her head. "Even the biggest storm couldn't overpower the anchor spell. Someone must have borrowed it. What awful timing!"

LISA McMANN

Alex's lips parted. And just as the wheels in his head started to turn, Simber looked straight at him.

"Have yourrr missing frrriends been found? Orrr arrre they playing hooky today, perrrhaps?"

Alex opened his mouth to deny it, but then he closed it again and slapped his hand to his forehead. "Ugh. I bet they did it. They said this morning that they were going to go have an adventure, but I had a meeting instead so I couldn't . . ." He trailed off, thinking, remembering now just how much he'd wanted to be with them.

Simber looked pointedly at Alex and tapped a paw. "Well?"

Alex startled. "Well what? *I* didn't do it." It was nice not to be the one in trouble for once.

Simber sighed. "I know that. What arrre you, as leaderrr, going to do about it?"

"Oh!" Alex said. *Sheesh, this whole leadership thing isn't coming very easily,* he thought. "Um . . . okay," he said, stalling. "Okay, well, Claire—" He blushed furiously. "I mean, Ms. Morning, will you stay on the island and watch over things while Simber and I go find the boat? Because he can, like, fly and stuff, so we should be able to . . . find it. Pretty easily.

Yeah." He felt very proud to have thought of that so quickly.

Ms. Morning, who had raised an eyebrow at Alex's familiarity, was secretly pleased that Simber was helping Alex in a way that her father hadn't thought to do. "That sounds like a great plan. If Father and I are gone to the peace meeting before you get back, just have some of the students help you load things up. You can leave it anchored out front overnight. Sound good?"

Alex nodded. "Whew," he said under his breath. "I mean, okay Simber, are you ready? That is, is that okay with you? I know you wanted a nap."

"Nap schmap," grumbled the giant cat. He leaped from his pedestal, causing the entire mansion to shake when he landed. "Nobody takes that boat out forrr months, and now all of a sudden everrrybody needs it."

Alex smiled, knowing that sometimes Simber just needed to get his crankies out, and it was better simply to listen than try to argue.

A few minutes later, on the shore, Alex hoisted himself onto Simber's back. "Any idea wherrre they may have gone?" Simber asked.

Alex had been trying desperately to set his brain to "leader" mode, thinking ahead to what Simber might be asking, and this time he'd succeeded. "They're probably either going around our island to see what things look like on the other side, or they've struck out to the west."

Immediately Simber took a powerful running leap and flew nearly straight up into the sky and over the center of Quill, leaving Alex dangling by his arms from Simber's neck. "Whoa! Whoa!" Alex shouted.

"Sorry," Simber muttered as he straightened out again, but Alex thought he could hear the big cat chuckling. "Therrre, we can see all the way arrround. Do you see them?"

Alex scanned all the way around. "No," he said.

"Neitherrr do I. All rrright. To the west, then."

Alex nodded and shifted on the cat's slippery back. "To the west!"

Paradise . . . Lost

Lani awoke to the sound of someone screaming. It was Meghan. And that made Lani almost start screaming too.

Her first thought was to jump to her feet and stop whatever it was that was making her friend scream. But instinctively Lani knew that would be foolish despite the enormous rush of panic inside her, so she remained deathly still. She squinted through mostly closed eyelids, remembering the beach but nothing else since then, trying to get an idea of where she was and what was happening. Her brain felt too groggy to make sense of everything.

Through slitted eyes she could see Samheed on a table next to her, still out cold. She was relieved to see him, and he appeared to be alive—his chest moved up and down. Lani turned her head to the other side, very slowly, toward the screaming, hoping she wasn't drawing attention her way. But a second later something caught her eye and she stopped moving. Lying in still-damp clothes, she broke into a cold sweat and tried to contain a clammy shiver, for a man and a woman in gauzy white shirts stood next to her, their backs to her, blocking her view of her friend's head.

They were bent over, focusing very hard on whatever horrible thing they were doing to Meghan. Lani swallowed hard, trying not to freak out and wondering what on earth she could possibly do to save Meghan and not make things worse.

There was no other sound except for Meghan's sobs and cries. It was hard for Lani to concentrate. She looked over at Samheed again, his face so calm and serene, willing him to wake up. She begged and pleaded silently with anyone who might be able to hear the thoughts in her head, and prayed desperately for Samheed's eyes to open so they could plan their imminent escape together. She wasn't sure she could do this alone.

Lani's heart raced. She'd have to startle them, then attack and disable them. And then somehow she and Meghan would have to drag Samheed out of here. Not impossible, she found herself thinking, and that thought calmed her. Unless, of course, Meghan was unable to move . . . but Lani couldn't let herself consider that option.

Slowly she slid her hand up her thigh to the opening of her pants pocket. Meghan's screams were growing hoarse now, and Lani turned her inner pleading toward Meghan to stay conscious, keep the white-shirted people occupied . . . and not die.

Lani wriggled her fingers into her wet pants pocket. There was nothing there. She tried the other pocket, but the only thing in there was the picture Alex had drawn and given to her. She bit her lip to keep the angry tears back. Someone had taken her spell components. Her heart pounded in her chest so loudly she was sure the people could hear it.

She lifted her head slightly to look around the room, knowing she shouldn't be moving so much, but unable to control herself now—she was starting to panic. And there, on a table across the room, she saw them. A pile of scatterclips and other assorted components, well out of reach. Lani let her head rest back on the table and squeezed her eyes shut, telling herself to calm down, to just stay cool and think. But Meghan's cries were totally unnerving her. Lani wasn't sure how much longer she could stand it. She needed a plan now.

An instant later Meghan's screams stopped; only the echo of them hung in the air for a second before fading. Lani tensed, her stomach clenching and churning. Had they killed her friend? With no more time to think, Lani pulled her knees up to her chin and kicked out at the man, striking him in the center of his back and knocking him off balance and to the floor. She leaped off the table and lunged for the components, managing only to knock them to the ground as the man grabbed her by the ankle and pulled her down.

Meghan, silent, struggled to her elbow. She kicked out weakly at the woman who had been holding her down on the table. Lani's eyes widened—Meghan was alive! Lani grabbed a handful of scatterclips and sent them soaring through the air at the woman, who was now wrestling with Meghan. The scatterclips caught the woman's clothing and dragged her several feet away from Meghan to the wall, pinning her there.

A look of shock and frustration crossed over her face as she struggled and failed to release herself from their grasp.

And then the man was getting up and grabbing for Lani's ankles again, trying to keep her from rising to her feet.

"Run, Meg! Get help!" she screamed, reaching blindly for components. "I'm coming!"

Meghan, dazed and no doubt in shock, staggered to the door obediently as Lani clawed at the dirt floor, trying to reach another scatterclip. "Go!" she yelled again, and Meghan, without looking back, disappeared from view.

The man yanked Lani by the ankles as Lani tried desperately to twist over to her stomach so she could see where the components were. "Sam, wake up!" Lani screamed. "Sam!" She wriggled one leg free from the man's grasp and kicked him hard in the jaw, sending him reeling once again. He hit his head on the corner of a table and fell to the ground, conscious but dazed, on top of the components.

Lani jumped to her feet and made a quick assessment. She looked at the door, which stood open now. Meghan was gone. She looked at Samheed, who hadn't moved. The woman was still stuck fast to the wall, she was sure of it.

The man was starting to struggle to his feet. There was no way Lani could risk going anywhere near him to grab another scatterclip. She scrambled to Samheed's side and slapped his face, tugging at his arm and screaming his name. "Sam! Wake up!" she sobbed. "Please . . ."

She looked at the man, who was standing now, grabbing a rope from a drawer and coming toward her. And then she looked at Samheed, lying helpless. Nothing barred her way to the door. She could still run.

But she couldn't leave him there.

She shoved her hands into her pockets once more in a desperate move to see if perhaps the strange captors had accidently missed one scatterclip or a bit of rubber in the fold of her pocket, but it was not to be. For the second time since they'd been captured, her fingers touched the picture Alex had drawn. But this time she drew in a sharp breath, and her eyes opened wide with the realization that there might indeed be one last hope. She gripped the drawing, her lips moving slightly as she mouthed the necessary word. *Seek.* With a fire-like blast, a ball of light burst from her pocket, not harming her in the least. It zigzagged to the doorway and disappeared.

A second later, dozens more silent people appeared as if from nowhere and flooded into the room, trapping Lani between the wall and the head of Samheed's table. She stood bravely facing them, gripping and pulling hard on Sam's hair, hoping the pain would wake him. But it didn't. *Go, Meghan!* she pleaded silently. *Come on, Alex!*

The man she'd fought now weaved his way through the crowd, most of whom were using a strange sort of sign language to communicate. Some stood on tiptoes trying to see what was happening. All of them wore scarves around their necks with symbols printed on them. Lani shrank back as the man with the rope approached. He signaled to another man, who roughly grabbed Lani by the shoulders and turned her around to face the wall, her cheek pressed up against the clammy coolness of it. The man took her wrists, pinning them at her sides. "Samheed!" she yelled once more, kicking backward and startling everyone, but not enough to allow her to escape.

The man with the rope pulled it around Lani's neck and held it tight. Lani struggled, but it was no use. First she saw spots dance before her eyes as she struggled to breathe, and then a wall of blackness. She could hang on to consciousness no longer. She slumped forward against the wall.

When Lani woke again, the screams she heard this time were her own. Her body was now tied to the same table she'd been on before. A different woman with strange, golden-orange eyes held Lani's head still while another painstakingly threaded metal thorns through the skin of her neck.

The Search

Simber soared toward the sun, which was just beginning its descent for the day. Alex shivered and wished he'd brought a jacket—it was much cooler flying this high over the middle of the ocean. And really, he had other things to do. He wished his friends hadn't chosen today of all days to mess around with Ms. Morning's boat. He wished . . .

Alex pulled himself up closer to the stone cheetah's neck, trying to hide his face from the wind that whipped his hair all around and stung his eyes. He had no idea how fast Simber was going, but it was much swifter than Alex had ever moved before, that was certain.

"Arrre you holding on all rrright?" Simber asked.

"Yes," Alex said. His arms ached.

Just then a glowing dot of light appeared in the distance, growing bigger by the second. At first Alex thought his eyes had gone buggy from staring at the sun, but as seconds turned into minutes, it didn't waver. Soon it reached Alex and Simber, and reversed its course to remain in a position just within Alex's grasp.

Alex, not knowing what else to do, held out his hand and grabbed the sphere from the air. It exploded, and a lighted image of a drawing of Lani—*his* drawing—appeared, then broke into tiny pieces of light and fell away. Instantly he remembered the spell Lani had created for Mr. Appleblossom.

"We're going the right way!" Alex cried out to Simber. "Lani sent a seek spell. So at least they're all right," he said, hope in his voice.

"Well," growled Simber, "at least *she* is, orrr was, wheneverrr she sent it."

The short blast of relief disappeared and fear returned to

Alex's belly. He didn't know how long it took for a seeking ball of light to travel. And who knew how far away his friends were? He leaned forward again, searching all the harder.

Within an hour they were closing in on the nearest island. Alex strained his eyes toward the water below, looking for the boat, but was fooled over and over again from this height by foaming whitecaps—the sea below was getting choppy. But he didn't need to worry. Simber's keen eyes soon spotted the boat without a problem.

The giant stone cheetah dove down to get a closer look, making Alex's stomach catch in his throat. They hovered over the boat for a moment. It was empty.

"Thrrree component vests on the seats, and no sign of theirrr ownerrrs," Simber growled, highly displeased.

Alex's eyes widened and his gaze darted from the boat to the shore to the lush green center and tall rocky points of the island. "Where are they?"

Simber flapped his powerful wings and headed for the island. "That's what we'rrre going to find out." His voice was gruffer than usual, and it made Alex feel like he should be worried.

They soared over the island, Simber flying swiftly and

277 « Island of Silence

carefully over the beach and the landscape. Alex shielded his eyes and peered around Simber's neck. He wasn't cold now. He didn't think about his discomfort or the annoying sun in his eyes. Simber was worried; therefore Alex was worried. Simber didn't worry about things unless they were big.

"Do you see anything?" Alex ventured after they'd combed a quarter of the island.

"Some footprrrints on the beach," Simber said. "I thought I saw a glint of metal orrr something else shiny a moment ago, but it was shorrrt-lived and I can't find it now." He went over the property again, but saw nothing.

Alex bit his lip and shifted on Simber's back, leaning far off to one side now, determined to find something. "Is it safe to land?" he asked.

"I'd rrratherrr not," Simber said gruffly. "Therrre's something strrrange about this place. Therrre's no noise at all. I don't trrrust it."

Alex swallowed hard. He tried not to let his panic overtake his senses. "Lani," he whispered. "Come on, you guys. The joke's over. Where are you?" But deep down, he had a feeling this wasn't a joke at all.

When they had cruised over the entire island, Simber made one last pass over the beach. "Okay, leaderrr. What now?"

Alex had been asking himself this very question. He tried to be as grown-up as possible, tried to think everything through like Mr. Today would do. Finally he said, "Do you think it's truly dangerous for us to go ashore and explore?"

"Forrr you, yes. Forrr me, prrrobably not."

Alex bit his lip. Could he rightfully ask Simber to risk going ashore alone?

Simber cleared his throat. He hovered over the beach, watching and sampling the air. Waiting.

"Would you . . . I mean, what do you think . . . ?" Alex couldn't ask such a thing.

Simber strained his neck and looked over his shoulder at Alex. "Do it, Alex," he said. "It's yourrr job."

Alex pushed his tangled hair out of his eyes and sighed. "Okay. Fine. Simber, please drop me into the boat, and go on shore to do a little exploring. But be very careful."

Simber nodded. "That's the best idea you've had all day," he said. He darted over the water to the boat and slowly lowered his body so Alex could safely drop into it.

LISA McMANN

"Be careful!" Alex repeated as Simber flew the short distance to the sand and landed gracefully.

Alex hung over the side of the boat, his knuckles turning white as he gripped the railing, watching Simber slink toward the trees like the hunter he truly was. "Please find them," he whispered over and over, his teeth chattering from nerves. "Please let them be okay."

His heart leaped when Simber started running through the trees, as if in pursuit of prey. Alex stood up straight, straining to hear something, anything, from the direction of the island. But as before, there was eerily no sound at all.

When he heard a small splash nearby, he jumped. He imagined a team of islanders coming up out of the water from underneath the boat to attack him, now that the beast was out of the way. Dizzy with self-imposed fright, he grabbed a paddle from the side compartment of the boat with one hand and a heart attack component with the other and looked quickly all around the water.

He heard another splash, and this time he could pinpoint it—it was coming from the back of the boat. Alex raised the paddle above his head with his right hand, and pulled his left hand back holding the heart attack component, ready to fight whatever it was. He carefully peered over the stern.

When he saw her, one arm slung loosely around the boat's ladder, he sucked in a breath, for indeed, he nearly didn't recognize her at first.

"Meg," he whispered.

He threw the paddle to the deck and reached out for her. She could barely lift a hand, she was so weak. The low sun caught Meghan's red hair on fire and glinted on the points of the metal thorn band around her neck.

Stationed Up and at the Ready

"Eva," Aaron called out when he had his plan for the next day's attack all figured out. "A word, please."

Eva rolled her eyes. "Now what?" She and the others had just sat down at the Halukis' dining table to eat a rather fine governor-type dinner.

Aaron tried to ignore her attitude. "I need you to sneak out of here and talk to Gondoleery—let her know what the plan is, and see what they've done with their weapons."

"What *is* the plan?"

"I'm about to tell you," Aaron said. "You can stop with the insolence now. I apologized for doubting you. It's over. Can't

LISA McMANN

we please move forward cohesively? We have a government to overtake, and we need to be together on this."

This time Eva didn't roll her eyes, but she wanted to. "Fine. Go ahead then."

"This is very important. I want you to tell Gondoleery's team to wait until it's fully dark, and then begin stealthily heading toward Artimé. They should bring all of their weapons with them, hide, and sit patiently outside Artimé's walls, watching who is going in and out overnight. They're not to attack until after you and Today leave in the morning."

"Okay," Eva said.

"And I want you to go inside and sleep in the mansion tonight as you normally would. Do you have your heart attack weapon?"

"I do," Eva said, patting her pocket. "And you have the rest of them." Eva stared at the ground, thinking. She'd have to fake not knowing the gate was back up. Hopefully there would still be a way into Artimé. She shifted nervously. If she couldn't release the gate spell herself and get into Artimé, she wouldn't be able to leave with Marcus in the morning.

"I'll have the rest of our team head toward the palace in the morning to try to delay Haluki in case he gets wind of this."

"Sounds good," Eva said. She glanced around at the others. "So you're camping out here tonight? All of you?"

"Yes. You'll be off with the old mage by the time we attack, so we'll see you after. Remember, just dump the body and say he went for a swim and drowned."

"I will."

"Be properly upset about it."

"I *will*." Eva was getting upset with Aaron now. "Maybe you should brave up and kill him yourself if you don't think I can do it right."

Aaron's face turned red. He pressed his lips together but said nothing.

Eva turned and looked longingly at the dinner table, where Liam, Bethesda, and Crawledge were making quick work of the food. "Is there anything else you want me to tell Gondoleery?"

"Just . . ." Aaron fidgeted. "Just tell her to hold off and stand down if she feels outnumbered. We aren't in a race."

"Okay." She took it upon herself to end their little meeting and went back to sit at the table and finish her food.

Aaron watched her, incredulous, and then cleared his throat loudly. "Eva?"

Eva turned to look at him, surprised. "Yes?"

"Now."

Eva and the other three paused simultaneously, hands to mouths, and stared at Aaron.

"Now," he said again, and pointed to the back door. "Go."

The former secretary to the High Priest Justine hesitated, and then slowly placed her spoon back into her full bowl of soup. She stood, infuriated, and without a word or a second glance, walked out the back door of the Haluki home, seething, and disappeared.

When she reached the home of Gondoleery Rattrapp, she entered quietly. Gondoleery sat at her table staring at the spell components, rolling them around in her fingers, deep in thought. She startled and stood up when Eva cleared her throat.

"I have a message for you," Eva announced. "Aaron Stowe requests that your team head over to Artimé now. There you'll find a gate up. Release the magic spell on it, or break it down if you have to," she said, looking at Gondoleery, "and attack immediately."

LISA McMANN

The Weekly Peace Meeting

As the sun set over the distant islands Marcus Today sat at his dressing table in his private chambers. He adjusted his robe on his shoulders and secured it, just so, around his neck. He doffed his favorite slippers and put on his walking shoes for the trip into Quill. But then he chuckled to himself, remembering he'd put the gate up again. Perhaps he wouldn't walk into Quill today after all.

The walk was one of his favorite parts of his new routine since the battle. Sometimes Claire accompanied him, and that gave him some lovely time to spend with his daughter. But he really favored the walk when he was alone. While the road was hot, and the odor and scenery left much to be desired along the way to the palace, it was often quite deserted for a good portion of the way, and it gave Mr. Today some much needed peace and quiet from the mostly friendly chaos that had overtaken Artimé. It was good for him to be alone sometimes, he knew. And occasional solitude was especially good for the creative mind. Some of his best ideas of the past months came out of that weekly walk. The greatest of which was Alex Stowe.

The boy was young, but Marcus had no doubt that he would flourish in the years ahead. And the old mage was set on helping Alex build his self-confidence and belief in himself as being worthy of the title of mage of Artimé. It would take time, but Alex would come around eventually.

As Marcus smoothed his flyaway shock of hair, he thought back on his meetings with Alex over the past months. How fun it was to surprise the boy with his eccentric ideas. How smart Alex was, and how capable. And how disappointed the boy could get when he wanted something so badly but was denied. He knew back then that Alex would feel incapable of being mage. He also knew, more than Alex himself, that Alex wouldn't want anyone else taking the job from him.

"Oh!" he said to his image in the mirror. "That reminds me. . . ."

He picked up a pencil and scribbled a note to himself for after the meeting:

Teach Alex Triad spells

He chuckled to himself as he put his pencil down. "Oh dear. Getting forgetful," he said. "It wouldn't do to leave out that little gem, now would it. In fact . . . I'll grab it now." He got up and walked out of his chambers and across the hall to the Museum of Large. Inside he gazed at the overflowing piles of books for a long moment, concentrating. Slowly he walked halfway down the library wall to the very center of the middle shelf, and pulled out a thin, handwritten diary simply called *The Triad: Live, Hide, Restore*.

He brought the book to his chambers and set it on his dressing table so he wouldn't forget to give it to Alex that night.

A moment later there was a light tapping on the door frame. Ms. Morning poked her head in.

"Hello, dear," Mr. Today said, smiling brightly.

"Ready, Father?"

"Just about," he said. "Has Alex returned with the boat?"

"Not yet," Ms. Morning said. She was starting to get worried, but she knew that there was no better companion for Alex to have than Simber. "I'm sure they'll be back before we get home after the meeting."

"Perhaps we should wait."

Claire smiled. "Father, you put us in charge. Alex is no doubt handling everything with utmost care. And if he and Simber are not back by morning, obviously you can cancel your trip."

Mr. Today nodded. "You're right. You know, Claire, this is very good for me, to let go of a few things now and then."

"I know," she said.

Mr. Today turned to Charlie, the gargoyle. "Charlie, can you let Gunnar know we're on the way?"

Charlie gave Mr. Today three thumbs-up. He'd always felt very lucky to have three thumbs, so he used them all whenever the opportunity arose.

Mr. Today and Ms. Morning left the mage's private chambers and walked across the hall to the kitchenette. Ms. Morning stepped to the side of the tube and flourished regally with her hand to her father. "Age before beauty, as they say."

Mr. Today chuckled softly and stepped into the tube.

Silence

"Meghan!" Alex hoisted Meghan's limp, sodden body into the boat, nearly toppling over when her foot caught on the ladder. He yanked her free and they both fell to the deck. "Meg!" he cried out again.

Her skin was blue-white and very cold except for the swollen red skin of her neck, where the thorny band was sewn, but her eyelids fluttered and she breathed shallowly. She focused on Alex for a second and tried to speak, but couldn't make a sound. Her fingers brushed past her throat and her face twisted up, lips quivering, tears leaking from her eyes in a silent chest-heaving sob.

Alex stared. And then he sprang to his feet. "Simber!" he shouted, leaning over the boat's edge and cupping his mouth. "Simber!" He scrambled around the boat to find towels, wrapping Meghan in them and giving her a pillow. Her eyes were closed now, and she didn't open them when Alex shook her arm. He stood again to shout the cheetah's name, but this time saw him coming.

The cheetah glided in and landed with his back paws precariously on the side railing of the boat, still flapping his wings to keep the majority of his weight from capsizing them all, but being careful not to touch the water. His eyes were eagle-sharp, his teeth bared. "What's happened to herrr? Wherrre'd she come frrrom?" he growled.

Alex, now fighting the wind from Simber's wings, shielded his face—he'd been accidentally knocked about by those wings before, and it wasn't fun, so he was cautious. "She was in the water, clinging to the ladder. I didn't know she was there until she splashed. She can't talk. They—" He choked up a little. Whoever "they" was Alex didn't know, which made it even more frightening. "They put that horrible metal thing on her neck." His own face threatened to twist up in emotion, but he gripped the captain's seatback, trying to control it. "I haven't seen Lani or Samheed." He dug his fingernails into the cushion and closed his eyes a moment, trying to compose himself. He was supposed to be in charge. And people in charge can't buckle. He knew he had to take his personal pain out of it for now and focus on what to do next. He took a deep breath and let it out. Then he looked at Simber, his face serious. "Did you see anything on the island?"

Simber nodded grimly. "Yes. Not Samheed orrr Lani, but I saw two natives with the necklaces made of thorrrns. I chased them until they disappearrred into a hole in the grrround, much smallerrr than I could get into." He looked at Meghan and then at Alex.

"A hole in the ground?" Alex echoed. He didn't have time to contemplate that right now—he knew he had another decision to make. But this one was beyond his ability. "Simber . . ." He stared at Meghan's limp body and looked up at Simber again. "I need your help," he said.

"I'm always herrre," he said softly.

Alex scanned the island once more, desperate to see Lani or Samheed. "It's going to be dark soon. Meghan's freezing—the water here is much colder than it is at Artimé. I don't know if she's injured more than just the neck thing, or what. She's . . . She won't wake up."

Simber nodded and waited.

"So . . . you're sure there's no sign of Sam and Lani?" Alex knew, of course, that Simber wouldn't have lied about it. He just had to get himself to accept that his friends were missing . . . and quite possibly worse off than Meghan. He couldn't bear to take it all in.

"I'm sorry. No sign. No scent. And, of courrrse, no sound."

Alex looked down at Meghan. "We need to leave them here . . . don't we." It wasn't really a question.

Simber's eyes softened. "Yes, Alex."

Alex blew out a breath and nodded. "Okay." That was the help he needed. "We need to save the one we know we can save." Hurriedly he grabbed more dry towels from the stack he'd found and began rewrapping Meghan in them.

"That's rrright."

Alex looked at the almost-setting sun, and then peered in the direction of Artimé. His heart pounded and he sat upright, leaning forward, squinting and worrying. "I can't see home."

LISA McMANN

"I can," Simber said. "We'll go togetherrr, as always."

Alex gave one last fleeting glance over his shoulder at the silent island, and then released the anchor spell and situated himself behind the wheel of the boat, straining his eyes to read the instructions in the dimming light. He started the boat and looked up at Simber. "Lead the way. Full speed."

"If we hurrry, we'll make it by darrrk," Simber said. He looked down at Alex. "I won't leave you."

Alex nodded. With a powerful flap, Simber rose and headed east toward home.

"Hang on, Meg," Alex whispered as he powered the boat to full speed. "You'll be safe soon." He clenched his hands around the steering wheel and followed Simber. He didn't look back again.

The Dark and Quiet Place

After the screaming came the silence, and then the burning eye drops, which were not nearly as bad as the thorny necklace surgery, but the drops still stung ferociously and made Lani blind. She ached everywhere. They brought her somewhere cool and dry, and left her there, free of ropes or tethers. But it didn't matter. She didn't feel like moving.

She had heard Samheed's cries for a while not far away, but she was too weak, too blind to even attempt to find him. And then Sam, like Meghan, and like herself, had gone silent without warning when the sharp device was connected in

LISA McMANN

place. There was nothing to be heard after that.

Later she felt a slight breeze, as if someone or something moved past her, and she swung her arms out weakly, but they didn't connect with anything but air. She crawled around, shaking with pain and weakness and fear, until the panic inside her finally shuddered its way out of her body. But no one who cared would ever see it.

Lani could do nothing but sit in this cave. She could see nothing but a sheet of black. And she couldn't hear anything at all—no noise transmitted anywhere on the island. Not through voice, or friction, or shuffle of feet.

Not even through dripping tears or cracking hearts.

Heart Attack

Aaron went back to worrying over the weapons on the desk in Haluki's office, having no stomach for food now. He sat in Haluki's chair, elbows on the desk and face in his hands. He was in over his head and he knew it. He had four dozen fighters at most . . . at most! How could they possibly prevail against hundreds of Artiméans, even if the Restorers did have a little magic? Artimé had more. They always had more.

Besides that, he was not playing it out right at all. What was he doing, getting Eva so mad at him? But he could feel it—the control he so desperately desired, flitting just out of his grasp, and it made him crazy. He should just call the whole thing off.

"It's too soon," he muttered, not for the first time that evening. He lifted his head and stared at the measly weaponry in front of him. And then he heard a noise.

When the closet on the wall across from him rattled, and the doors unlatched, he first thought that his stressed-out mind was playing tricks on him. But then the doors opened further, and before Aaron could make a sound Mr. Today emerged from the closet into the office through the enormous glass tube.

Mr. Today took a few steps before he noticed the strange weapons strewn over the top of Gunnar's desk, and then he looked up and saw Aaron slowly rising to his feet.

They stood stock-still, both completely startled, facing each other just a few feet apart. Neither moved a muscle, and thoughts flooded both of their minds.

Mr. Today's first instinct was to warn his daughter. But before he could do anything to stop Claire from coming through the tube, Aaron Stowe jerked out his arm and grabbed a handful of heart attack components from the desk.

Without hesitation, Mr. Today whipped a pen from his

robe pocket and shot a blinding highlighter spell into Aaron's eyes. But Aaron, unfazed and spurred on by Eva Fathom's dare, didn't need his eyes to know where the mage was. As he reeled backward, he flung all of the components at once toward the man, shouting, "Heart attack!"

Five clay hearts sprouted wings and flew at Mr. Today. The old mage tried to dodge them, but the components had locked in on their target. They slammed into his chest, knocking the mage to the floor as they found their mark.

Shocked by the impact, Mr. Today gasped and clutched his robe. The pain seared through him, from his chest outward in all directions, stopping his breath. He closed his eyes, sending one last message as the heart attack spells stabbed deep into him, five times the power and intensity of one. He writhed on the floor, shaking.

Aaron, blinded, called out to his team, unsure what had happened. "Help!" he called out. "I can't see!"

A second later Aaron heard another noise from the cabinet. "Help!" he cried out again. "They're attacking!" His housemates came thundering in. By the time Claire Morning stepped out of the closet and saw her father on the floor, Mr. Today had stopped shaking and lay completely still.

Crawledge and Bethesda seized Claire, and Liam clamped his hand over her mouth. He grabbed a rusty knife from the desk and held it to her throat. "Not one word," he said.

Everyone stood transfixed by the strange, horrific situation as one by one they realized what Aaron had just done.

"What's happening?" Aaron called out anxiously, but then his sight miraculously cleared. He scrambled to his feet, ready to attack, but everyone's attention was diverted to the closet, where the strange glass tube faded away before the Restorers' eyes.

From the Vast Ocean

Alex never loosened his grip on the wheel, and he urged the boat on faster and faster. Simber stayed steady, ahead and to the right, so he could look over his shoulder now and then and make sure Alex was okay.

And Alex kept looking down at Meghan, glad she was shielded from the wind, hoping she was still alive, still hanging on.

Regret and fear pounded through his body in waves. He wished he'd stopped his friends. He wished he'd known what they were about to do. How foolish! What were they thinking?

LISA McMANN

But he remembered his first glance at the beautiful island, thinking how serene and lovely it appeared. "Why'd you do it, Meg?" he asked, knowing she couldn't hear him.

It was what he couldn't say that crushed him. He couldn't even think it, it was too horrible to imagine. *Lani.*

And Samheed, too, but it was different with Lani. She was his . . . sort of . . . oh, this was all so horrible. He had to stop thinking about it. He glanced at their component vests, folded neatly on the seat next to him, the top one fluttering slightly whenever a gust of wind slipped under it. They'd had no protection. Why on earth would they take their vests off? They were smarter than that! Alex didn't understand it.

And now he and Simber had left them there . . . wherever they were. Underground in a hole? That was crazy.

Maybe he should have had Simber carry Meghan and him home, and left the boat for Sam and Lani, just in case. He glanced over his shoulder and bit his lip, wishing he'd thought of that. Maybe they should turn back. But they were almost home now. In the dim light Alex could see the mansion all lit up. It was beautiful from this angle. He'd never noticed it like this before.

By the time they grew close to Artimé, Alex had decided it. He'd drop Meghan off in care of the nurses, and then he and Simber would go back to the island and leave the boat for Samheed and Lani, just in case. He doubted the natives of that island could know how to dismantle the anchor spell, so there was little worry of it being stolen. What if Samheed and Lani had watched him and Simber leave with the boat, and they'd been unable to make a sound, like Meghan? It tore Alex apart to think about it. He cursed the boat for not going faster, and Simber flapped onward, never tiring. Always there, faithfully at Alex's side.

Until suddenly, he wasn't.

Without warning the boat sputtered loudly and stopped running. Alex and Meghan pitched forward, Alex hitting the windshield and cutting his lip open, Meghan slamming lifelessly into a seat and stopping there. As he was about to use the magical verbal component to get the boat started again, he noticed, out of the corner of his eye, Simber frozen mid-flap in the air. The giant cat tipped forward sharply and began falling, falling, falling. "Simber!" Alex yelled, but the giant stone statue didn't respond. *"Simber!"*

Simber slammed face-first into the water with an enormous splash, sending a giant wave that nearly capsized the boat. Alex and Meghan flew out over the side like weightless rag dolls being tossed across a room, and plunged headlong into the sea. When Alex surfaced, coughing and sputtering, he saw the tip of Simber's tail disappearing under the water. "Simber!" Alex cried out again. But he had no time to think about Simber now. He twisted in the water, looking frantically in all directions.

"Meghan!" he screamed.

She was nowhere to be found.

Gone

Aaron watched in amazement, and then came to his senses. He grabbed a pistol from the table and pointed it at Claire Morning. "If you speak, you will die," he said.

Ms. Morning couldn't make a sound. She didn't even look at Aaron. She could only stare at the body of her father, crumpled and unmoving on the floor. He looked so helpless.

Keeping the gun trained on Claire, Aaron turned back to Mr. Today. He stepped carefully over to the mage and nudged him with his foot. The magician didn't respond.

LISA McMANN

"Is he dead?" Bethesda asked. "What did you do to him?"

"Quiet," Aaron barked. His heart raced. Had he killed Mr. Today? Had it really been so easy? He turned to Crawledge and Bethesda. "Take her to the pantry and lock her up. Bar the door. Liam, give her a little something to help her remember not to give us any trouble."

Liam's eyes widened. "Like what?"

Aaron shoved his hands into his pockets to keep them from trembling. "Just . . . whatever. Threaten her. Think of something! I don't care."

Claire turned her head back to Liam now, her eyes filled with hatred and unshed tears. She glared at him, and he couldn't look at her.

"Come on," Liam said roughly. He picked his way over Mr. Today and around furniture and led them to the kitchen pantry, Claire struggling slightly, but not enough to get herself shot. "Just throw her in there," he mumbled. "I need to help Aaron with the body."

Crawledge and Bethesda shoved Claire into the space under the bottom shelf, tied her wrists and ankles, stuffed a

LISA McMANN

dusty cloth in her mouth, and closed the door. When they had secured the pantry, and the sounds of their voices grew distant, Claire Morning closed her eyes and let her head fall back against the wall.

The Restorers

Once Eva had delivered the false message, Gondoleery Rattrapp wasted no time. She'd been waiting weeks for this moment, and her teams and weapons were ready. They slithered toward Quill, staying in whatever late afternoon shadows they could find along the way. They arrived at dusk. Gondoleery tried to release the spell on the gate, but it didn't work. She tried again, and then realized it must be a very strong spell— more powerful than she was at the moment.

"We'll have to break it down," she said. But first she gathered her troops around her to go over the plan one last time. They were all in agreement to wait until the moon was high overhead so they could have some advantage of light when the Artiméans came pouring out of the mansion to fight.

But before the plan could be enacted, a strange cry rose up from inside Artimé. Gondoleery and her team could hear it, plain as day. As far as she knew, that had never happened before—Artimé had a sound barrier around it, which had helped to keep it from being discovered all those years. But now they could hear people shrieking and crying out. Something chaotic had clearly happened. And then the gate clicked and popped open an inch.

Gondoleery was happy to take advantage of that.

"Ready?" she whispered harshly. "Charge!" She opened the gate and her team streamed in behind her. But it wasn't long before they were all nearly trampled or swept up by the crowd of people that flooded out of Artimé.

"After them!" Gondoleery cried. She wasn't pleased that no one seemed to even notice her ferocious team amid all the chaos. Still, they managed to take down a few straggling Unwanteds as they chased after them.

Out in the road around Quill, the Artiméans, realizing they

were under attack, struggled to pull themselves together. Soon they began to fight back. Gondoleery flinched as an Artiméan sent a rubber sphere flying toward her, hitting her in the shoulder.

But nothing happened. The spell component bounced harmlessly to the ground and rolled in the dirt. As the look of surprise came over the face of the Unwanted who'd thrown it, Gondoleery picked up the ball and stared at it, then shoved it in her pocket. There was no time to ponder this latest development now. She had a battle to win.

To the Depths of Despair

Alex sucked in a breath and dove down, eyes wide open, looking for any flash of color, any sign of Meghan. It was dark down there, and mentally he scrambled for all of the possible spells he could use to help him in a situation like this, but he could think of none. Even his origami dragons would be of no use now to light up the night, for they were a sopping wet mess in his component vest pocket.

Desperately he searched for Meghan, waving his hands around through the water. His lungs felt like they were going to burst. He came up for air and whipped his head around, looking for any sign of her, but there was nothing. Then down he went again. *Please!* he screamed in his mind, thinking of Lani and Samheed. *I can't lose everyone.*

That thought nearly made him break apart, but it also gave him the strength to dive deeper, to search harder. He surfaced once more, panting, and looked everywhere. Only the boat, upright again and drifting toward the shore, was visible. He knew there was no time to waste.

He sucked in an enormous breath and down he went a third time, deeper, farther, until his ears ached and popped. He strained to reach anything he could touch in the murky water. Just when he was about to give up he kicked his feet, and his toes got tangled up in something.

It was hair.

He turned sharply and reached for her hair, grasping it with his hand, and yanked as hard as he could, rushing, kicking, with all of his might, pulling her up alongside him and then pushing her above him to the surface. When they broke through, Alex gasped and sucked in air, flipping on his back and holding Meghan tightly to his chest, trying to float, and unable to do another thing until he had replenished his oxygen stores.

He squeezed Meghan's stomach and started kicking toward the shore. "Breathe!" he cried. And then, between ragged breaths, he chanted to keep himself focused. "Breathe. Please breathe."

Meghan choked and silently coughed up water. She took a raking breath in and coughed some more.

"Come on," Alex said. "Breathe! That's it!"

Meghan struggled. The sharp thorns around her neck cut into Alex's chest like lethal scatterclips hitting their mark, but he couldn't do anything to adjust his pain or hers right now. Waves constantly washed over their faces, causing them to feel like they were drowning over and over again.

"Come on, now," Alex said again, barely whispering. "We're going to make it. We're going to make it." He put everything he had into getting through the next second, and the next, and the next.

It took almost an hour to reach the shore of Artimé. When Alex could touch the bottom, he stumbled, dragged Meghan to the measure of sand, and collapsed. They rested there for several minutes in the dark, Alex just feeling the solid wet earth beneath him, Meghan not feeling anything at all. Alex didn't let go of her. The only way he knew she was alive was by feeling her stomach rise and fall beneath his arm.

Finally, when he was able, he called out in a hoarse voice. "Help—anyone? Is anyone out here?"

No one answered.

No one? On a beautiful evening like this? Carefully he rolled Meghan off of him and staggered to his feet, his legs wobbly and his arms feeling like seaweed. He picked up Meghan under her arms and walked backward, dragging her up the shore, and then when he could go no farther, he set her down gently and turned toward the mansion to go and find help.

But there was no mansion there.

There was no mansion, no trees, no water fountains, no beautiful colors. No happy little creatures wandering about. No brightly lit lawn to sit on.

There was only a gray shack, sitting on a slab of broken cement. Burned-looking weeds grew out of the cracks. A stark wall stood in the distance, with a gate standing open. And strewn across the cement were the lifeless bodies of squirrelicorns and beavops and owlbats.

Alex felt his head spinning. Was he hallucinating? Had

he landed on the wrong island? He stumbled forward in the moonlight, leaving Meghan lying on the sand. He went past lifeless body after lifeless body, not comprehending anything, until he saw a familiar lump with seven and a half quiet legs, none of them floating about at all. A pair of vanity glasses had fallen from her snout and lay next to her. "Ms. Octavia?" he whispered.

He kneeled at her side, feeling panic bubbling up inside. "Ms. Octavia!" he shouted in her face, but she didn't blink or move. He touched her. Her face felt like cloth. Like she was some ridiculous patchwork doll.

Alex looked up. "Florence," he murmured. "Florence!" He got up and started to run toward the gray shack, where Florence stood unmoving, in full stride, as if she were heading for the entrance. Alex went up to her and tugged on her arm. "Florence!" he shouted, but by now he knew.

Everything Mr. Today had created was dead.

But what about the humans?

"Mr. Today! Ms. Morning!" he screamed, his voice failing him. "Mr. Appleblossom! Sean? Eva? *Anybody?*"

He ran to the gate now, watching the path carefully so as

not to step on any platyprots or other creatures. "Tina," he whispered, not even bothering to yell anymore. The three girrinos were giant heaps in the dark. From somewhere beyond the gate he could hear voices—angry ones—and the sound of weapons clashing. He ran into Quill, encouraged to have heard some hint of life. But then out of the shadows someone strong reached out and grabbed Alex, clamped a hand over his mouth, and pushed him up against the wall.

To the Next Frontier

Aaron couldn't stop the heart palpitations that apparently came packaged with the honor of killing the great mage of Artimé. When everyone had left the room, he sank weakly to High Priest Haluki's desk chair and mopped his face with his hands. He rubbed his eyes and took a deep breath.

It didn't matter that it had been pure luck. An accidental ambush. A surprise attack from both perspectives. It didn't matter that he was young and rash and quick, and that the old man wasn't willing—or intelligent enough—to kill on first draw. This wasn't some planned duel where each had the advantage of fairness. This was the enemy, without warning, entering Aaron's own private quarters. Or, at least this place *felt* like Aaron's home now. It was self-defense.

Then why did he feel like he had cheated somehow? He thought briefly of his brother, and how this would hurt him. Aaron was surprised to feel little satisfaction from this. Perhaps because the battle was not nearly over. The mage's death may well get him the chaos he wanted in Artimé, which would surely bring the Necessaries back home, but Aaron was no closer to the throne. Or perhaps it was because Aaron had felt this same pain that Alex would soon know. He scowled and banished the pity from his mind. His brother deserved so much more pain than this. It was just the beginning.

Aaron turned and looked through the open closet door. It was empty, though Aaron *knew* there had been a giant glass tube in there a short time ago. Where had it gone? It was too much for Aaron's mind to grasp. But one thing was clear. The glass tube had been a passageway to Artimé. And since it was here in Haluki's home, there was no doubt that the new high priest knew exactly how it worked. All Aaron cared about right now was that High Priest Haluki didn't know it was gone.

When Liam Healy stepped into the office, Aaron looked up. His team needed direction. This was his moment to get it right.

"Is the woman securely imprisoned?" Aaron asked.

"Yes."

Aaron nodded and looked over at Mr. Today. He still couldn't believe he'd killed the man. Aaron felt numb, not powerful. "Take the body to the Ancients Sector and bury it yourself."

"Just me?"

"Yes. I need the others. We have to take over Quill now while we've got the chance."

Liam hesitated. When Aaron gave him a sharp look, he went over to the body and tentatively picked it up, hoisting it over his shoulder.

Aaron couldn't look at the mage. He chided himself for the weakness, but he told himself that he had other things to do besides wasting time staring at dead people. As Liam walked to the door Aaron stood up. "Wait," he said.

Liam stopped and looked back at Aaron.

"Give me the old geezer's robe. It'll be our . . . reward." He hesitated. "Perhaps we'll cut it up and make ridiculous flags from it in memory of this day." His eyes shifted, anxious to avoid the body.

Liam laughed hollowly and obliged. When Liam finally left the Haluki house in the thick of darkness, Aaron took the colorful robe, folded it into a neat square, and placed it solemnly on the corner of the desk.

"We've a slight change of plans," Aaron said, addressing the two allies that remained, Bethesda and Crawledge. "Eva and the others have started their secret mission to Artimé now. They are too far away to fetch. However, the opportunity is ripe to seize the palace. No doubt Haluki was planning on Today's visit. When he doesn't arrive, Haluki will come looking for him. And we will be lying in wait."

While Aaron plotted against Haluki, Haluki went in search of Matilda to find out why his friend Marcus had not yet arrived for the peace meeting. When he found her crouching on a windowsill, she was uncharacteristically unresponsive. It was almost as if she'd never been alive at all.

He glanced out the window, down the long driveway. "Guards," he said quietly, and immediately his four guards appeared. "Take a vehicle to Artimé and see if anything is amiss. Go swiftly, now."

The Clash

Alex, his mouth covered and his back against the wall, kicked with all his might, but his foot was anticipated and blocked by his captor.

"Alex, stop. It's me. Stay quiet!"

Alex's eyes widened but that didn't help him see. It was black as pitch in the shadow of the wall. He didn't know who "me" was and he wasn't going to trust anybody until he found out. He struggled again, and tried biting the hand that covered his mouth and pressed painfully against his cut, swollen lip. When that didn't work, he stuck his tongue out and licked the hand. It did the trick, and at last Alex's mouth was free.

LISA McMANN

"Ew, sick!" the voice said. "What the—?"

Alex could hear the person furiously wiping his hand on his pants. "Who . . . wait. Sean? Is that you?"

"Yes, you dolt. Gak. That was disgusting."

"Well, you didn't have the worst end of it." Alex spat on the ground, trying to get the taste of dirt and sweat out of his mouth. "Blech." He wiped his tongue with his sleeve and in an instant, everything came flooding back to him. He gripped Sean's arm and grew solemn. "What happened to Artimé?"

Sean didn't answer at first, as if he were contemplating what to say. Then he sighed and said, "Come on. Back into Artimé. Don't close the gate, mind you—it might lock us in, and we've no magic at all."

No magic at all.

Alex remembered how suspicious Sean had seemed over the past weeks, and he almost hesitated, wondering if he was being trapped. But there was something else Alex had to say before Sean could begin talking, no matter where Sean's loyalties lay. "Sean . . . first we need to save your sister."

"What?" Sean's whisper grew loud. "Where is she? Is she okay?"

"She's on the beach. Come on." They ran in the moonlight, dodging bodies.

When they reached her, Sean kneeled down and picked her up, wrapped his jacket around her, and cradled her in his arms. "Oh, Meggy . . ." He looked around helplessly. "There's no hospital wing, no nurses around . . . Everyone who could move took off, and most of them have been fighting since the attack." He touched the metal thorn necklace, a look of horror on his face. "I can't even believe this."

Alex squinched his eyes shut. "The attack?" he said in a hollow voice.

"Yes."

It was almost as if those words were enough to answer all the questions that were swimming around in Alex's head, unable to form complete sentences. Everything around him made absolutely no sense—and he didn't even want to make sense of it. Because that would mean admitting the truth of what Alex was already quite sure.

The two young men stood together on the beach with an unresponsive sister and best friend, the waves crashing on the shore as if the whole sea were at war with itself. And both quite nearly wished to be swallowed up in it rather than face the insurmountable truths before them.

Wearily they sat down and took turns filling each other in.

"Simber and I went after them, and found the boat at the island," Alex said.

"There's a group in Quill called the Restorers," Sean said.

"Samheed and Lani are still . . . out there. Somewhere."

"Your brother, Aaron, is in charge, and he's been building his followers."

"We had to leave them—to try and save Meg, and then—"

"Mr. Today went to his peace meeting, and the next thing we knew, Artimé was gone and the Restorers had managed to open the gate. The girrinos went down when Artimé did. The Restorers stormed us in all the confusion and our spells wouldn't work. . . ."

"Out of nowhere the boat died, and then Simber . . ." Alex choked and couldn't go on as he remembered the cheetah's frozen descent, and the crash into the water. He demonstrated Simber's ride into the water with his hand. "He's out there. Somewhere at the bottom of the ocean." A cough-sob escaped, and he cursed himself. If he lost it now, he'd never get through this.

It was quiet for a moment. Alex looked at Sean, and even in the small light from the sky, he could tell they needed to address one last thing.

Alex bit his lip, accidentally reopening the cut and feeling the sting. He tasted blood, and it made him queasy. "Is Mr. Today . . . gone?" He couldn't say "dead."

Sean looked out over the water. His jaw quivered and he broke down, shielding his face with his hand. It took him several minutes to contain himself, and then he choked out, "He has to be. For this to have happened—" Sean waved his hand around. "There's no other explanation." Sean couldn't hold in his sorrow. He looked at Meghan's pale face. "It's all such a disaster."

Alex was numb. "What about Ms. Morning?"

"She went with Mr. Today. And she's not here. I suspect she's dead too."

The blood tasted like metal in his mouth. Alex couldn't comprehend anything. He felt like he was going to faint. Finally he whispered, "What are we going to do?"

The Throne

igh Priest Haluki checked his timepiece and looked out the window again. All was quiet. But where was Marcus? And where were the guards? He called out to his chef, who was cleaning up the kitchen, "I'm going for a walk down to the house."

"Yes sir," the chef said.

The high priest slipped outside as he sometimes did after dark to enjoy the coolness of the evening. If it were light out, he'd be able to see the roof of his house from here. It wasn't far.

He hadn't been back since his move to the palace; Marcus had always made the trip to see him, as was the mage's preference. And while there hadn't been any violence in Quill since he took over, he picked his way carefully down the driveway toward the palace gate, looking left and right. Everything seemed perfectly normal.

He opened the gate, nodded to the guards that stood there.

"Shall we accompany you, sir?" one said.

"No thank you, Frederick." He didn't want to be *that* kind of high priest. "I'm just going down to the house. If Marcus Today comes to call, ask him to wait inside. I won't be long."

"We shall do just that, sir."

"Thank you." The high priest continued down the slight hill for several minutes, trying not to notice the heavy stench of garbage in the air. He wished for a light breeze, and perhaps there was one, but the walls stopped it from permeating their land. He would have to fix that one of these days. Tear the walls down. Ah, but that was a job for another day, once the Wanteds had quite gotten used to manual labor.

When he reached his home, he went up the steps and pulled a small key from his pocket, unlocked the front door, and then went in.

It was dark and stuffy inside, the house having been shut

up for months. It felt smaller than he remembered. He turned down the hallway to his office. All was as it had been when he left it—his desk empty, the chair just so. He reached for the closet doorknob and pulled it open to get to the tube that would take him to Marcus's office.

Without a sound Aaron Stowe reached out, grabbed Haluki by the neck, and put him in a choke hold. Crawledge Prize captured the surprised high priest's wrists, wrenching them behind his back and tying a long, thin rope around them, and then he did the same around his ankles. Bethesda Dia Gloria shoved a towel in Haluki's mouth, but it wasn't necessary. He had already passed out from Aaron's grip.

The three hoisted his body into the closet, then nailed the doors shut.

"Well done, everyone," Aaron said in a low voice, breathing hard. "We are working together quite well now, aren't we?"

Then, from the back door, a sound. Aaron grabbed a pistol and stealthily slipped down the hallway to the kitchen. When he saw who it was, he put his gun down. Liam and Eva entered together, talking softly. Eva had a stricken look on her face when she turned to Aaron. "You killed Marcus?"

Aaron smiled now. "Indeed," he said. "Liam's just been out to bury him." He watched her face. "Disappointed?"

Eva just stared at him. "Yes," she said. "I was so looking forward to doing it." But she didn't sound very convincing.

Liam interrupted. "What about the high priest? I saw him enter. We heard the pounding and waited before we came in."

"You were wise to wait. Haluki is in our possession. He's a bit tied up," Aaron said. No one laughed.

Just then Dred Crandall burst through the back door, breathing hard. "There's a major fight going on in the street with the Unwanteds," he said, gasping. "Down by their gate. All of Artimé has disappeared and there are bodies everywhere! Several of our Restorers are down and so are many of theirs."

Aaron grew alarmed. "What? What were you doing down there tonight?"

"We attacked at your command, sir!"

Aaron stared at him. And then, slowly, he turned and looked at the frozen Eva Fathom. She shook her head as if she didn't understand a word Dred was saying.

In the pantry, Claire Morning's eyes opened wider at every revelation. Artimé gone? Bodies everywhere? Gunnar captured, her father buried . . . She stared at the dark shelf above her, not seeing it, and worked at the ropes around her wrists until her arms burned and her fingers bled.

The Weight of the World

Sean picked up the sleeve of his jacket, which was still wrapped around Meghan, and wiped his eyes with it. He looked at Alex. "It's up to you, man. You've got to fix this."

Alex's throat ached. He couldn't fathom it. "I can't," he whispered. "I don't know how. He never taught me all of that."

Sean turned and faced Alex. "He's told you a lot more than anyone else here," he said. "You're the only one who can do it."

Alex shook his head. "No. You don't get it. It was just supposed to be for a few days. I can't even wrap my mind around this." He looked at Meghan. "We need to worry about her. And Sam and Lani . . . Simber . . ." *Mr. Today is dead. Mr. Today is dead. Dead.* "And find . . . everybody else."

"Oh! Blast it." Sean's face turned to panic. "Speaking of everybody else, I have to go. They're still out there fighting. I have to get back and help." It was as though he'd just realized the entire world hadn't stopped when he found Alex and saw his sister. He struggled to his feet, still carrying her. "Get up," he said to Alex, an anxious tone in his voice. "This isn't over. But you—you need to stay here. And stay hidden. If you die, we have no chance at all. Here, take Meghan."

Alex scrambled up on weak legs and Sean placed his sister into Alex's arms.

"Go hide in the shack. Bolt the door. Try to find something to eat and get some rest—you look . . . wow. You look terrible."

Alex watched, slack-jawed and completely overwhelmed, as Sean turned and ran, jumping over the creatures that littered the lawn. Carrying Meghan, he picked his way carefully to the gray shack, struggling in the dark and unsure of his footing, exhausted from his ordeal.

When he reached the shack, his arms were trembling. He pushed the door open and stumbled in, straining to see in the shadows. He'd never been in here before. Not as a shack—only in its mansion form. He peered around the darkness and saw some furniture-like blobs. He staggered over and laid Meghan on a couch, then caught the back of it with his hand to steady himself and stop the black spots that swam before his eyes, like one of the paintings in Mr. Today's office. *Mr. Today is dead*, he thought once again. *He's dead. The man who saved us all . . . is dead.* But it just wasn't registering. He sucked in a deep breath and let it out. Then another, slower, until the spots went away. He thought about what Sean said, about eating something, and realized that might really be part of his problem. He hadn't eaten a thing since lunch.

And then he heard the creak of a door opening.

He whirled around and searched the dark room without success. "Who's there!" he said. "I have a weapon and I will kill you."

He sidestepped into the familiarly shaped kitchen—familiar to Quill homes, not to the mansion—wondering how on earth there were no lights here, and then he remembered how things used to be. He reached into the kitchen drawer and pulled out the required candles and flint. He lit one, only a little bit rusty at using the flint after not having had to light a candle in well over a year. It flared up, and the chicken-grease-soaked string stayed lit. Alex held it in front of him. "Who's there?" he said again. He walked toward the bedroom and pushed the door open.

Inside, the light reflected on two sets of orange eyes.

Alex gasped. Their beds had disappeared along with all of the other lovely things from the mansion, though it was clear Mr. Today had had some kitchen goods and furniture in this shack for the purpose of the governors' visits. Now there was merely a small single bed that looked quite precarious. The two huddled instead on the floor, looking terribly harmless. Was it really just earlier today that the girl had spit in his face?

"Sheesh," he said, when he could breathe properly again. "You scared me. I'd forgotten about you guys." He took a few steps closer and got down on his haunches. "What a time to wake up, little boy. Don't be scared," he said. "I won't hurt you. I was, um, just lying about the weapon." He didn't know if they understood him. "But don't tell anyone," he added. "Get it? Heh." It was a terrible joke, he knew, and totally inappropriate. But he wasn't exactly thinking properly at the moment.

The eyes moved, and as he leaned forward he could see the outlines of their bodies. Their neck bands glinted in the candlelight. The two drew back against the wall, so Alex stood again and backed up a few steps.

"Okay, guys, look. This is crazy. You don't trust me. I don't want to get spit on again. But I want you to know that I don't plan to hurt you, not ever, and you can leave anytime you want. Your raft is . . . probably outside somewhere." He scratched his head. "How about this: I'll stay over here in the living room with Meghan," he said, "and you two just do whatever you want. You're really the least of my worries right now." Alex fought off a violent yawn. "Though it would be really nice if you'd tell me what's up with the thornaments." He laughed a little at coining the phrase and realized he was growing delirious with exhaustion. "Just . . . don't kill me, all right? I'm sort of valuable right now, it seems."

He looked at the door, remembering Sean's suggestion to lock it. Sighing deeply, he pulled a rickety chair to the door and wedged it under the knob, securing them in for the night. Then he rummaged through the kitchen cabinets for water and brought some over to Meghan, trying to rouse her, but unable to do so. He dripped a bit into her mouth to moisten it, drank some himself, and left the rest on the counter for the Silents. Then he collapsed in a softish chair nearby, too tired to scrounge around for something to eat, and fell asleep.

When he awoke, it was a bright new day. But everything came flooding back too fast. Meghan was still unconscious, Sam and Lani were still missing, Simber was still at the bottom of the ocean, and Mr. Today was still dead.

Alex sat up, disheveled. He looked at his best friend, who hadn't moved, and felt completely lost without his other friends. He wandered all around the little gray shack, looking at the meager, colorless furnishings and focusing his gaze out the windows at the bodies strewn about. His eyes landed on the footpath, where Jim the winged tortoise had fallen, probably just like Simber—without warning.

Alex leaned against a window, buried his face in his hands, and realized two things:

There was no cure for this pain.

And his life would never be the same again.

In the Middle of the Night

In the middle of the night Sean Ranger had found Eva Fathom lurking on the outskirts of the fighting. She seemed relieved to see him, though he was never quite sure if she was faking it. She pulled him aside.

They walked together a few steps, and then Eva whispered, "Aaron killed Marcus and he's holding Haluki hostage—they're in Haluki's governor's house." Her voice was urgent. "He's planning his takeover of the palace. He has weapons and guards."

"What about Ms. Morning?"

"I haven't seen her."

Sean let out a held breath. "Where could she be?"

Eva shook her head. "No idea. Who is down among the Artiméans?"

"Alex's friends Samheed and Lani—Haluki's daughter—are missing, unrelated to this conflict. Several of our older Unwanteds have been slain . . . and Mrs. Haluki is seriously injured. I'm afraid she won't make it—not without magic. And then there's my sister . . ." Sean squeezed his eyes shut and massaged his lids with his fingers. It felt like his eyes were filled with sand. There was so much wrong, it was almost beyond measure.

Eva squeezed Sean's arm. "I'm sorry for you," she said. "Everything has gone horribly wrong. I never expected . . . this. We just need to press on." She hesitated, and asked, "What about Alex?"

"He's okay, as far as I know," Sean said. "Can you get word to Haluki about his wife and Lani somehow?"

Eva pressed her lips together, thinking hard. "I'm not sure Aaron trusts me enough at the moment to let me in. But I'll try." She turned to go, and then looked back. "I heard there's nothing left of Artimé . . . ," she said, trailing off with the hint of a question in her voice.

"There's the gray shack. Not much else, though."

"My daughter, Carina . . . ?"

"Still fighting."

Eva turned again and nodded, nothing else to say, and began walking. Exhausted from running back and forth, she limped through the shadows back to Haluki's house once more, hoping rest was somehow in her near future.

As the clash in Quill between Aaron's Restorers and Artimé's spell-less Unwanteds lost steam overnight, the injured finally limped home, dragging or carrying their fallen with them, while the strong fought on.

Most of the Necessaries who had made Artimé home over the recent months witnessed what had become of Artimé, and now watched the Unwanteds fall. Sadly, it wasn't hard for them to turn their loyalties again. They avoided the fighting and went back to their homes in Quill, frightened of being punished, but having nowhere else to go. All of them were more than willing to do whatever it took to allow them to stay in Quill.

Aaron had lost seven Restorers so far in the skirmish.

Artimé lost more than thirty. Without magic, Artimé was woefully unprepared in the way of weapons. The night wore on with no relief, both sides seemingly fighting without any real leader present. Finally, when Gondoleery had lost two of her strongest fighters and several of her weapons, and Mr. Appleblossom could stand it all no more, they came together and called for a truce. Most of the Restorers wondered bitterly where Aaron Stowe had been all this time. And most of Artimé had the sinking suspicion that they had lost a lot more than just magic and some fighters.

Eva made her way to Haluki's house once again. At the door she reported to Aaron that Mrs. Haluki was barely clinging to life and that Lani was missing. She hoped that the information would gain her some more credibility with Aaron—she needed to be on his good side again. And it worked, at least for now. He let her in.

When the palace guards knocked on Haluki's front door a few hours before dawn, concerned and looking for their high priest, Gunnar answered it.

"I'm fine—thank you for checking in with me," he told

them as Aaron, hidden, trained the pistol at his head. "I have a family emergency and some things to take care of here. But I've appointed an associate high priest—you know him. Aaron Stowe, former assistant secretary to the High Priest Justine."

The guards glanced at each other uneasily.

But Gunnar continued with an air of authority. "He'll be moving into the palace and will be running things for me from there. Please show him your utmost loyalty. And prepare an announcement to be delivered to all of Quill at daybreak. The entire community must meet at the amphitheater at noon."

The guards looked puzzled, but it was not their place to question the high priest.

"Hurry along now," Haluki said. "That's a lot to do before morning."

"Whatever pleases the high priest," they murmured. Frederick, the gate guard, gave one last glance over his shoulder as they walked away. Gunnar, sweat pouring down his neck, merely waved them onward. And then he closed the door and turned to his captor.

"What about my son, Henry?" he asked Aaron. His eyes

flitted to Eva Fathom, who had emerged from her hiding place in the hallway, and he raised an eyebrow in surprise. She shook her head the slightest bit.

Aaron kept the pistol pointed at the high priest, but turned to look at Eva. "Have you seen the Haluki boy?"

"No," she said. She'd passed many of the injured as she traveled back and forth, and the boy had definitely not been among them. But she wasn't about to say anything about that now. She had another agenda.

"I thought I saw Claire Morning out there fighting," she said carefully.

Aaron Stowe laughed. "I doubt that."

A noise came from the kitchen, like somebody dropping a box or bumping against a door. Liam shot a look of alarm at Aaron, which Eva noticed. *Aha*, she thought. Aloud she said, "I'm sure you're right. It was dark, and we both know my eyes aren't as good as they used to be. Is she dead, then?" She wondered if Aaron would lie to her.

Aaron hesitated. "Enough," he said, changing the subject. "Haluki, if you keep playing your part this well, you will live. Perhaps even long enough to keep your son from being an orphan, now that your wife isn't long for this world." His voice was so cold, he cringed at his own words.

Haluki stared at Aaron, giving him no indication of how Aaron's declaration shocked or hurt him. "I will follow your wishes for the sake of my family," he said with utmost dignity. And then, unable to contain himself, he added, "Aaron, you truly have some redeeming qualities, but they are growing more invisible at each passing day."

Aaron glared at him, his face growing hot. "Tie him back up," he said to Liam.

Haluki ventured further. "There is a natural path to success, Aaron. But you're too angry and bitter to follow it." He held his arms obediently behind his back for Liam. "You just flail around stubbornly in the brush alongside it, angry with the world for not making the path exactly where you wish to walk."

Aaron, unsure what the high priest was talking about, felt his mouth twitch and his breath quicken. "Gag him!" he said to Liam. He put the gun down on the table and stormed out the back door, not caring now who saw or heard him.

He took a deep breath of the rank night air and coughed,

and then he determined that getting the Necessaries back to cleaning would be his first act now that he was in charge of Quill. That's right—*he was in charge of Quill!* Not Haluki! And Associate High Priest Aaron Stowe didn't need some stupid former high priest telling him how to act, as if he were a child.

A New Day

Alex heard a soft tapping noise. When he looked up at the window next to the door, he saw a face staring back at him. He turned quickly, knocking over a small side table and sending it clattering to the floor, and hurried to the door, shoving the chair out of the way and opening it wide.

"Henry," he said. He was glad to see the boy. But then his heart fell, knowing he'd have to tell Henry that his sister, Lani, was missing.

Henry came inside, a strange look on his face. "My mother is dead," he said.

Alex gripped the door handle. "What?"

"She died," he said. "I can't really . . . you know. Can't believe it. She was fighting for Artimé. She's a hero." He shook his head. "That's what my dad would say. That's what the nurses said too."

"I'm so sorry," Alex murmured.

Henry looked around, a dazed expression on his face. "I'm really seriously so thirsty, Alex. There's no water anywhere. It's so hot here now. . . ."

Alex, taken aback by Henry's strange reaction, worried that the boy was in shock, or dehydrated, or a perhaps both. Quickly he closed the door and urged Henry toward the kitchen. The jug on the counter was empty. He scrounged around in the pantry and realized there were several more jugs of water in there. He puzzled over them at first, wondering why Mr. Today would have so many here in this shack, but then he guessed that Mr. Today must have gotten a large supply of water every time the governors came, so that no one had to cart it all the way out to the Death Farm each week. Mr. Today had no use for it after he transformed the world again once the governors left, so clearly he stored it. It was a relief to see it.

Alex opened a jug and poured Henry a glass. He watched Henry slam it down and he filled the glass again, not really knowing how to hold all the grim news. "I'm . . . I'm really sorry about your mother," he said finally, and his chest ached as he wished he didn't have to tell Henry about Lani. Alex felt like he needed a second body to hold all of the extra sorrow. "Are you sad?"

"Yeah. But everything is so sad, you know? Mostly it just feels weird." Henry gulped his second glass of water down, a little slower this time, and caught his breath before continuing. "Before she died she told me that she wanted to fight for Artimé even though it's all gone, because she knew that you would be able to fix things."

"Oh," Alex said. "Oh . . . wow." He didn't know what else to say. He ripped his fingers through his tangled hair. "Buddy, I don't know . . ."

Henry looked at Alex. "Where's Lani? I thought she'd be with you and Meghan. Hey, Meghan," he said, looking over at her. He waved.

Alex turned sharply. His eyes widened. "Meg," he breathed. He rushed over to her. "You're awake." He grabbed her hand

LISA McMANN

and held it, held her gaze. Her eyes flooded. "Don't be sad," he said. "Don't worry. We'll fix you. I promise."

She nodded her head, touched the spikes around her neck, and mouthed, "I can't speak."

"I know. Here, can you drink some water? Henry, grab that glass of water and bring it over." Gently he hoisted Meghan up and took the glass that Henry brought. He put it to her lips and she swallowed, wincing, but she drank it all.

"Phew," he said. "Okay, good. That's one good thing. No, two. We're on a roll," Alex said, looking at Henry. "You guys are both alive. Finally some good news."

Meghan gave Alex a quizzical look.

Alex hesitated, but he knew Meghan was wondering where on earth they were. So he gave both Henry and Meghan the full story as he knew it, leaving out nothing. He didn't notice that the two Silents, as he'd begun calling them, had come out of the bedroom to listen as well.

When Alex finished, Henry was as quiet as the others. He looked up at Alex with solemn eyes—the same blue as Lani's. "So you have kind of a lot of things to fix," Henry said.

The overwhelming feeling took hold of Alex again. He

stood up quickly, startling the Silents, and walked over to the window that faced the gate, letting his forehead rest against the glass. His breath steamed it up, and after staring through the fog it made, he wiped it all away with his sleeve. There was no way Alex could do all the things people were expecting him to do.

Fix Artimé? How? Mr. Today hadn't told him this could happen. He probably didn't even know it was possible, or surely he would have prepared him. All of those books in the Museum of Large—and an extra set of copies, even, for the library. . . . Mr. Today had been sure to make it possible to solve any problem, even though his organizing system left something to be desired. But could Alex get to the books? Of course not! They were in the mansion. And the mansion was gone.

He thought back to his times with Mr. Today. He remembered asking him how to bring creatures to life, and Mr. Today telling him no, that only his successor would get to know that.

"Well, here I am," Alex muttered. "Thanks for stupid nothing." He glanced over his shoulder to see if anyone had heard him, but Henry was talking quietly to Meghan and examining her necklace of thorns.

Alex surprised himself at how angry he felt toward Mr. Today. How could he leave him like this? How could he have done this to his world, and his people? The only conclusion Alex could come to was that Mr. Today couldn't possibly have known that the world would end upon his death. Or maybe he was just so certain he wouldn't die.

And maybe he'd told Ms. Morning.

A fat lot of good that did him right now. Where in the world was she when everything was falling apart around him?

He stood at the window for several minutes more. Soon the previously embattled warriors trickled into Artimé—or whatever this place was called when there was nothing artful about it anymore. Do they go back to calling it the Death Farm? It felt that way now, anyway. Death surrounded them.

Alex watched anxiously as people returned. He didn't know where they planned to go, exactly. They could fit some people in this shack but certainly not more than thirty without everyone stepping on everyone else. He was just glad to see so many alive. He saw Carina Fathom—the one he'd made the extra-strength heart attack spells for. Too bad she hadn't been able to use them.

A few minutes later Sean Ranger came jogging through the gate. He went straight to the shack when he saw Alex in the window. Alex opened the door. "Shh," he said. "Meghan woke up earlier—she's just sleeping now."

Sean's relief was visible. But he had other things on his mind too. He looked around the shack, and then he looked at Alex. "What in the world have you been doing all this time? Napping? Having tea?" His face was scratched and smudged with dirt and his arm was bleeding. "I thought you'd at least have water ready for your people."

Alex blinked. "My people? What?"

Sean stared at him like he was an idiot. "Alex, everybody knows Mr. Today was training you to take over for his vacation. Come on. You need to step up and lead. Just because he's dead doesn't mean you get a mourning holiday."

The words dug in and pinched. Alex swallowed hard. "Um . . ."

Sean's green eyes flared. "Look, Alex. These people outside have been fighting all night without sleep. If you don't have anything to offer them, I guarantee they will go back into Quill and find people who do." He shook his head at Alex. "Think, man! Come *on*! Do you really want them leaving here and going back to Quill? All the Necessaries have gone already! They can't wait to get back to work for your brother. They're practically salivating to go clean up piles of garbage and ask for seconds, just so they can get out of this burned-out, wasted mess of a place."

Alex turned away. The words stung. But he knew Sean was right. Where was his head? All these people coming through the gate had lost family and friends too. And now it was up to him to rally them . . . or Aaron would win, and all would be doomed. "I'm sorry," he whispered. "You're right, Sean."

Sean's face softened. "Okay. We're all dying of thirst. That would be a good thing to start with. Is there any water in here at all?"

"Yeah, some." Alex looked around at his meager surroundings and took a deep breath. "Give me a few minutes to come up with a plan."

Sean nodded. He punched Alex in the arm. "That's the way. I can hold them off that long." He turned and went back

LISA McMANN

outside, calling people to line up and organize into rows. Alex watched him almost naturally, fluidly, taking over for Claire and Florence.

And now Alex had to take over for Mr. Today.

He turned when he heard a noise. In the kitchen, the female Silent was struggling to pull water jugs out of the pantry cupboard. She was still a bit weak, but she was doing well, all things considered.

Alex caught her glance and reached to take the jug. "Thank you," he said softly, not wanting to scare her. Her strange golden-orange eyes reminded him of the way the sun set over the silent Warbler Island and shimmered on the water. Then he cocked his head to the side and realized what she was doing. "Can you . . . understand me? Us?"

She hesitated, and then looked away and pulled out another jug of water. When she set it on the counter in front of Alex, she bit her lip and nodded.

Alex stared.

Sean pounded on the window and held up four fingers. Alex nodded to Sean and then flashed a quick grin at the girl. She could understand them! That offered him a small ray of hope. She hid her face and grabbed another jug.

Energized, Alex called to Henry. "Hey, little buddy, I need your help."

Henry patted Meghan on the shoulder comfortingly, and a moment later he was by Alex's side. Alex handed him two jugs of water, grabbed four jugs for himself, and pulled the door open with his foot. He held the water up in the air. A murmur of hope rippled through the haggard ranks of Unwanteds—at least they had water. For now.

May Quill Prevail

Once the palace guards had left, Aaron and his team took turns sleeping and watching over the prisoners. By midmorning, Aaron had moved his meager book bag full of things into the palace and cleaned himself up, putting on his best clothes and topping them reverently, Justine-style, with a black cloak he found in a closet of the palace. He found paper and a pencil on the high priest's desk, next to a strange little gargoyle statue, and went back to Haluki's house to prepare his speech, making High Priest Haluki sit at his own desk to write everything as Aaron demanded him to.

LISA McMANN

At eleven thirty, the high priest's vehicle stood outside waiting for Aaron.

The new associate high priest, looking at his reflection in the window, smoothed his hair down. Then he gathered his team together. "Crawledge and Eva will stand with me as I deliver the speech. They are both well-known and trusted faces in the community, and those who loved Justine will feel confident in their presence alongside me." He turned. "Liam and Bethesda, you stay here and keep watch over the prisoners." Then he regarded the entire small group. "I've spoken with Gondoleery, and we believe it's best to keep her and the rest of the Restorers out of sight for now. But they will act as eyes and ears, and report back to me the reaction to these interesting events."

"What about the governors?" Liam asked. "Are they in support of this?"

"Haluki dismissed them weeks ago. No wonder it's been dead as the Ancients Sector around here—they're all sulking in their houses. Which means their support or opposition simply doesn't matter," Aaron said. "There's no law against the high priest appointing a new role. And associate high priest trumps governor." He tilted his head and shrugged. He'd once aspired to be senior governor. Now he'd surpassed that goal. "So there you go. I've got it all—on paper, even."

Their eyes perked up at this. Only a few select people in Quill were allowed to write things down. Teachers, mostly, and the governors and high priest, of course. "That's pretty clever," Liam said.

Aaron didn't reply. He thought the comment stood alone just fine. He glanced at Eva Fathom to see if she was going to give him any trouble.

She wasn't, and instead smiled at him. "Shall we go, then? If we leave now, we'll be just a few moments late. That's what the High Priest Justine always preferred."

Aaron nodded. His stomach stirred as the others wished him well, and before he knew it, they were on their way to the amphitheater.

Aaron Stowe, the new self-appointed associate high priest of Quill, looked at the crowd standing in the hot sunshine. They were quiet as always. His parents stood in the same spot where he and Alex had stood with them at their Purge. A year and a half had passed since then. It seemed like forever. Mr. and

Mrs. Stowe stood alone now. Aaron squinted. His mother was obviously very pregnant. He hadn't known. Not that he cared about such trivial things—it would be seven or eight years before the baby would be of any use. It could easily die by then. He frowned and shook the thought away.

Aaron turned his musings back to the past several months, from his ousting at university to his building up of the Restorers to his killing of the mage of Artimé. It was an incredible journey—if only Justine could see him now. His hard work and vision had paid off, not to mention his cunning. No one here needed to know how he'd done it. Just *that* he'd done it. He focused on the complacent faces before him, cleared his throat, and spoke.

"Greetings, people of Quill. I am Aaron Stowe, newly appointed associate high priest." His words carried beautifully in the amphitheater, and he sounded noble and ominous—two very important traits of a leader.

He continued. "My friend Gunnar Haluki sends his regards and regrets that he cannot be here at this time. Unfortunately, his wife was murdered by a gang of ruthless Artiméans in a street squabble last night. Even though she'd been living peacefully among them, they turned on her. One never knows whom one can trust. Does one?"

He felt like he'd said the word "one" too many times now, and he faltered for a moment, but then he pulled the paper from his pocket. When the crowd murmured at the sight of it, his confidence returned.

"Here is a letter from High Priest Haluki's own hand," he said, holding it up. He called forth a scholar and showed it to him, who then verified it before the crowd.

Aaron cleared his throat. "The letter reads: 'Dearest people of Quill, I am pleased to announce the creation of the associate high priest position, allowing a second ruler equal power over Quill. I am proud to fill this appointment with a capable young man—someone whom the High Priest Justine held in high esteem, and someone I hold great respect for as well. I have worked with him extensively and have the utmost confidence in his ability to lead Quill while I am unable to carry out my duties during this unfortunate time.

"'To avoid punishment, you will give Associate High Priest Aaron your dedication from this moment forward until further notice. I am certain that with your unquestioning support he will lead you to the pinnacle of the world in strength and intelligence.

"Very sincerely yours,

"High Priest Gunnar Haluki.'"

"Quill prevails when the strong survive," said the crowd in monotone unison, almost as if they approved of Mrs. Haluki's death. There was no backlash, no surprised faces, no shock or horror.

Aaron folded the paper and placed it into his pocket, satisfaction warming him from the inside to match the outside heat of the day. It had gone as smoothly as he could have possibly imagined.

"Now," he said, "my first declaration as associate high priest is regarding all Necessaries who have realized their heinous mistakes and have returned home from the disaster called Artimé." He paused to see how many people shifted eyes and shuffled feet. It was a large number. "You will have a chance to redeem yourselves. Report to me at the palace gate at daybreak tomorrow, ready to work, and I will grant you the right to live here once again." He could almost feel the relief flooding over the crowd, and he knew he had won many points from both Wanteds and Necessaries alike.

"And," he continued, "for every Unwanted of Artimé whom any of you recruits to Quill's quest to be world pinnacle, I offer you a bonus food item of your choice once per month. And you will continue to receive this benefit for as long as that Unwanted works his hardest for the greater good of Quill—and does not reproduce. That could be months of extra food on your table, or even years."

The crowd's silence was different this time. No longer did they wear the bland looks of sleeping fish on their faces. Now they stood straighter, their eyes opened wider. Never before had they been given an incentive for anything. Never had they been granted a choice in things to eat. A small murmur buzzed through the crowd of Quillens, especially from those who had lived in Artimé and had relaxed their stiff personalities a bit over time. Those Necessaries began to think of all the possible Unwanteds they could convince to come to Quill, now that Artimé was a mess. And though these Necessaries weren't nearly as hungry right now as the ones who'd stayed in Quill, they had been back in Quill several hours now—long enough to have heard the rumors and whispers about life under Haluki's rule.

To them it almost felt like this new leader was going to share some of the wealth . . . not just with the Wanteds, but with the Necessaries who were willing to work for it. And that was unheard of.

Aaron didn't fear their reaction. He allowed the murmur of the crowd to build and settle again on its own. He smiled a rare smile at them, and they seemed to move toward him just slightly, as if they wanted to hear more.

That was precisely how Aaron wanted to leave them.

Back in the Haluki home, with Haluki closeted and Bethesda nodding off to sleep, Liam Healy, hands shaking in light of what he was about to do, quietly opened the pantry door and knelt down. He removed Claire's gag and held a cup of water to her mouth. Weak, she didn't argue. She drank it down.

He replaced the gag, looser this time, closed the door, and locked it again just as Bethesda stirred and looked up. "Everything all right?" she asked, smacking her lips together in a disgusting sort of way.

"Same as always," Liam said as calmly as he could, his heart in his throat.

She yawned and laid her head on the table to sleep again.

Inside the closet, for the first time since she'd entered the house, Claire Morning felt the faintest glimmer of hope.

Two rooms away, Haluki mourned for his family and his dearest friend alone.

On the way to the palace after the speech, Eva Fathom turned to Aaron from her usual spot in the high priest's vehicle. "You were very well-received, as expected, Associate High Priest Aaron Stowe," she said evenly, as the old Secretary might have said to Justine.

"Quite," Aaron said. "And we'll be cutting the 'Associate' part. For simplicity's sake, of course." Secretly he was enormously pleased. "And as for you," he began, turning to her with an eyebrow raised. He regarded her for a long moment.

Eva froze. It brought back the memory of Justine telling her she'd be eliminated soon. She watched the barbed-wire shadows flying over her skin and felt a frightening sense of déjà vu. "Yes," she said.

"I promised you that your loyalty would be rewarded with getting your old job back."

LISA McMANN

"I remember," Eva said. She waited in deepest dread for him to say, "*But . . .*"

But he didn't. Instead he said evenly, "I'd like to take you on as my secretary if you are willing."

Eva felt a flood of relief build up inside of her, aching to be let out with a large sigh or a laugh or a whoop. Instead she answered affirmatively in the traditional way of Quill. "May Quill prevail with all I have in me."

Aaron Stowe, the Wanted—former assistant secretary to the High Priest Justine; former future senior governor; former outcast, conniver, and head of the Restorers; murderer of the highly acclaimed Mr. Marcus Today; and current not-really-associate high priest of Quill through despicable means—looked out his window at the tops of cornstalks and coconut trees and enormous berry bushes of the flourishing Favored Farm as the Quillitary vehicle sputtered and chugged along. And he smiled.

He had just one final visit to make today.

Alex's Message

He couldn't think of a time when he'd been more nervous, except maybe at his Purge. Now Alex stood before the tired faces of hundreds of despondent Unwanteds, crammed into a small plot of cement and weeds, all the way down to the shoreline and spilling out the gate into Quill. All of them, filled with respect for the land and the fallen leaders they once served, were loyal despite the dire circumstances. They waited, exhausted but patient, to hear a single word of hope that would help them get through the day and keep them from desperate measures—like looking for shelter in the place that once sentenced them to death.

LISA McMANN

As the water was passed around, each Artiméan took a few swallows, no more, without having to be told, everyone confident in their fellow Unwanted to be reasonable. Sean Ranger pulled Alex aside and gave him the latest news, confirming that Mrs. Haluki had indeed died as Henry reported, and that the rest of the injured had found secret respite in a sympathetic Necessary's home on the outskirts of one of the quadrants. "And then there's the high priest," Sean said. "Aaron's got him captured, but we're not supposed to know that. Most of Quill doesn't know that. Aaron has just declared that Haluki appointed him as some sort of associate high priest, with equal power."

Alex stared at Sean. "You're not serious."

"I am."

Alex stared thoughtfully at the gate, not really seeing it. "Wow."

"I know."

"Well," Alex said, clearing his head. "I guess he's really going after it. I'm pretty sure he'll go full speed ahead and do everything he can to keep us from existing, then." He was surprised at how calm he felt about it. Maybe it could be chalked up to knowing where Aaron was and what he was doing that gave Alex a bit of serenity. "How are you getting this information?"

Sean hesitated. "I'd rather not say at this moment."

Alex frowned. He got an uneasy feeling in the pit of his stomach again. Sean was up to something, always sneaking into Quill and not telling Meghan what he was doing, but Alex didn't have time to worry about him right now. He remembered what Mr. Today once said about being honest if you wish to prevail, so he looked Sean in the eye. "Sometimes I wonder if I can trust you."

Sean held his gaze. "I swear you can trust me, Alex. I swear it on Meghan's life."

Alex regarded him for a long moment, and Sean's gaze didn't waver. Alex held out his hand and Sean took it, shaking it firmly. No further word was needed. With that, Alex turned to the crowd, stood on a chair that Henry had brought from inside, and requested silence by holding up his hands. They shook the slightest bit.

Alex waited for the news to travel that he was about to speak. And without an amphitheater or the magic of Artimé

LISA McMANN

to help his voice carry, he knew he'd have to take it slowly and speak as loudly as possible so everyone could hear.

A wave of emotion rolled through him as he looked over the bruised and battered people. When it was quiet, he set his jaw and began.

His voice didn't crack. He didn't break down. He just spoke from the heart, like Mr. Today would have.

"Greetings, warriors," he said. "You're all so brave and loyal, just like our fearless leader, Marcus Today, taught us all to be. And, well, just like he was until . . . the end. Let's all take a minute to remember the moment we first met him."

The Artiméans bowed their heads, remembering the day they'd been saved by the eccentric magician with that electric shock of white hair, who had come out of the gray shack to greet them and had said those fateful words: "How does it feel to be eliminated?" Year after year he did it the same way, always delighted beyond measure to save the lives of the creative and artistic, and to not only save them, but to make them, mold them, into amazing people. He taught them to think and to live and to create. To fight for what they believed, and stand up for their rights, and not fear the unknown. To feel love and warmth and acceptance after being told so often, so much, that they were useless trash, not even good enough to line the roadway of Quill.

Alex embraced the numbness he felt inside him—he was thankful for it, for once, because it allowed him to do the job he had to do now.

"Friends," he said, breaking into the memories of hundreds of people. "Mr. Today is gone, and so is our world. We don't have any other choice except to ask for one another's help now." He paused, scanning the crowd. "We've lost members of our families at the hands of the people of Quill, and some of our residents are missing. We also can't forget our Silent visitors, who, by chance or by fate or whatever, have joined us under some pretty weird circumstances, and we need to continue to treat them as family, despite our, um, momentary lack of lavish decor."

A few in the crowd nodded, and Alex caught the eye of Mr. Appleblossom, who touched his fist to his heart and nodded encouragingly. That gave Alex a surge of confidence to go on. He repeated the act back to Mr. Appleblossom, finishing the nonverbal rhyming couplet.

And then he went on. "Friends, my brother, Aaron, has taken control of Quill and has announced his position as associate high priest, supposedly working in tandem with High Priest Haluki." Alex looked down, not wanting to see the skeptical looks from the crowd that he expected there to be. But then he looked up again, knowing he needed to stand strong. "But I don't believe he'd ever work side by side with anyone as good as High Priest Haluki. I admit it's hard to speak badly of my brother. But I have to—I can't think of any reason why I should protect him anymore. He chose his own way, and it's the opposite of everything I believe in. And now I'll just repeat what you already know: Aaron has all this evil junk in his heart, and I know he won't stop his attacks until he can figure out how to take control of us. It would be his best day ever to finish what Justine thought she'd started with the Purge. And Unwanteds," Alex said, his voice growing louder, "we can't let that happen. We've got to stick together so we can stay strong." He pointed at the shocking starkness of their land and said, "This is what Mr. Today saw when he first dreamed of Artimé. Now we have to begin from scratch, just like Mr. Today did—from this plot of land, this little gray shack—only we're not alone. There are hundreds of us! We have each other, don't we? Surely we can hold together."

Alex looked slowly at the silent crowd, from the edge of the water to the wall to the gate and beyond. "Surely we can honor our leader by building up a bigger, stronger Artimé—something just as grand and wonderful as he could ever imagine."

Alex had no idea how they'd do it. But he was determined to succeed or die trying. He knew he didn't have much time.

The crowd murmured. Alex felt the ownership of Mr. Today's vision and of their beloved Artimé emanating from the pores of the Unwanteds that surrounded him. What other choice did they have but to embrace this? For most of them, going back to Quill couldn't possibly be an option. Alex leaned forward on the chair, a most intense look on his face, fearing rejection, but forging ahead—it was now or never. "People of Artimé," he shouted at the top of his voice, wanting everyone to hear him. "Are you with me?"

When a rousing chorus of yeses greeted his ears, something surged inside of him, giving him goose bumps. He repeated it, pumping his fist. "People of Artimé! Are! You! With! Me!"

This time the shout rang out, loud and clear, hundreds of voices as one.

Alex grinned and waited for them to quiet down once again. And then he said earnestly, "I really want to hear it from each one of you. When I'm done, I'll stay standing here. And I'm going to ask you, if you would, to come up here so that we can look one another in the eye and agree to go along together on this. Despite how hard it's going to be, despite the fact that we don't have much, despite that we've lost our leader and our friends and we're scared to lose more. So, will you do this for me?"

Another thick wave of yeses greeted him in response.

"Okay." Alex blew out a breath of relief. "That's great. Thank you. When you come by, I'll assign you a duty so that we can begin to take care of our most basic needs right away—water, shelter, that kind of stuff. People of Artimé, do you accept that challenge?"

"Yes!" came the reply. Each time they grew louder and louder.

Alex paused now and waited for the crowd to settle. He had one last important item to discuss.

"Finally, friends," he said, "we need to talk about the gate.

I've decided that despite the threat of attack from Quill, we need to leave our gate open for now." He paused, letting the words sink in. "It was a really hard decision to make, but I have three reasons for making it."

People remained quiet, straining to hear every word. "One, because Ms. Morning is missing, maybe even captured, but, basically, we just don't know where she is. If she's able to escape, we'd want her to get in. Also because of our injured, who are camping out in the home of a very generous Necessary. She's hiding them and caring for them along with our nurses. If we close the gate, we risk locking everyone out until we—um . . . I mean until I—can figure out how to restore our world. And I'm not willing to write off anybody who wants or needs to get back in here.

"Two, because we need water, and frankly, there's no other place to get it but Quill at the moment." People looked at one another and nodded.

"And three, because someone, somewhere in Quill, has a key. And we don't want any one person in Quill to hold that kind of power over us." Alex looked at his people and said, "Are we in agreement?"

This time the agreement was quieter, but no less important. The truth was that the people of Artimé understood so much more than anyone about risk and safety, life and death, because of what they'd endured to this point. There was unity, mostly. Alex would soon find out if anyone stood against him. So far, everyone seemed to be willing to give Alex a chance.

"Excellent!" Alex said, trying to sound as upbeat and as competent as possible. "You can always come to me with your questions any time, and I promise you I will be going to work immediately to get Artimé back on its feet once again." He surveyed them from his height once again, and then he said simply, "Thanks, everyone. Thanks for your loyalty. Together we can remain strong—strong hearts and strong wills, right? And we'll get through it." He made a fist and touched it to his chest, as Mr. Appleblossom had done earlier, trying to express his deepest and sincerest loyalty to Artimé. Several repeated the motion in return.

Alex stepped off the chair and soon an organized line had formed. As the members of Artimé approached, looked Alex in the eye, and said, "I'm with you, Alex," Alex repeated the phrase back to them, "I'm with you, too." He then created teams of workers. The most industrial and architecturally creative he appointed to clean out the shack. They needed to make as much room on the floors as possible, and to expand the little house by removing all the doors from the cupboards and rooms and making a sort of lean-to out the back door from the wood and paneling.

Alex sent the stealthiest and most robust Artiméans to sneak into the Quillitary Sector to steal barrels of water, and to collect food from the Favored Farm.

And Alex sent the most able-bodied to move the lifeless creatures out of the way of foot traffic, standing them against the wall or around the exterior of the shack like yard ornaments, so that the living could make prime use of the little space they had.

As the day wore on, Alex also set up a guard schedule for the gate, and a six-hour sleeping rotation for the shack. Finally, he sent a team of Artiméans out to see if they could find the boat and physically bring it to their little plot of land and tie it to shore.

It was exactly what Alex needed. Putting his mind to work and his body, too—it felt like he was doing something

375 « Island of Silence

important. And indeed, he was. As he worked, his subconscious went to work too, trying to figure out how he was going to follow through on his promise to restore Artimé.

It was nearly evening when someone approached him from behind and tapped his arm. It was the Silent girl. She'd been helping the team that cleared out the shack as best as she could, and she held what looked like a dollhouse sitting on a board. She held it out to Alex.

He sat up and squinted, looking at it. Then he wiped his hands on his pants and took it from her, peering at every detail. It was a miniature replica of the mansion, in all its glory. "Wow, cool," he said, lifting up the roof to peer inside at the hallways, staircase, and adorable miniatures of Simber and Florence at the front entrance. His heart clutched when he thought of the cheetah. He swallowed hard and said, "Where did you find this?"

She pointed at the shack and beckoned him to come with her. Inside, she pointed to a cupboard under the kitchen counter.

"Huh. No kidding," Alex said softly. He could picture Mr.

Today standing at this counter years ago, dreaming about his future home, making plans, creating this replica, and then slowly re-creating it life-size with magic, bits at a time. It felt like Mr. Today was right here with them, in spirit at least. Something Mr. Today's hand had actually created was now in Alex's hand. There was a good deal of comfort in that.

He turned to the Silent girl and smiled, grateful she'd thought to bring it out to him. She must have known instinctively that it would be important, even though she knew so little about what was going on here—she barely knew Mr. Today at all, and she'd seen very little of the mansion except for the hospital wing where she stayed. "Thank you," he said. He crouched down and slid the mansion back into place in the cupboard.

She crouched down next to him, brought her fist to her chest, and smiled back.

The Way It Is with Twins—Threedux

There was something strangely fulfilling about the new High Priest Aaron's ride to Artimé, knowing what a disaster was there now, and knowing he'd caused it. Truly a lot had happened since the last time he'd seen his brother at this gate.

He'd managed to batten down his fleeting feelings of pity for his brother, though he didn't feel entirely like gloating to him about his new position. Something Haluki had said kept gnawing at him, but he wasn't sure why. Besides, there would be plenty of time for gloating later.

Still, he found himself being driven here at his own request by his new faithful guards. Also accompanying him was his newly appointed secretary, Eva Fathom. He still didn't entirely trust her, but he knew the ancient saying: Keep your enemies at your side to learn their every move. So this would be the perfect situation to put Eva in. Face-to-face with the people who trusted her in the midst of the mess she helped create.

As they drew close, Aaron pulled a pistol from his cloak and laid it on his lap so that whatever guards were protecting Artimé could see it. He wasn't looking for trouble. Not today. His Restorers needed a bit of a break.

"What do you want?" the Artiméan guard asked when the jalopy pulled up.

"I wish to speak with Alex Stowe. I presume someone here might know who that is." Aaron didn't mean it as a joke.

The other guards laughed bitterly. "Apparently you don't, though," one of them muttered. It made them all the more loyal to Alex when they caught whiff of Aaron's haughtiness. Who would want to follow a leader like that?

One of the guards found Alex carrying a lifeless beavop. "Alex, your brother is here. He says he wants to talk to you."

LISA McMANN

Alex narrowed his eyes and ignored the fear that sparked in his gut. "How many are with him?"

"Just his driver and another guard, and his secretary."

"All right," he said. He set the beavop down and walked to the gate, greeted his own guards, and said to them, "Can you please tell Aaron to approach alone? I'll speak with him in the road. And tell him to leave his weapons behind."

The guards stepped back to the gate, eyeing the Quillitary vehicle suspiciously, ready to attack and defend their new young leader if they had to.

Alex walked to the center of the road and clasped his hands in front of him, waiting. Aaron took his time getting out of the jalopy, smoothed the wrinkles in his cloak, and walked up to Alex. He carried a small bundle wrapped in a burlap peanut sack.

Alex narrowed his eyes. "What's that?"

Aaron flashed a patronizing smile. "Greetings to you as well, dear brother. It's been a long time." He held out his hand in a lazy fashion like the High Priest Justine might have done. But Alex didn't take it, bow over it, kiss it, or otherwise acknowledge it in any way.

In fact, Alex's deep brown eyes held none of the warmth they'd held a few moments earlier, inside the shack with the Silent girl. "I don't have time for chitchat, Aaron. As you can see, we're quite busy here."

Aaron glanced into Artimé, but his eyes didn't linger. He seemed bored. "That's why we're giving you a bit of a reprieve to get your things together. I wanted to invite you and your . . . people . . . ," he said with a sneer, "to live in Quill. We have several jobs available where they can earn their keep."

"Get out of my sight," Alex said. "No one here wishes to be a slave to you."

Aaron shrugged. "That's fine. I thought you'd appreciate the gesture. It's a lot easier to get water delivered to your home than it is to steal it by the barrelful," he said.

Alex glared at him and said nothing.

"But I've let your workers get away with it this time."

Alex didn't waver. "Is there anything else?"

"Just this." Aaron held out the package. "Though with the way you're treating me now, I'm hardly inclined to give it. Ah, but I'm here. And I certainly don't want it."

Alex held the glare a moment longer, and took the package.

LISA McMANN

"When Mr. Today died, he didn't say a word, by the way."

Alex worked his jaw. He wasn't prepared for this. He knew he was showing weakness, but he had to ask. "How did you kill him?" He'd been wondering, and no one seemed to know.

"Oh, I didn't kill him," Aaron said, as if he was delighted Alex asked. "He died of a heart attack. Five of them, to be exact—all at once. Pity."

Alex's own heart nearly stopped. He squeezed his tired, red-rimmed eyes shut for a moment and then opened them again. His voice was barely above a whisper. "You killed Mr. Today with my own spell?"

"Oh! That was one of yours?" Aaron feigned surprise.

Alex couldn't believe it. "How did you get the components?" he demanded. "No one has access to them."

"Oh, ho, ho, perhaps not. But my secretary did."

Alex shot a glance at the vehicle. He shielded his eyes and peered in through the window. Looking back at him was Eva Fathom.

His lips parted and he sucked in a little breath of recognition. And then everything came together. He'd given Carina Fathom twelve heart attack components. Eva Fathom, whom Mr.

Today trusted, was working for Aaron, not for Artimé. All this time . . . Alex felt a huge wave of disappointment flood over him. He was too trusting again. When would he stop thinking the best of people?

Eva caught Alex's stricken glance. Her eyes widened just slightly at his disappointment. She'd been expecting it. She didn't react further. A moment later she averted her eyes and faced the front of the vehicle.

Alex felt the blood rush out of his head. His own amazing spell, the one that had gotten raves, had killed Mr. Today. He took a second to compose his anger. Finally he looked at Aaron and said evenly, "Where's Ms. Morning?"

Aaron smiled again. "Wouldn't you like to know."

That vague sentence was more info than Alex had expected. Almost too much. "Haluki?"

"Tch," Aaron said. "Now you're getting desperate. Not attractive, Alex. Especially not from where you stand in this disaster area."

Alex gripped the package and shook his head as if he pitied his brother. "You've taken everything I love. What else could you possibly want from me?"

"Ahh," Aaron said with a grin. "I thought you'd never ask. But the answer is nothing." He pushed a lock of hair off his forehead. "Not today, anyway. Perhaps in a week or even ten days, when your water runs out and your people are getting shot for stealing, you'll be anxious to talk again. But for now? Not one more thing."

Alex folded his arms across his chest, the package still dangling from his fingers. "Then go."

"Aren't you going to open it?" Aaron pointed to the sack.

Alex, disgusted, didn't give him the satisfaction of a response. He turned on his heel and walked away.

Aaron stayed where he was, watching Alex walk back into the dreck of Artimé, the hollow smile never leaving his face. When his brother was out of sight, he got back into his vehicle and signaled the driver to go.

"That seemed to go well," Eva said.

"Silence!" Aaron said. He wanted to brood alone.

Coming to Terms

By midnight things had settled down in Artimé. The exhausted teams had worked hard, fed by inspiration and adrenaline, and now more than fifty of them were able to find floor space in the shack to lie down for their six-hour sleep shift. The un-shacked sat in small groups on the hard cement or in the sand along the water. Most dozed, a few talked, some mourned family, friends, and Artimé.

The tide was out and the moon full, and a couple of clever teams were out gathering oysters, clams, prawns, and anything else they could find to eat, while another tireless group worked at making a fire from remnants of the Silent kids' raft and the flint Alex had found inside the shack.

The team that had found the boat, unharmed and bumping up against the east wall of Quill, pulled it onto the beach. They'd been clever enough to bring back the net and fishing gear they'd found inside, and now that team stood as far out as they could, casting the net over and over, catching a few fish now and then.

Inside the shack Henry Haluki babbled on and on to the Silent boy about Quill and Artimé and the big battle, and then he pulled his magnifying glass from his pocket and made his eyeball enormous. The Silent boy smiled, seeming to enjoy all of it. Sean snored lightly on the floor next to Meghan, who slept as well.

It was as harmonious as it could be, under the circumstances.

Alex, carrying the unopened package from Aaron in his component vest's interior pocket, picked up one last stiff platyprot and brought it over to the wall, next to Ms. Octavia.

He got down on his haunches and turned to her, adjusting her glasses to where she liked them, just so. "I'm trying," he said wearily to her. "I wish you were here." He pinched the bridge of his nose, trying to stop the sorrow and hunger headache from getting any worse. Then he went over to the creatures that couldn't be moved because of their weight, namely Jim and Florence, both near the shack.

He kneeled next to Jim and petted his mosaic shell, noticing its intricacies for the first time. *What a lot of work went into that*, he thought. Mr. Today always pointed out others' abilities, but he rarely spoke about his own amazing talent as a sculptor. Alex traced his finger along the pattern. "So much detail," he whispered into the night. "What I wouldn't give to hear your exceedingly slow speech right about now, Jim."

The winged tortoise didn't answer.

Alex moved to Florence. She was twice his height and frozen in full, glorious stride. Perhaps she had been running when it happened, making Artimé shake with her steps. She was sleek and ebony and beautiful, just as she always looked. Alex almost expected her to turn when he reached up and touched

LISA McMANN

her arm. "I'm so sorry," he said to her. "If there's anything you can do to fix things here . . . well, just let me know." But he didn't expect an answer.

He turned, considering taking a walk down by the water to process his thoughts, but there were Unwanteds everywhere. There was no place as far as the eye could see to sit and think and be alone.

Then, from somewhere above his head, he heard a scraping sound.

He looked up above Florence to the roof. There sat the Silent girl. She froze when Alex saw her, as if she were caught doing something wrong.

"Hey," Alex whispered. "How did you get up there?"

She pointed to Florence.

Alex's eyes widened. The thought of climbing up Florence's body freaked him out a little. It seemed so . . . so wrong. But she was just a statue now. And her bent knees and elbows did offer a lot of hand- and footholds. He considered his path, and then started climbing quickly, in case she woke up. Which he'd be thankful for, but she'd kill him anyway, probably. "I hope you have no memory of this," he muttered. It was an easy climb, and seconds later he hoisted himself to the roof and sat next to the girl.

"Clever," he said. "I like this. I can breathe again."

She nodded and looked down, suddenly self-conscious.

Alex looked out over the sea and thought of Lani and Samheed again, wondering where they could be, and if they were alive. He had to believe they were okay—he couldn't handle anything more than that right now. His throat tightened and he moved his eyes to the place where Simber had gone down, well beyond the edge of low tide. There was no way to get to him, Alex knew. And there never would be.

Alex couldn't get the image out of his head—Simber's downward crash into the water. The scene had been in his nightmare last night, and it lurked in the back of his brain whenever he had a few extra minutes to think. "We'll go togetherrr, as always," Simber had said as they'd left the silent island. "I won't leave you."

Alex covered his face with his hands, overcome. He didn't know what would happen now. All he knew was that Simber was made of sand. Sand dissolved in water. Even if Alex could bring back Artimé, he didn't think he'd ever see Simber again.

LISA McMANN

Mr. Today had once said the giant statue was "virtually" indestructible. Simber had taken many hits with bullets and other weapons, and they bounced right off of him, or at worst left a tiny mark. But "virtually"—that meant there could be a way to destroy him. And if so . . . well, he'd never seen Simber venture near the water. Alex remembered how the great statue would hover forever above the water, but was careful never to let his wings touch. And maybe now Alex knew why.

He couldn't bear to think of it. Simber, gone forever, his body dissolved like a sugar cube in tea, sandy bits of him sloshing around at the bottom of the ocean.

And here Alex sat with nothing. Aaron was ready to pounce on them when they got desperate enough, and all of Artimé looked to Alex to fix everything, to restore the world. Alex had not one single clue how to do it. All of Mr. Today's books were gone. When Alex failed to fix things, what would happen to them all? Would they turn to Aaron to be slaves in exchange for food and a place to sleep?

Alex had no doubt some of them would.

"Please help me," he choked out in a whisper. "Anybody."

When his shoulders began shaking, the Silent girl put her

hand on Alex's back to comfort him. After a while Alex sniffed and looked up, eyelashes wet.

He pulled the package from his pocket and looked at it, wondering what Aaron could have possibly found to torture Alex with. He took a deep, shuddering breath and unrolled it, reached inside, and pulled out something lightweight and soft and brightly colored.

It was Mr. Today's robe.

In a Very Small House

J ust past midnight at a table in a very small house in Quill sat Gondoleery Rattrapp, thinking for the umpteenth time about how she had once been magical, and then wasn't for the longest time, and then was again for a few short months. And now, because the man who created the magic had died, she had lost the ability once more. And here she sat, puzzling over it, because something clearly wasn't right.

She studied the components as she had done many times recently, and tried them out on a skinny stray dog she'd captured in a trap in her backyard.

"Die a thousand deaths!" she cried, flinging a metal clip at the dog, but the clip bounced off the dog's back. He came up to the woman and licked her hand.

She pushed him away and picked up a clay heart. "Heart attack!" she said, throwing it at the mutt. It struck his side and did nothing, though he whimpered a bit and recoiled at the sting.

The woman scrunched her eyelids tightly together.

She scrunched her fists, too, and dragged her arthritic knuckles along her eyebrows, stopping them at her temples and pressing in hard. This wasn't right. Not at all.

"When I was a girl," she said softly, trying hard to remember the creakiest of thoughts from a very, very long time ago. Trying to remember how things were back then. "When I was a girl."

She opened her eyes and looked at her hands, and at the useless components. She looked at the dog, who whined at her, and then she stood up. "Go on," she snapped. She opened the door and shoved the dog outside. "Run off now."

The dog stopped to lap water from the bucket that had been recently filled on the woman's front step.

"Get!" she said, kicking at the dog, and the dog got.

And then the woman looked at the water in the light of the moon.

She dipped her hand into the water and lifted it up, watching it drip from her fingers to the dusty step. "When I was a girl," she whispered, staring as the water made a stain in the dirt.

She looked up into the sky at the thousands of stars that twinkled above. She hadn't noticed them in years. All she knew was that there were no clouds—there were almost never clouds in Quill.

She looked at the water in the bucket again, and the element seemed to whisper to her. "When I was a girl," it said.

The old woman looked around, but there was no one anywhere to be seen at this late hour. She cupped her hand and dipped it into the water to take a drink of it. It was warm. Warm, like the rain had been on a hot summer day on Warbler Island, more than fifty years ago. She'd been on the jutting rocks, on a plateau halfway up to the peak, playing with her friends who were magical too, but there was no Marcus Today there. She was sure of that. She remembered the fun of it, standing on the slick stone as rain poured in sheets around her and her friends. How they'd shrieked and danced in it.

She took another scoop of water in her hand and stepped into the yard, the water carelessly dripping from her fingers. She was wasting it, by Quill's standards.

In the dark of the night and the light of the moon, she held her hand to the sky and watched the shimmering droplets cling and quiver on the back of her hand, then fall to the parched earth. And she remembered.

Finally. She remembered.

She brought her hand down, and then flung the water that remained into the sky with all her might. As the drops flew through the air, she envisioned the scene and the words she'd abandoned for more than fifty years.

She cried out to the water, "Make it rain!"

A moment passed, and the cloudless sky above the little house rumbled and sparked with light and life. The woman stood in the dirt yard in the center of the desert island of Quill, hands raised to the sky, eyes closed.

The sky opened up above her tiny house, like that day on the rocks when she was happy and young and with friends. A triumphant cackle built and grew in her throat, filling the air. For now, pouring down on her and her small plot of land and her bucket of water on the front step of her little house in Quill, was all the rain of half a hundred years.

In a Dark Cave

Weak and blind, Samheed sat in total deafening silence. He pounded his hands on the dirt floor of the cave, scratched his fingernails on his pants, kicked his feet against the wall. There was no sound at all. He felt like he didn't exist, except for the constant waves of pain around his neck.

Now and then he'd open his mouth to yell for Lani and Meghan, but no noise left him, no matter how hard he tried. He felt utterly helpless. He couldn't see, couldn't make a sound, and his friends were gone.

Every now and then he could feel a small breeze, as if

someone walked past him, but he could never catch that person in time. There was no way to tell when the breeze was coming, no way to tell how many minutes or hours or days were passing. After the second breeze Samheed crawled around and touched a tray of food quite by accident. Next to it was a cup of water. He ate and drank, and then stayed exactly there so that when the breeze came, he'd be able to reach out and grab it.

But the breeze brought the next food and water to a different spot.

By the fourth time, Samheed had determined that the breeze could see him, and would only go where he wasn't.

His entire existence was pointless.

All he could think of now was that Lani and Meghan had gotten away. And deep down, beneath the pain of abandonment, he hoped for it, he really did. Not just for their sakes, but for his—if they'd escaped, maybe they'd get Mr. Today to come and rescue him . . . and he could take this pain away. It was so hard to bear when there were no distractions anywhere.

"Please, please, please," he said from silent lips, over and over again. "Is anybody there? Can anybody help me?"

Time passed, and nothing changed.

When he drifted off into a hard sleep, he dreamed he was lying in the sun on the beach in Artimé, listening to the creatures singing softly on the lawn and the murmurs from conversations nearby while he dozed. He was free from the dark and silent cave, free from the painful thorny collar around his neck. In his dream a cool hand touched his cheek, and he smiled, realizing he wasn't alone. He reached for the hand, traced his fingers up the arm, and touched the face of the girl who was touching his. It was the most comfort he'd had since the piercing sleep arrow embedded in his back.

But then something bumped his foot, jarring him from the dream. Someone was shaking him awake, grasping and pulling his shirt, almost ripping it. He sat up, alarmed, plunged once again into the darkness and silence and pain of the cave. He pulled his hand back to throw a punch, but the person pushed him down to the floor on his back once more, pinning him. He struggled to get free.

Even when he felt her fingers touch his cheek, his lips, he fought her, though he was weak. She pushed mightily to keep him on his back, then sat down hard on his chest, knocking the wind from him, and pinned one of his arms to the floor with her foot. With both hands she grabbed his other arm and pulled it close to her body. She brought his hand up to her head and squeezed his fingers around her hair. She forced his hand to travel down the length of it, and held it there. Then she touched his lips and felt his chest heave a sigh of relief.

"Lani." His lips moved against her finger, and he was overcome.

She scrambled off of him. He rose up to his elbow and grabbed blindly for her hand, trying to let her know that he understood now. He held her fingers to his cheek and nodded, then put his hand on her face as well. She did the same. He could feel her relax next to him, both of them exhausted and aching. Breathing hard, not making a sound.

And then she started to shake. Samheed reached out and wrapped his arms gently around her shoulders, and she slid closer to him, gripping his shirt and burying her face in it. They held on to each other, trying to survive a minute at a time, until somebody . . . anybody . . . came to rescue them.

One Last Message

n the roof of the gray shack Alex gripped the colorful cloth like it was a lifeline. "This is his robe," he whispered to the girl.

She nodded, pushed her fingers through her hair, and lifted them, making her hair stand up.

"Yes," Alex said, laughing a little. "Yes, the man with the hair. Mr. Today." He paused and grew somber again. "He's dead now."

The girl put a finger to her eye and traced an invisible tear down it.

"Yeah," Alex said. He was a little embarrassed now that he'd cried so hard in front of a stranger. Not because he was

LISA McMANN

male, since men and women in Artimé cried freely whenever they felt like crying, but because unexpected sobbing might make a stranger feel awkward. But she didn't seem to mind.

"And Simber," he said. "You probably never saw him. He's huge and scary-looking, so I'm sure they kept him away from you once you woke up. But he was really nice, deep down."

He looked sidelong at her now, remembering their first meeting face-to-face. "You totally spit all over me," he reminded her, trying not to smile.

She raised her hand to her mouth, eyes wide and mischievous. Then she acted out the scene from her perspective. Alex tried to narrate—it was like doing pantomimes in Actors' Studio.

"You were scared," he guessed. "Everyone was staring at you."

She nodded. She looked around, forlorn.

"You didn't know where you were," he said. "And the boy—is he your brother?"

She nodded.

"Ah, okay, that's what I thought. Anyway, you're saying he was sleeping and wouldn't wake up, and you didn't know what was happening."

The Silent girl nodded again.

"And so you spit water on me. Makes perfect sense."

She laughed a silent laugh. Then she made a sorry face.

Alex smiled sadly. "Aw. It's okay. It was just a little spit." He reached out absentmindedly and touched the metal thorns around her neck. She shrank back slightly and Alex looked up. "Oh, geez, I'm sorry." He pulled his hand away. "You saw my friend Meghan inside, right?" he asked.

She nodded, her face turning serious again.

"I guess that's your island, huh. Did you and your brother escape?"

She narrowed her eyes and looked away quickly, focusing on the ocean.

"What—did I say something bad?"

She didn't respond or react in any way.

"Okay, sorry," he said. "You don't want to talk about it."

She gave him a measured sidelong glance, and then rolled her eyes.

"Oops," he said. He was quiet for a moment. "But don't you want that neck thing taken off? I'm just worried what will happen—like, to your neck, and your voice and stuff if it comes off. Plus, we don't exactly have the right tools here."

The girl raised her hands and put them in front of Alex's face, pushing him away. He took her wrists and gently moved them apart so he could see her face. "I don't understand," he said.

She bit her lip and turned her face away, and now it was her turn to cry.

"Dang it," he said under his breath. "I'm sorry. I'll shut up now. I didn't mean to make you cry."

He dropped her wrists and scrambled to his knees, sinking his hands deep into his pockets to see if he had a hankie, forgetting that all of his clothes had been soaked in the ocean, along with everything in his pockets. He pulled out a few bits of wadded-up tissue, some useless scatterclips, and a marble from one pocket. From the other he pulled out something he didn't recognize at first. It was a folded piece of paper.

And then he gasped, his heart thudding in his chest. He recognized the colorful border design.

It had to be a spell from Mr. Today.

Why hadn't he thought to check his pockets earlier? His hands shook violently as he tried to unfold it, begging to catch a break—pleading that the ocean water hadn't washed the magical words away.

He didn't notice the Silent girl watching him, startled from her tears by his sudden strange behavior. Finally he got the paper open and he smoothed it carefully. The words were there. They'd not been washed away at all. Each letter was bright and clear as the morning sky.

He held the note up to the light of the moon and read:

To whom it may concern:
Follow the dots as the traveling sun,
Magnify, focus, every one.
Stand enrobed where you first saw me,
Utter in order; repeat times three.

I apologize for the cryptic nature of this note, but I know you'll understand. I'm sorry, my boy—so very sorry. I've left you what you need in my chambers, but if something unexpected happens, follow the above.

Yours,
Marcus Today

P.S. Five heart attack components, what a waste! He could've done the deed with three. Ha-ha! Ouch.

P.P.S. In case you're curious, he's got two left on the desk. Remember for later.

Farewell. I do believe in you.

Alex stared at the note. He read it once, and a second time. His heart ached, remembering the amazing Mr. Today, and it made him feel a little bit better to know that the old mage was jolly enough to make a joke, even at the end.

But Alex's eyes kept going back to the spell, which made almost no sense at all.

The only word that stuck out was "enrobed." He knew what that meant. He clutched Mr. Today's robe like it was a gift made of gold, and he delighted in the ease of its acquisition. "Ha!" he said aloud, looking up. Aaron had given him something invaluable and he hadn't even meant to!

All Alex had to do was figure out what the rest of it meant, then wear the robe, and ta-da—Artimé would be back.

Alex's blood surged. To have such a valuable clue put him about a hundred times closer to saving Artimé than he'd been five minutes ago. He was so excited that he nearly lost his balance and fell off the roof, but the Silent girl grabbed his shirt just in time. He steadied himself, sat back down, and squeezed her hand, thanking her.

He scratched his head through the mess of tangled hair and stared at the note. "This is it," he whispered reverently. "This is the help I've been begging for." He looked at the girl and said, "You know what? We just might live through this after all."

He looked out to the west where Warbler was. And even though he couldn't see it from here in the darkest hours, and even though there was no magic to be found in all of Artimé, still Alex concentrated with all his might and whispered to his friends a world away, "Hold on."

Alex's and Aaron's stories continue in

THE UNWANTEDS

BOOK THREE

Island of Fire

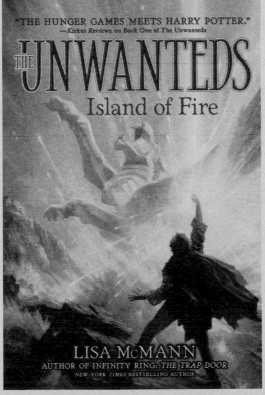

"THE HUNGER GAMES MEETS HARRY POTTER."
—*Kirkus Reviews*, on Book One of The Unwanteds

THE UNWANTEDS
Island of Fire

LISA McMANN

AUTHOR OF INFINITY RING: *THE TRAP DOOR*
NEW YORK TIMES BESTSELLING AUTHOR

Turn the page for a sneak peek. . . .

Death Farm

I t was as if Artimé had never existed.

In the weeks since the death of Marcus Today, Alexander Stowe was often seen sitting on a rickety stool, staring out the window of the gray shack, clouding the glass with his breath. Sometimes he leaned his head of dark tangled curls or pressed a dirty cheek against the pane to catch a few moments of sleep when he could stay awake no longer.

Today was no different. He stared even now, but he wasn't seeing anything at all.

In his hand he gripped a piece of paper with a colorful border, which was beginning to smudge, and he never let it go even though he'd memorized the words on it. It was his last message from Mr. Today, a cryptic, poetic spell that would fix all of Alex's problems if only he could decipher the clues. He went over the words for the millionth time in his mind.

> *Follow the dots as the traveling sun,*
> *Magnify, focus, every one.*
> *Stand enrobed where you first saw me,*
> *Utter in order; repeat times three.*

The only thing Alex truly understood about the clue was the "enrobed" part. Mr. Today had been famous for his colorful robes, and Alex imagined there was some hint of magic to the robes themselves—there must be if Alex had to wear one to make the world of Artimé come back. Alex had the good fortune of possessing the only robe in existence at this moment—the one Mr. Today had been wearing when Alex's Wanted twin brother, Aaron, killed him. The robe was Alex's only symbol of hope in a time that could not possibly be any darker.

"You should eat something," said a voice at Alex's shoulder. It was Henry Haluki, Lani's younger brother, and next to him stood the Silent boy, a ring of thorns threaded through the skin around his neck. When Alex turned and focused his bleary eyes on the boys, Henry held out a good-sized half shell he'd been using as a small bowl.

Alex smiled and took it. "Thanks," he said, breathing in the faint smell of a weak seafood broth. His empty stomach snarled, begging for it, but Alex hesitated. The Unwanteds were beginning to starve. He handed it back to Henry and shook his head. "Give it to Meg," he said. "No, wait . . . to Carina Fathom and her baby. They need it most." Alex swallowed hard and turned away so he wouldn't be tempted to grab it back again. It would be a sign of acceptance to Carina, who was so mortified that her mother Eva had turned against Artimé that she couldn't bear to look Alex in the eye.

Henry frowned, but he shuffled away obediently and left the shack carrying the soup. The Silent boy followed him, both of them careful not to disturb any sleeping bodies on the floor. After a minute Alex stood up, stretched his tired limbs, and left too. He walked around to the front of the shack, maneuvering over the still body of Jim, the winged tortoise, whose mosaic back sparkled in the sunshine, until he reached Florence, frozen in full stride. Nimbly he climbed, using Florence's legs and arms as a ladder, and he swung his body up to the roof as if he'd done it dozens of times.

He lifted a hand to shield his eyes and looked west, in the direction of the two islands that dotted the ocean. "Follow the dots as the traveling sun," he muttered. "The dots have got to mean the islands, but . . ." He didn't finish the sentence because there were so many unknowns. The phrase didn't even make sense. And then the next line—"magnify, focus, every one." How could Alex magnify and focus on the islands? He was stuck on *this* island. He couldn't get any closer. He had no binoculars. Sometimes, when conditions were less favorable, he couldn't even see the more distant one. And "every one"? There were only two visible, though Simber had told him once that there were actually three in that direction. Mr. Today certainly would've said "both" if he meant only the two he could see, but the clue said "every one." Could Mr. Today have meant to include the island of Quill, too? And what about the rest of the chain that they couldn't see, to the east? There were seven islands in all, with Quill in the center, Simber had said. . . .

Oh, Simber. A wave of grief flooded Alex. He closed his eyes for a moment. Nightmares had plagued him since Simber had plunged into the sea, deadweight. All the rest of the creatures Mr. Today had created in Artimé had ceased to be alive then too, from the moment of the mage's death. The mansion and every wonderful thing in it was gone. Worse, two of Alex's best friends remained missing on Warbler Island, where the Silents had come from, and Alex had no means by which to search for them.

Alex shook his head. "I don't know what to do," he whispered.

Just then he heard a shout from the gate that led to Quill. He stood up on the roof to see what was happening. The shout had come from Henry, who lay sprawled on the dusty ground. Two other Unwanteds ran off through the gate and disappeared into Quill, with the Silent boy giving chase. Henry didn't move.

Broken Harmony

lex scrambled down to the ground and ran to see what had happened. By the time he got to Henry's side, Sean Ranger and the Silent girl had arrived on the scene, and Meghan Ranger ran from the water's edge. The girrinos sat near the gate, unmoving, in heaps like boulders.

"What happened?" Alex demanded. "Did you guys see anything?" He looked from the Silent girl to Meghan to Sean, who knelt next to the boy.

Henry rolled to his side, curled up, and sucked in a few sharp breaths, as if he'd fallen hard and had the wind knocked out of him. After a minute, he waved Sean away and rose to his feet, dusting off his pants. There was a trickle of blood coming from his nose. He wiped it gingerly on his sleeve and scowled. "They stole the broth," he said. His lip quivered for an instant, and then it stopped. "Crow ran after them."

Sean raised an eyebrow as Meghan took a closer look at Henry's injuries. "Crow?"

"The Silent boy," Alex said. "Henry named him."

"That *is* his name," Henry said. "He showed me. He drew a bird in the sand and I guessed it."

"I'm going after him," Alex said, finding it a little easier now to take charge than he had just a few short weeks ago. "Sean, you want to get the story?"

Sean nodded. Alex started off toward the gate and then stopped, turned, and called back, "We need to have a meeting. You, me, Meg, Henry, and the Silents. See if you guys can find out if Mr. Appleblossom and Carina are available too. They've had their hands full with the fish catchers the last few days."

"Got it," Sean said.

Alex's best friend, Meghan, whose skin was mostly healed

around the band of metal thorns on her neck, could only nod in response.

Alex didn't have to go far before he saw Crow walking back toward the gate. He caught up with the boy and turned around, walking with him. "You okay, little guy?" Alex asked.

Crow nodded and punched his fist into his other palm.

"I know," Alex said. "But I don't want you to fight. I shouldn't have sent you guys out in the open with food like that. People are mean when they get desperate." He pressed his hand into his own stomach, trying to batten down the hunger. He knew he didn't have much time before the little plot of land that had once been Artimé became a battleground of infighting. And if that happened, the Unwanteds were doomed.

Who was Alex trying to fool? If he didn't do something quick, they were already doomed.

Crow kicked the dusty road with his bare foot as they turned in at the gate.

"We're going to have a meeting. I'd like you to be there, okay?"

The Silent boy made a fist and tapped it to his chest. It was the new Artiméan symbol of loyalty, which meant "I am with you."

Alex smiled. "Good."

They made their way to the shack. Alex poked his head in and spied Henry sitting in the midst of dozens of other Unwanteds, most of whom were trying to get their six-hour shift of sleep. "Meet by Florence," Alex whispered, trying not to disturb the slumbering masses. The roof was the only private place around.

The small team of Unwanteds assembled one by one around Florence. It was a strange group, since three among them were unable to make a sound, and a fourth, Carina's baby boy, spoke only gibberish.

Henry scrambled up Florence's limbs to the roof and then reached down to take the baby. Alex, Meghan, Crow, the Silent girl, and Carina all climbed up too, and they sat in the shade—for the moment—of Quill's forty-foot-tall stone wall.

Alex looked at the Silents. "So, your name is really Crow?" he asked the boy.

The boy nodded.

Alex smiled. "Nice." He looked at the girl. "I wish I knew your name," he said.

She tilted her head and both she and Crow pointed upward.

Island of Fire

Alex frowned and looked up. "Cloud?" he guessed. "Blue? Sunny? Star? Rain?"

The girl shook her head and pointed again.

Carina and Henry looked on, and then Henry piped up. "Is it Sky?"

The Silent girl nodded, her face breaking into a bright smile.

"Sky," Alex said, gazing at her. He liked the sound of that. And then he blushed and looked down to see if Sean was coming.

On the ground, Sean appeared, along with Mr. Appleblossom. "Um . . . ," Sean said, looking first at the man, who was one of the original Unwanteds Mr. Today had saved, then glancing up at the roof. "Is this going to be a problem, Sigfried?" he asked the theater instructor.

"Oh my," Mr. Appleblossom murmured, "what a predicament indeed." He gazed imploringly at Florence's ebony face. "It's not the height that bothers me, of course. I'm nimble quite enough, though lacking speed. But think of when she wakes! Severe remorse—without our gentle mage to intercede. I may as well attempt a pommel horse." Instead he drew back a few steps and gave Sean a measuring glance. "Or vault," he murmured, suddenly thoughtful. "At that I may perchance succeed." He brought a finger to his chin, calculating his odds of running and vaulting to the roof using Sean's back, rather than disrespecting the enormous warrior trainer.

"She'll never know. We won't tell her, I promise," said Sean, his eyes widening in alarm when he realized what Mr. Appleblossom was considering. "There's really no other way to get up there—I'm not nearly big enough to be used as a gymnastics apparatus. Besides, I'm sure Florence would be glad she helped us in her own way."

The theater instructor shuddered, then set his shoulders and carefully climbed up the statue to the roof, where he settled next to the others. Sean followed.

"Well then, everyone," Alex began, and then he cleared his throat a little. "It seems things are beginning to crumble."

Meghan's eyes shot open wide.